Water Fire Steam

Mitzi Zilka

MAXFIGGY PRESS

First U. S. Edition, 2022

Published by Maxfiggy Press
Distributed by IngramSpark, Amazon and AppleBooks
Audible recording to follow

ISBN 978-0-578-26682-4

Cover art: Adria @ Mandi. Inc., mandi.nodorft@gmail.com

Acknowledgments

To my dear husband Gary, thank you for your endless support, patience, And most of all, your unconditional love.
To my sister Sara, thank you for saving my life and for putting your trust in me, you've taught me so much.
To my dear friend Julie, thank you for your writing wisdom and the many happy hours together. Never give up the fight.
To my father, thank you for your gentle way and artistic eye.
Finally, to my mother, thank you for showing me the magic in words.

Chapter One

Aftermath - August 5, 1889

Thick smoke filled the morning air. Each breath unavoidably fouled with it was followed by an explosion of painful hacks. Overhead, a woolly orange ball labored through the gauzy sky as if it was shouldering against a jammed door. Ashy particles fell, dusting every object in grayish crumbs. Fir tree bows heavy with the powdery material could almost pass for snow. Black charred remains lay blanketed with it, and chunks of jagged brick took on softer shapes. Squinting against strands of hovering smoke, a handful of townspeople wandered through the ruins, their gaze pitched low. One woman with braids tied across her head picked up a melted souvenir and wept. A short distance away, another found a photo album only to fall in pieces to the ground. Someone was responsible for this catastrophe. Finding him would change nothing, but the people of Spokane would want the guilty punished.

Down on the waterfront, hordes of people stood huddled beside the muscular Spokane River, which originated from the northern part of Lake Coeur d'Alene in the Idaho Panhandle emptying into the Columbia River more than a hundred miles downstream. This mighty river held the promise of a good life to all who settled at its banks. Its life force gave the land and its people the vitality to prosper. But, on this Monday morning, the promise had, by all accounts, gone up in smoke. Townspeople sifted through the few possessions they managed to save from their boarding house rooms and hotels. Some had blankets, others carried bundles on their backs, but most were scantily attired and bankrupt of all personal effects.

Smoke trailed off the building remnants like steam from a pan of boiling water. Sawtoothed sections of walls, chimney fragments, and roofs; structure after structure reduced to black cubes and dust. Everything said death: a naked armless doll, a mangled brass doorknob, melted glass puddled in the dirt. This once-booming city of twenty-thousand people with more than thirty-two blocks of banks, saloons, dress shops, and livery stables had succumbed to the canines of fire.

The sun had punished Washington's Inland Empire with a prolonged drought that summer. Forest fires were witnessed east of town in the Idaho territory. Every shrub, every tree, every fence post was dustbowl-dry, dry like long-forgotten creek beds and the water that once cascaded freely down them. In a rush to settle the West, stick-built storefronts, shanties, and boarding houses had been thrown together alongside wood sidewalks, all of it built with pine. Pine was abundant, and its generous use was akin to leaving a box of matches in reach of precocious children or someone out to wreak havoc on innocent lives.

One thirty-three-year-old man, Rolla Alan Jones, soot-smeared and light-eyed, staggered across a footbridge from Crystal Island where the water pump station was located. He had injured his left leg when jumping from the train last night. The gash was deep and made it impossible for him to bear weight. He grabbed at the rail, took a step forward with his good leg, and pulled the other through the brittle embers that were casted over the ground. His throat was raw and chaffed from the air's abrasiveness. The acrid odor of fire, a scent usually associated with campfires and cozy homes, permeated everything. He fingered his waxed mustache. One side flared like the end of an ornate scroll, the other a burned stub. It would take months to grow it back, a consequence of little importance, fore he was lucky to have escaped with his life like so many others that night.

Rolla, his pregnant wife Sadie, and their three-year-old son Daniel returned from Lake Coeur d'Alene that evening. A much-needed getaway from the brutal heat. It was nine at night when they rounded the bend to find the entire downtown burning like a chamber in hell. Without a moment's thought, Rolla jumped from the moving train.

Tumbling down the steep terrain, he tripped and hit his knee on a jagged rock, breaking the cap in two. Determined to get to the pump house located on the other side of the torrential river, he pushed through the wrenching pain. Stopping once to help a woman waiting for her husband in the middle of the street with her children and dining room table get to safety before the raging fire devoured them.

When Rolla and the young family reached the Howard Street bridge it was chock-full of hysterical men, women, and children, fleeing from the fire and skin blistering heat. His only option was to scale the bridge on its outer flank hand over hand.

Once across, his assistant, Andrew Akin, and he could push the water pumps to its utmost proportions. This morning as the sun squeezed through the phlegm of smoky air exhaustion moved through Rolla like the last drops of a near-empty jug of molasses. Drop by drop, his energy dribbled out. The guilt of leaving his family on the train gnawed at him. Sadie and Daniel had waited all night not knowing if he was dead or alive. He hobbled along on his good leg, bracing himself against street poles, posts, and blackened tree trunks. Dragging his bum leg was as excruciating as pulling one's own tooth. He tried hopping, but that sent shock waves of debilitating pain. He needed a crutch to keep his leg from touching the ground. A nearby board, still smoldering on one end, was the answer, just as rebuilding was the answer for Spokane. He tucked the unburned section of the board under his arm, a bit short, but sufficient enough.

Up ahead, a wooden sign lay face down in the baked earth. He lifted the board and wiped the debris away only to discover it was his store sign: R. A. Jones Jewelry Shoppe. The rest of it was gone like all the other storefronts. Sadie will be crushed. The shop was her endeavor.

At the corner of Main and Stevens Street, a gust of hot wind whipped around his legs and further dried his chapped mouth. At the far end of town, a crowd of people was headed his way. Drawing nearer, he spotted Mayor Fred Nicholls, his supervisor; Councilmen

Frank Rossiter and Jeb Thomas; Police Captain Everett, two of his officers; and a handful of townspeople. Rolla tried to hurry his pace, eager to find out what they knew, but the leg choked his zeal.

Rossiter burst out from the crowd, shaking his fist, and shouting over the distance.

Spittle flew from his mouth. "Jones, where the hell were you?" screamed Rossiter, a barrel-chested man with thick mutton chops, beard and demonic eyebrows.

"What?" called Rolla, dragging himself closer.

Frank Rossiter's words met his ears as gibberish, utterances thrown together in a foreign tongue, "We trusted you."

"Speak clearly, man?" Rolla said, closing the distance between them, his jaw tightening evermore.

"This is all your fault," said Rossiter.

Fault, a word Rolla held in much disdain, clanged loudly in his ears. Son-of-a-bitch, always the first to point fingers. A bolt of energy shot through his depleted muscles, stripping away much of his exhaustion.

Three townsmen charged at Rolla. Their eyes were red, their lips snarled up high. Seth Bos, a giant of a man, got hold of Rolla by the neck and dragged him to a telegraph pole. He felt like a boy about to get a whooping until he was slammed against it.

"String him up," yelled Francis from the livery stable.

Francis's betrayal was crushing. He had been his first friend in Spokane.

Another fierce pain jolted through his leg, "It was Sunday, my day off. I wasn't even in town," shouted Rolla.

A young woman, holding a toddler with raccoon eyes, charged over and scratched his arm bloody, "Where's my baby going to sleep tonight?"

Rolla reeled against the sting as the blood seeped onto his salty skin.

"Hang the bastard," choked an old-timer.

Had he awakened into a world of dragons and burning catapults? Yesterday he was everyone's favorite son who had brought running water to every home and business. Today they wanted him dead. Thoughts piled up behind his teeth like caustic stomach acid.

Captain Everett blew his whistle and directed his officers to intercede. They rushed in and pulled two of the men off but Seth wouldn't budge.

"Seth, let him go," commanded the captain.

Rolla raged against the lynching stake. His good foot slid forward in the hot dirt, setting him askew. His broken knee throbbing. An image of Sadie and Daniel flashed before him. He was suddenly thankful that they would not witness his hanging.

Seth's rancid breath spread over Rolla's face, "I'm gonna kill you."

"Seth," shouted Captain Everett in a parental voice.

Mayor Nicholls, a stately man with a long tapered beard and a fashionable handlebar mustache, pointed at the crowd with scorn, "No one's gettin' strung up, not in my town."

Seth finally let go, but not before throwing Rolla onto his knee. He screamed in pain and in embarrassment.

An elderly man with a burned straw hat elbowed through, "By God, we should hang him, the morgue's fillin' up."

Rolla squeezed his eyes closed and ground down on the ash in his teeth. "People have died?" When he came out west from New York, five years prior, he made promises to be successful. Failure was not an option. A kind of naivety held by someone as young and ambitious as Rolla. He dropped his head and muttered, "If this is my fault, kill me now."

Mayor Nicholls stepped forward and turned to the crowd. "Now you listen here," shaking his fist, "I will find who is responsible for this disaster, but," he paused glaring at their faces, "we will not stoop to such lawlessness."

"Criminy sakes, why wait," insisted Rossiter, "we know who's responsible?"

Nicholls sneered at Rossiter and commanded with clenched fists, "Captain, move these people out of here."

Councilman Thomas threw a hostile stare at Rossiter, "Don't be an idiot." Thomas was a tall, athletic man with an Abe Lincoln beard. "We assume innocence until proven otherwise. You being an attorney know that."

Rossiter backed off, his eyes shifting, his mouth smirking in disregard. Only days prior, Rolla warned the city council that the volunteer fire department was not prepared for a three-alarm fire. Yet as was often the case with Rossiter leading the dissension, they rejected his assertion.

Rolla got to his feet with the aid of his flimsy board, "I warned you about the fire department. My system worked like a savage all night long."

Townspeople booed and spit at him.

Thomas spoke under his breath, "Be thankful you have a home to go to."

Rolla brushed off his clothes, picked up the sign, and fought back his rage. "I've been at the pumps since half-past nine. There's nothing wrong with my system."

Mayor Nicholls looked over his fire-torn city, and resignation settled in his face, "Go home, Jones."

Rolla, still hungering for the truth to come out, raised his fist, "How can you blame me? It doesn't make sense."

Captain Everett and his officers pushed the crowd onward. Rolla's mind cleared as they got out of earshot. He thought of other things he wished he had said, things that would have made their accusations even more ludicrous. But, his words withered on his tongue while he hoped for fairness.

****

Three-year-old Daniel spotted his father from a distance and ran to him, a tail of ash swirling behind.

"Daddy," his eyes were as big as fifty-cent pieces, his arms stretched wide. Daniel hurled himself at his father.

Breathing a deep sigh of relief, Rolla smoothed down the boy's ash-imbued hair now the color of sand and said, ”Careful, son, don't touch the leg.”

Daniel frowned at his bleeding flesh visible through his torn pant, "Eww."

Sadie rushed over, her mouth covered with a handkerchief, "I was so worried. My God, what has happened to your leg?"

Rolla grasped her shoulder, “Are you all right?”

“We’re fine. Tell me what has happened,” pleaded Sadie.

“I was so worried about you,” said Rolla. He then dropped his gaze, fought the urge to cry, and carefully collected himself, "They're blaming the fire on me."

Sadie stiffened, her eyes flared as she wrestled with his statement. "Oh, poppycock! Give them a few days. They'll come around,” she said rubbing his hand.

Rolla raised his chin and drew her into his eyes. It was the same look he held that bitterly cold day last February when the three of them stood over a dark rainy hole in the ground. A spot where their second baby, a son, was laid to rest.

Rolla gently swept the strands of hair floating across her face and tucked them behind one ear. With false confidence he said, "Don't worry, there will be a full investigation and I will be exonerated."

Water

"Most people...are like a falling leaf that drifts and turns in the air, flutters, and falls to the ground. But a few others are like stars which travel one defined path: no wind reaches them, they have within themselves their guide and path."
— Hermann Hesse

Chapter Two

Five years before - September 1884

Looking out across the broad expanse of the Hudson River with the many skyscrapers of Manhattan, Rolla stood tall on the riverbank in his polished shoes and fitted suit. The air was crisp. It smelled of river, a concoction of mud and brine and boats billowing coal dust. It smelled of seagulls devouring discarded catch and trees dropping their latent summer foliage on the lapping shore below. He drew in deep gulps of it, determined to remember the smell of the great city. To squirrel it away in a secure place, a place where it would forever remain in memory. He was about to embark from all he'd known and travel to a new world.

He admired New York, marveled at its energy, as exciting as a combustion engine, but Rolla felt drawn elsewhere. That somewhere pulled on him hard. It seemed there was no choice but to commit to this gnawing urge, to brave the unknown even though the thought of it made him sweat. Rolla would go west. A rugged, mostly unchartered part of the nation offering boundless opportunities to those with the nerve.

He had not dreamed this up yesterday. He'd been mapping the West since he was a boy. His father made it impossible to resist such desires. After dinner, he'd crouch beside his father and his older brother Renaldo to study the scant maps available at the time. They imagined what it was like out in the Wild West. By the glow of their river stone fireplace and beeswax candles, his father spun tales around excerpts from newspaper stories penned by Meriwether Lewis who wrote to Thomas Jefferson on the expedition, as well as from citations in the private journal of William Clark. A favorite passage of Meriwether's letters read:

"*As our vessels are small and the current of the river much more moderate, we calculate on traveling at the rate of 20 or 25 miles per day as far as the falls of Missouri. Beyond this point, or the first range of the Rocky Mountains situated about 100 miles further, any calculation with respect to our daily progress, can be little more than bare conjecture.*"

Rolla ached to bear witness to such a moment. Although his father had not ventured far from New York, where his great-grandfather settled after arriving from Wales in 1773, he was an adventurer at heart. Rolla believed his father had sown the seeds of wanderlust in them, most especially Renaldo. But, Renaldo had died in a barn fire at twelve when Rolla was five. With a broken heart and a badge of guilt that it should have been him, his father passed the baton to Rolla, "It's up to you, son," he said, his hand laying heavy on his small shoulder. Even now, he could feel his pressing fingers.

When his baby sisters Cora and Clara died from diphtheria the very same month, the burden of his dead siblings' lives fell on Rolla like a gargoyle guarding purgatory. On the one hand, every breath he drew was guilt-ridden. On the other, he glistened with purpose.

After graduating from Cornell University, he received a bona fide offer from a town out west to build a water system—to bring running water to every home and business in Spokane Falls. At last, his youthful yearning for adventure had found a destination, a proving ground for his right to be called a man. A platform to honor his siblings and his parents.

His father's eyes had teared when he told him. An unmissable look of pride rose in his face. Moreover, Rolla saw regret of an inevitable chasm resulting from being thousands of miles apart. Rolla tried to assure him he'd be back. His father squeezed his shoulder just as he had when he was a child, then strolled onto the front porch. His countenance changed as the golden glow of the setting sun surrounded him like spun taffy. Rolla bowed his head in gratitude for his parent's sacrifices and vowed never to relinquish his promise.

Rolla wanted more than anything to build wealth, earn respect, and create a lasting legacy for his father, his mother, Renaldo, and his baby sisters. To make something that would forever be a recognition of their lives. The Civil War was over. All people were legally free, but freedom often meant that no one belonged anywhere. Many roamed the country, searching for their place on earth, their home. You'd see them in the cities rolling by waving like flags. They had no ties. They knew nobody. They owned nothing. When one of them died, people scarcely knew where to bury them. Strangers they'd casually met; the hotel clerk, the baker, the stable boy were the only mourners. They left nothing behind except possibly a hat well-cast in their head shape or a pair of old leather lace-up boots. They lived in the streets, in the town square, in the dance halls. They sat in sidewalk cafes and concert halls and looked about at the hundreds of others like them. But, Rolla was different. He saw his destiny. It was right there before him. The journey occupied a permanent place in his heart, and he vowed to follow it wherever the road shall lead.

Call it romantic, call it naive, but nothing short of death was going to stop Rolla from finding his home and reaching his goals. However, venturing out west alone was not preferred. Many settlers married Indian women to bridge the gap of loneliness and establish a family. He, on the other hand, had met and fallen in love with Sadie Withers, a woman of strength and conviction who was in accord with his utopian ideas. She was an intelligent, progressive woman up to the challenge and hardships that would surely come their way.

He fingered an envelope containing a deed for 160 acres of public land within his coat pocket. The Homestead Act signed into law by Abraham Lincoln in 1862, granted homesteaders to pay a small filing fee if they completed five years of continuous residence before receiving legal ownership of the land. After six months of residency, homesteaders had the option of purchasing the land from the government at $1.25 per acre. Conversely, they could buy it outright for a slightly higher price per acre. In his outside pocket, he clasped a small box containing a ring. He hoped to give her a grand setting with diamonds and gold one day. Today, a plain circle of silver would have to suffice.

Rolla dashed along the river trail of sedimentary rock and brackish sand leading to Manhattan's cobblestone streets. When he reached Broadway Street, he tipped his hat gallantly to the many decorated carriages pulled by grand horses transporting well-to-do New Yorkers, gentlemen who came by their wealth through inheritance or long-standing family connections. They were in stark opposition to dreamers such as himself, who insisted on forging their bearing. He believed the pursuit of happiness was not dependent on a family legacy but on vision and the strength of one’s back. With the promise of Sadie Wither's hand in marriage, a guarantee of employment, and land of their own —he would conquer the world.

He hitched a ride on the back of a wagon as it rumbled across the street, then skipped across a pedestrian median and bounded off to catch the clanging streetcar, which brought him within a block of the famous Delmonico's Restaurant. He and Sadie were confident this would provide the perfect setting for proposing marriage. With a hopeful heart and clammy hands, he hot-footed up the marble steps to the mahogany-and-beveled-glass doors of Delmonico's. The light inside glowed through the polished glass and reflected off each bevel. The honeyed tones of sweet violins escaped through the gaps of the thick double doors.

Renaldo's face floated past his mind's eye as he stopped to catch his breath. He removed his handkerchief and wiped his hands dry as the memory of Renaldo faded. Rolla would have given anything to have Renaldo by his side. He pushed through the heavy brass-handled door feeling reasonably self-assured. He removed his wool coat, straightened his vest, adjusted his starched collar, and with a quick twist of his mustache, was ready to meet his future in-laws. Candles and chandeliers cast a glow of golden light on the many coiffed guests. A string quartet played in one corner. Moments before the maitre d' reached him, his gaze landed on Sadie. For a brief uninterrupted moment, he admired her beauty. Her brown satin ribbon nestled among a crown of dark pin curls; her light blue eyes and perfect nose were accentuated by an alluring overbite.

His nerves skittered between heartbeats. He drew in his breath to settle himself, yet the anticipation of proposing marriage was unequivocally rattling.

The maitre d'—dignified and conscientious—queried, "Mr. Jones?"

Rolla cocked his head, “That’s me."

Bowing the maitre d' said, "Your party is expecting you. Follow me."

As Rolla crossed the room, he saw Sadie's father, a man in his late fifties with dark thin hair parted in the middle, pull out his watch from his vest pocket and flip it open. Sadie turned toward the front foyer with searching eyes. She wore a delicate lace blouse and high collar, fashionable among young women. A cameo that hung from a satin ribbon laid perfectly against her décolletage.

"Rolla," said Sadie grinning from ear to ear, her hand extended. "You're here."

He hurried forward, took her hand, and kissed it.

"Father, Mother, may I introduce Rolla Alan Jones. Rolla, these are my parents, Mr. and Mrs. James Withers."

His heart, now in his throat, revved.

Mrs. Withers put out her gloved hand, "Of the Ohio Hayes family, President Hayes, you know. You can call me Mrs. Harriet."

"Mrs. Harriet," he said in acknowledgment. Sadie had neglected to tell him of her family background. Caught off guard by this declaration, he turned to Sadie and whispered, "You never told me."

She covered her mouth with two fingers and whispered, "Far too gauche darling."

Still perplexed, he kissed Mrs. Harriet's hand, shook hands with Mr. Withers, and wondered what other details he was not privy too.

"A pleasure to meet you both," said Rolla, bowing.

The maitre d' pulled out a chair, unfolded a cloth napkin, and as in a practiced danced he snapped his wrist. Rolla lowered himself onto the chair as the serviette floated onto his lap.

The maitre d' leaned forward. "May I bring you an aperitif?"

Spying what the others were having, he said, "I'll have what he's having."

"Very well," said the maitre d,' padding away.

An uneasy silence fell upon them as her parents looked him over. "Have you been here before?" asked Rolla, antsy to end the awkwardness.

Mr. Withers shifted. "We don't get out much, but of course, everyone knows of Delmonico's," He picked up his crystal tumbler half-filled with an amber-colored liquid. "Mr. Jones, my daughter tells me you are an engineer?"

Right down to business, he was. "Yes, sir, a civil engineer from Cornell University."

Sadie touched his hand and addressed her father. "He graduated top of his class."

Mr. Withers glanced at her with slight annoyance. "So, you've said."

Sadie cleared her throat and quieted.

The maitre d' removed a crystal glass from the tray held by one of his underlings and set it before Rolla.

"Are you considering many offers?" said Mr. Withers.

Rolla sat up a little taller. "It does seem my credentials are in demand."

Mr. Withers raised an eyebrow and cocked his head. "Does that surprise you?"

Desperate to wet his mouth, Rolla took several sips from his glass and shrugged. "I merely chose the field that interests me."

Mr. Withers crossed one leg over the other and brushed a speck from his pant, "I would have thought it was the plan all along. After all, are we not in an industrial revolution? Have we not a duty as American's to consider the good of the nation? If everyone chose professions based on self-satisfaction, how would we prosper?"

It was clear that Sadie's father was used to being the focal point of every discussion. A glimpse of understanding came to Rolla as to why Sadie was a keen advocate for women's rights—and why she was eager to leave home. "You sound much like my father. But, I ask you, can't both objectives be present in a decision? Cannot a man chose a field because of its benefit to the nation as well as his skills and interest?"

"And what about engineering interests you?" interjected Mrs. Harriet, a well-groomed woman with one lazy eye and a placid smile.

"I am intrigued by how things work," he said, pulling a matchbox from his vest. "Here, let me show you. The candle on the table has been lighted by a match, much like the one I hold." He dragged the match head along the striking surface. “A surface consisting of sand and powdered glass. It causes friction and heat, enough to convert some of the red phosphorus to white phosphorus—a chemical so volatile it ignites in the air." He slid the match across the surface. The flame ignited blue in a controlled blast and soon settled to yellow.

Their eyes widened at the brilliance of the flame.

"Oh my, that is fascinating," said Sadie gesturing to her parents for consensus.

Rolla hoped she didn't appear too eager, fearing it would not sit well with her scrutinizing father. He focused on the flame to avoid any detection of his nervousness. "The match is dipped in wax so that the fire will spread evenly over the entire surface of the match head."

"Who knew a simple match had so much complexity?" said Mrs. Harriet looking to her husband, "Did you, darling?"

James Withers leaned back in his chair with a piercing look. "So, you're one of those who believes a man should follow his heart?"

His words cut. He was testing Rolla? As with most of his father's generation, a man must repeatedly prove himself.

"We must be true to ourselves, do you not agree?" Rolla asked.

A smirk came over Mr. Wither's face. "My father would argue that premise. We were taught to think practically, to follow what makes the most money."

"I don't disagree, and yet, some of the most profitable ideas come from pursuing curiosity," said Rolla.

"Benjamin Franklin discovered electricity not to change the world, but to first satisfy his fascination. If a man is unhappy with his lot in life —it's up to him to change his circumstances. And, if one is content, would he not do a better job?"

"Hmm," said Mr. Withers, another skeptical expression set at his brow.

Thankfully, Mrs. Harriet interjected once again. "Tell us about the opportunity you're most interested in."

"Gadly," said Rolla, "I would be designing and building a booming town's water system. Currently, they collect their water from small towers around the city."

Mr. Withers looked astonished, "Clearly behind the times."

"Indeed," said Rolla. "However, water is plentiful. A massive river runs through the north end of town. A citywide plumbing system is necessary to distribute water to homes and businesses, and, of course, for fire prevention," he said. "A modern system is key for any growing city." That statement made Rolla realize he believed in the project. It felt good to claim it.

"Quite the undertaking, especially for someone with no practical experience," said Mr. Withers.

A pang of agitation flicked in Rolla. He clenched one hand under the table to not reveal his lack of ease. "I've worked on similar projects over the past three summers with one of the most reputable engineering firms in America."

Mr. Withers thumped his fingers on his hollow-sounding belly and yielded with a nod. "Dare I ask, where would you be building such a system?"

Sadie sat up. Rolla cleared his throat. Their gazes darted back and forth between them.

Rolla drew a breath, "In a town—a city—called Spokane Falls, in the Washington Territory."

"On the West Coast?" said Mrs. Harriet, with alarm in her voice.

"No, madame, Spokane Falls is four-hundred miles east of the Pacific Ocean in a region called the Inland Empire."

"Still, it's a long way from New York," she said, letting go of an exasperated snort.

"True, and it will be rugged. But the contract is lucrative, and a great many other opportunities are possible." He looked to Sadie. "Spokane Falls is earmarked to be the next financial hub of the Northwest. We want to be part of it."

"Couldn't you have found something nearby?" said Mr. Withers. "New York is teeming with opportunity, especially for an aspiring young man such as yourself."

Rolla steadied himself, hoping what he was about to say wouldn't result in an outburst. "I believe—he said, locking eyes with Sadie—we believe our destiny is in the West."

James Withers stiffened and raised a brow, "That's the first I've heard of it." His neck reddened.

Rolla tried to sound confident yet sensitive to this man's perspective. He should have known Sadie's rapid acceptance would not be reciprocated with parental enthusiasm. He laid his hands flat on the table and gathered his thoughts. "Jefferson believes, as do we, the

West must be developed for the good of the country. For someone with my credentials, the West holds great promise."

Then Sadie did what he hoped she wouldn't do. She got mad. Her upper lip tightened. "I do have thoughts of my own, many of which I do not share with you."

Mrs. Harriet lifted her index finger, "Young lady." Her good eye was wide, the other less so, at her daughter's impertinence.

A look of irritation flamed across her father's face. "What about the Indian problem? Moreover, how do you plan to get out there, the Oregon Trail in a covered wagon?"

Sadie and Rolla burst into a laughter. Could James Withers be interjecting some much-needed levity? His austere expression said no.

Rolla quieted. Those were questions he could answer even if they were rhetorical. It was common knowledge that the Northern Pacific Railroad had finally connected the East to the West in 1883 after many years of struggle. The Indian's had been forced onto reservations or obligated to accept below-market compensation for their lands. "As you know, the Northern Pacific Railroad reached Spokane last year. It takes about a week to train across the country. The Palouse Indians have their reservations and have been reported to have settled in well."

James Withers smirked, "Nevertheless, it's risky."

"We're going to plant a fruit and nut orchard," said Sadie with buoyancy, "and sell seedling trees."

"Oh, bully for you," said Mrs. Harriet, an apparent attempt to stir the conversation into milder waters. Rolla wondered what her true feelings were if her controlling husband weren't overshadowing her every word. He remembered his mother's tears when he told her. Now Mrs. Harriet had to face her youngest daughter moving away, leaving with someone she barely knew, for a destination fraught with dangers and thousands of miles away from her protective wing.

"We could visit you one year, and you could visit us the next," said Sadie now with compassionate eyes.

James Withers pressed on. "Have you been to the West?"

An irksomeness simmered in Rolla, "No—but my information comes from reliable sources. I also have first rights to one hundred and sixty acres of fertile land." Rolla took out the papers from his inside pocket and laid them on the table upon that declaration.

Mr. Withers reached over and turned the top page out.

"I promise to provide Sadie with everything she'll ever want," said Rolla, "to meet every challenge, to provide a prosperous life for the woman I love."

Sadie and her mother squeezed hands.

Her father reached for his glass. "You don't let up, do you?" He swallowed the last bit of his drink.

Rolla watched the excitement fall from Sadie's face.

"What if things don't go to plan?" said Mr. Withers.

Rolla raised his head. "I have everything worked out, every detail."

With sternness in his jaw, Mr. Withers leaned in, "It'll take some real sand to carry out such an endeavor. There's always a chance for failure."

Rolla stiffened and locked eyes with him. "I am not afraid." He held his stare until Mr. Withers blinked.

"Maybe you should be." After a breathless moment, Mr. Withers drew a fist down on the table, causing the settings to jump. Mrs. Harriet flinched. Sadie's eyes narrowed.

"No, I cannot allow my daughter to embark on such a journey without being certain of her safety. My God, man, we've only just met."

Rolla's breath let go like a punctured sack of flour. His front teeth moved back, and his jaw came forward. He would have walked out if it weren't for Sadie. "Do you think it proper for an unmarried woman to travel alone?"

"Of course not, which is why the better plan is for you to go out and settle yourself. After you've ironed out the details, and if my daughter is still intent," Mr. Withers turned to face Sadie, "her mother and I will escort you out."

Sadie crossed her arms in a huff. "I am not a child."

James Withers stared at the candle flame and tugged at his collar.

Sadie glared at her father indignantly.

Her mother patted their hands. "Settle down, you two."

Rolla could tell Sadie and her father had tangled before.

Exhaling, Mr. Withers spoke. "I have to do what I believe is best, as I have for her sisters."

Sadie lowered her gaze. Her countenance changed to one of resignation.

"All right, I'll get settled," said Rolla smiling faintly and swallowing hard, "and call for Sadie as soon as I am situated. At that time, I would prefer to return and collect her myself." Thinking about the scalawags who might descend upon her.

"No, not necessary, I am eager to see a bit of the Wild West for myself," said Mr. Withers. "I should think the spring of '85 would be a prime time to travel across the country."

"Spring," said Rolla and Sadie in unison. It was only September, and the thought of spending most of the fall and winter alone was not a welcome realization. Her father had bullyragged them into his plan —a plan not of their choice or of their liking. His heart plunged as the upheaval of their plans fell like a jigsaw puzzle on a lopsided table. He wished Sadie had forewarned him; her father was as insistent and opinionated as anyone he'd ever met. He turned to Sadie, gallantly reserving his nerves. "Is that acceptable, darling?"

Sadie dropped her gaze and yielded with a sad nod.

Studying her eyes, Rolla said, "I'd like to ask for her hand now."

One corner of Sadie's mouth lifted.

Mr. Withers thumped the tabletop. "Go ahead, son, but I'll hold you to your promises. Fail, and you'll have me to answer to."

Rolla would have argued his warning but thought it best to let it go for now.

Sadie reached across the table, squeezed her father's hand, and smiled. To Rolla's surprise, James Wither's chin wobbled.

Rolla stood up, nearly tipped over the chair, removed the ring box from his pocket, and kneeled on one knee. A wave of soft voices bubbled from the other guests in the restaurant.

"Sarah Elizabeth Millar Withers, will you give me the honor of becoming my wife?"

Mrs. Harriet dabbed her long-lashed eyes and hugged her husband's arm.

Mr. Withers's mouth lifted slightly on one side.

Sadie threw back her head and trumpeted, "I do."

The many onlookers clapped.

Adrenalin shot through the two of them as he slipped on the ring. They kissed softly, and for a single blissful second, they were adrift in each other's wanting.

Mr. Withers called out, "Waiter, two more bourbons and champagne for the ladies," rapping on the tabletop. "Take note, young man. This is how a man takes charge."

Rolla conceded with a you-don't-say tilt of his head.

"I guess it's plausible the West could be a suitable place for retirement," said Mr. Withers. "Most especially if we want to know our future grandchildren, right, Mother?"

"Indeed," she said, now laughing in a strange honking manner.

Rolla cleared his throat and diverted his gaze so as not to call attention to the shock of her boisterous laughter. He looked at Sadie. "I did warn you about that," whispered Sadie.

With glasses lifted high, the four of them touched the crystal rims together, setting off a clarion chime.

"I think a cigar is in order," said Mr. Withers. He turned and snapped his fingers. "Waiter, two cigars, if you please."

The waiter flagged another, who hurried over with two hand-rolled cigars. He clipped the ends and handed them to the men. Rolla drew in too long and coughed. They laughed; so did he. It was a good moment. It wasn't long before several dining guests began coughing at the smoke.

Mrs. Harriet pushed the ashtray between the two men. "Why not save those for after dinner?" They looked about and promptly set down the cigars in the glass basin.

"Now that's settled, let's order dinner?" said Mr. Withers, turning to hail the waiter, who by now had come to stand behind his left shoulder. "Good man," he said, smoke still seeping from his nose.

The waiter opened the cartes du jour and handed them to the ladies first. Candlelight illuminated a splendid set of choices on butter-colored cotton paper. Like threads of honey, the recent turn of events stuck to Rolla. He would be going west without Sadie. Rolla couldn't help from worrying how the many months apart would be endured before the distance became a recipe for fading hearts.

Chapter Three

What's the matter Sadie," said Rolla, pulling her through the crowd at New York's Grand Central Depot, "The train departs at half past the hour?"

Sadie waffled.

Rolla turned back, "I can't miss this train."

The terminal had massive domed ceilings tiled in stone that arched above yards of steel tracks that ran in and out of daylight. Hordes of travelers rushed about often colliding into one another, people from every walk of life. Indian braves and their squaws wrapped in animal skins, Chinese donned in silk garments, and black Americans dressed in the days current fashions. Immigrants from European countries, the rich, the middle-class and the working class. Nowhere else in America did this kind of diversity exist. Sadie bit her lip and took a conciliatory step forward. Rolla grew annoyed, stopped and pulled her close. Her woeful eyes cast to one side.

"I've got to get on the train, don't you understand?" His eyes were wide, his neck elongated and jaw was held tight.

Sadie teared up, "Don't leave me. Stay in New York."

"The decision has been made," said Rolla, "and, I am expected in a week."

"You could get a job around here just as easily as you did in Spokane."

Though saying goodbye to Sadie tore at Rolla, he was too excited to think of little else. The more he tugged, the more she pulled back. It was one of their favorite coquettish games, but this morning, the gaiety of it became irksome. He didn't think it was a conscious decision to delay him so much as she just couldn't make herself feel exuberant about the long separation. This was an optimum time to train across the country before the plains and mountain pass filled with snow and ice. The passage through North Dakota was known to have an average snowfall of forty-five inches a year. Crossing the Rocky Mountains, however, where the snowfall exceeds 150 inches would be far treacherous, if not impossible. If he delayed, his opportunity would be forfeited.

Rolla planted a peck on her cheek and continued marching toward the platform. When they reached it, her tears broke loose. "I won't see you for more than half a year. It's just too long," mewled Sadie. "You'll find someone new."

Rolla felt her worry, reached into his pocket, pulled out his handkerchief, and dabbed her tears, "Our love is forever. No one could ever replace you. Believe in us, in our future."

Sadie's downcast eyes ascended, "Promise?"

"I have promised," said Rolla, pulling her left hand to his mouth and kissing the thin band around her finger.

Sadie took a small step back and confessed," I do trust you. It's just wrong to put our lives on hold. How I wish my father would stop treating me like a child."

Rolla checked the platform number. "This is it," he said, he climbed onto the metal step and pivoted back, "Spring will be here before we know it. I'll send telegraphs and write often, don't worry. I love you."

"One last kiss before you go," said Sadie, tears pooled in her aqua eyes. Rolla jumped back into her arms and kissed her fervently. The next second he was back on the step just as the train jerked forward. Clutching his handkerchief, Sadie wiped her nose and waved the cloth in the air as the P.A.—short for Pennsylvania—moved slowly down the track. Rolla remained on the steps. Their eyes fixed on each other until a porter forced him inside. Once inside, he rushed to an open window seat and planted his hands on the glass for one last long gaze.

Chapter Four

Rolla had purchased a second-class ticket at $152 one way. A tidy sum, nearly as much as the cost of the one hundred and sixty acres of land purchased through the Homestead Act. He had intended to travel third class, but his mother wouldn't hear of it, "Arriving unwashed and sleep deprived is no way for a young man of your promise to start a career." Though he would not have a real sleeper. Instead, he would have an upholstered bench, a footstool, and a curtain to draw across at night for privacy, accommodations otherwise known as compartments.

The price of his ticket afforded shared bath accommodations and a seat in the dining car where he would be waited on during meal times. Whether first, second, or even third class, one hundred and sixty hours on a train would be an arduous. He kept his spirits high holding on to the promise of the scheduled layovers—one as long as four hours—where he could suspend the monotony, stretch his legs, and explore the immediate surroundings.

Traveling from New York to Philadelphia, onto Pittsburgh to Columbus to Indianapolis, and finally into Chicago on the P.A. would be fairly mundane as the train moved through industrial areas and skirted ordinary towns. Once in Chicago, he would change trains onto the CMSTP&P, otherwise known as The Milwaukee Road, into Milwaukee, Wisconsin, and St. Paul, Minnesota. The Northern Pacific Railway picked up in St. Paul and headed straight west, crossing the

Great Plains of North Dakota and Montana, and Idaho, then rode into Spokane Falls in the Washington Territory, his final destination. The N. P. was the last leg of the line to open up. It would take three day's ride. The N. P. was the first of the northern transcontinental railways, created by an Act of Congress signed by President Abraham Lincoln on July 2, 1864. The route was to closely follow the Lewis and Clark Expedition explorations of 1804 and allow for settlement of the northern territories between Lake Superior and the Pacific Ocean. Chinese and American workers built the road from opposite ends of the line until they met on September 8, 1883, at Gold Creek, Montana, President Ulysses S. Grant drove the last spike into the ground.

Rolla stored his bags in his compartment and watched the train rumble along from New York's central business district into shanty neighborhoods and on to stately homes. Once patches of open land began appearing, he made his way to the dining car. It was eleven in the morning, and he was famished. Making himself comfortable in a wine-colored velvet booth where a gentleman in his mid-forties with a comb-over that tucked around one ear like some kind of horn approached.

"How do you do, Roy Thursdell is the name." Roy, a professional vagabond, rode the rails between the Pacific and the Atlantic, worming his way into the good graces of unsuspecting passengers. Roy was a master at filling people with enchanting stories in exchange for drinks and food. And quite eager were those travelers to hear him spin tales. An equitable exchange, he thoroughly believed.

He would pontificate about settlers who first rode out in wagons by the hundreds in 1843 from Missouri pulled by mule and oxen on what is was known as the Oregon Trail. He told of the hardships they encountered, the many who died along the way and were buried where they fell. The Civil War had been fought and won, and the industrial revolution was rapidly changing the world. The advancement of connecting railroads and locomotives where travelers could board and be at their destination within a few days with little threat of death was nothing short of miraculous. His tales were rich in folklore. These were stories he felt confident would be brought home and shared, tales to retell over supper by the glow of oil lamps or, in many cases, incandescent bulbs. This scamp was a genius at spotting idealists from afar, just as the fox does the rabbit hiding in the underbrush. Rolla was one such idealist.

Roy twisted his feeble excuse for a mustache. "Aren't you Jeb Sorey's boy?" He placed his other hand in his hip pocket.

Rolla, taken aback, even questioned himself for a moment.

"Yes, I knew it when I saw you. How is your father getting along? Have your sisters found proper suiters?"

Rolla smiled politely at the stranger's mistake. "I beg your pardon. My name is Jones, Rolla Jones. My father is a merchant, and my only sister is already wed."

"Oh, my word, but you do favor Mr. Sorey, with your flaxen panache and square chin," said Roy, "mind if I sit a spell?"

"Be my guest," said Rolla, thinking it would be pleasant to talk with someone as the train made its way to Philadelphia's Broad Street Station and the Pittsburg rail yard. A passage he had ridden a half a dozen times before for job interviews and summer employment. It would be agreeable to share a celebratory drink commemorating his first big adventure out West, "May I offer you a drink Mr. Thursdell?"

Roy pulled out his pocket watch and raised an eye of doubt," Why not, thank you," said Roy hiking his trousers as he sat.

Rolla raised a finger to summon the waiter. A Black man in a starched white jacket with Abe stitched on the pocket in blue thread approached from behind Roy. The waiter shook his head and rolled his eyes, trying to tip off Rolla to his sort—Rolla missed the cue.

"The gentlemen and I would like a drink and a lunch menu if you please."

The waiter nodded and turned to Roy, "Your regular bullet with a beer chaser?"

Roy smirked." My reputation precedes me." He stared dead-eyed at the cheeky attendant. Thursdell seemed the proper gentlemen at first glance. His apparel appeared superbly clean and pressed. His fingernails were clean and white. His shoes polished high. Yet, on closer examination, his right shirt cuff was frayed. A small amber stain sat in a wrinkle halfway down his starched shirt. One collar button was missing and had been replaced by a lady's hatpin and two hanging threads at his lapel suggested things were amiss. If the man's drink choice was a bit hefty for the time of day, Rolla didn't seem to care. He was too excited to concern himself with such trivial matters. Roy polished off the first drink and ordered a second, all the while filling Rolla with fabricated stories of mystery and subterfuge.

"My first experience on any train was the P.A. This very same train. I was on my way to Indianapolis," said Roy. "My word, what an unfortunate education did I gain."

"Do tell," said Rolla, his eyes big, his attention riveted.

"There I was, just a young man of twenty-five, traveling to courier an important proposal for my father's textile business. Women's garments were his specialty. The proposal was to be delivered to none other than his arch-rival, Paramatta Textiles. I, of course, was elated to be entrusted to carry such a pivotal document. Every thump of my heart beat with pride," said Roy, his hand placed squarely on his chest. "If things went well, I would likely be awarded other important assignments." Roy leaned in and spoke from one corner of his mouth. "My father was a brute of a man, but I did so want to please him." Roy sat back and gazed out the window for a moment in plaintive repose. "Things went well until I arrived in Indianapolis. I hired a driver to take me directly to the front steps of the textile giant. A cost I should have forgone. Nevertheless, off I went. Pennywise, pound foolish is the young. Along the way, unknown to both the driver and myself, thieves stole my luggage right out of the boot." His hands flew up in exclamation. "I had nothing to give the chairman of the board—Dexter, I believe his name was. And since I had only glanced at the documents, I was in no position to negotiate. I begged him to give us another chance. In the end, I went home empty-handed. Parramatta Textiles went with another firm. Subsequently, I was thrown out on my ear."

"Why I just had my twenty-seven birthday," said Rolla. "How absurd, and dare I say, unfair. Surely your father came around after cooling off?"

"One would think so, but no. My father was not the sort of man to retract a decision. So let this be a lesson to you. Keep your valuables close at hand, said Roy with a glister in his eye. They're those out to do no good."

"I should say so," said Rolla, taking a sip of sherry and patting the deed in his breast pocket as he imagined a similar fate for himself.

Roy rested back. "Where may I ask is your final destination?"

Rolla was careful not to boast after such a heart-wrenching story, "I'm traveling to Spokane Falls to work for the city."

"You don't say?" said Roy, his eyes widening.

"I plan on building a homestead on a piece of land my father helped me purchase. I carry the papers with me now."

"Bully for you," said Roy, lifting his glass and toasting Rolla's good fortune. His pleased expression changed ever so slightly to a scheming glance. "So you're going to settle the Wild West by your own two hands. This nation needs more men like you, but don't expect too much of little Spokane. Settlements out west are mostly unsophisticated, and conditions are, shall we say, common."

Rolla squirmed, imagining Spokane as a dust bowl. "How about yourself? What venture employs you?"

"I'm afraid my purpose is not so grand. I am on my way to visit my ailing mother in Sand Point, Idaho. I hope to get there before she passes."

"How dreadful! Godspeed to you, sir," said Rolla, his face flush with sincerity.

Roy looked away and sniffled. Roy's web of unfortunate mishaps and life consequences had snared Rolla by the heartstrings. The first step of Roy's plan was in place—the critical sympathy bone well within Rolla's mouth—his next caper on track.

****

Like most of the depots he'd seen on the East Coast, Philadelphia's Broad Street Station was massive brick buildings covering several acres with tall towers. The rails fanned out in all directions as far as one could see. Free government money and an open country offered boundless opportunities to enterprising men emboldened to connect the nation from coast to coast. A great urgency had ballooned across the nation to distribute commerce by railcar: grain, silver and gold, beef, and timber. There was a great push in the American psyche to seize lands and resources away before the British and Europeans cherry-picked the best opportunities.

Once they pulled out of Philadelphia, the thought of sitting through another slow march across the industrial area, where coal dust clouded the air and people lived in squalor, was unbearable. Rolla moved forward in his chair and hailed the waiter. "If you'll excuse me, Mr. Thursdell, I'm going to retreat to my compartment to catch up on some reading."

Roy got to his feet, "I completely understand." He grasped the chair as he stood to disguise his inebriation. He twisted his thin mustache and clicked his heels, "A pleasure to meet you. Shall we catch up later?"

"The pleasure would be mine," said Rolla, paying for the meal and pausing to gaze out the window as the train headed into the waning westward sunlight.

****

By the time the train was twenty minutes from Chicago, it was past lunchtime the next day. They had been traveling for forty-two hours, and boredom had set in. Being a voracious reader, Rolla discovered he had not packed adequate reading material. He had picked up a two-day-old newspaper section and begun scanning it when Roy strolled up the aisle in the same plaid suit he had worn yesterday.

"Mr. Jones, I trust you slept well?"

"Mostly," muttered Rolla, "My compartment is rather restrictive."

"Indeed," said Roy, looking away so Rolla could not see him roll his eyes as he pulled at his stiff neck. The result of sleeping in a chair in third-class, where he was ticketed. Roy put aside his irritation and slid next to him in the observation car. Leaning back and twisting his neck from side to side, he said, "You know we change trains in Chicago and have a lengthy layover?"

"Yes, I planned to wander around a bit. Care to join me?" said Rolla.

"I know the city well and can act as your tour guide. So tell me, what interests a young man such as yourself?" said Roy.

"Anything regarding architecture, industry, and a book store would be wonderful," said Rolla.

"I think I know a few places that may satisfy your predilections," said Roy.

It was a quarter past four when they disembarked. Enthusiastically stepping off the train on a late September afternoon Rolla followed Roy with gusto.

"We must be back before eight, or we'll miss the train," Rolla said.

"Don't worry, we'll be back in plenty of time," said Roy, preparing to launch into his rehearsed tour guide persona. "When in Chicago, one must start by visiting Lake Michigan; it is, after all, why they call it the W*indy City*. The wind whips off the water streaking through the streets like a tornado blowing hats and lifting skirts. Some say it the city's embrace of visitors and locals alike."

"A rather romantic notion, no doubt," smiled Rolla.

"Indeed. More often than not, the wind is bone penetrating."

"May I ask, how many times have you traveled across this great country of ours?" asked Rolla.

"Oh, my word, more times than I can count," said Roy.

Rolla nodded knowingly.

"The last seventy-five miles had to be taken by wagon. Still, between my mother and my professional demands, I am on the road continually." The breeze whipped through the trees ahead. “Here it comes. Hold on to your hat," said Roy, just as a gale streaked between them. Roy kept talking." My poor wife has had to learn to get along without me, dear woman that she is. The children consume most of her time." Roy stuck his hands in his trouser pockets and rounded his shoulders, "I doubt she thinks of me more than once a week."

Rolla's face dropped as he felt the hardships this poor man endures. Once they reached the stone wall separating the shoreline from the promenade, Rolla gazed upon Lake Michigan in earnest admiration. It was immense. He could discern no difference between its vastness and the Atlantic Ocean. It was an expansive body of water the color of faded work jeans woven with threads of silver. The wind blew again, pulling their clothes into funnels that whistled lowly up their pant legs and arm sleeves.

"Chicago is the place where many come to see the future in all its advancing splendor since the Great Chicago Fire of 1871. It killed more than three hundred people, you know, and consumed over three miles of homes and businesses. One hundred thousand people were left homeless."

"All because of a cow?" Rolla smirked wittingly.

Roy chuckled, "A myth, dear boy, merely a folktale."

They held tight to their hats as another mighty gale from behind lifted their knees.

Rolla wanted to know more. "The conditions must have been right for a fire to spread so fast."

"Oh, yes, a long hot, and windy summer had primed the pump. Wooden construction— including sidewalks prevalent in those days—fed the fire. Afterward, the city underwent unbelievable reconstruction and grew from its base of 300,000 people to over a half a million."

"You don't say," said Rolla, his neck set back, his eyes wide.

“Indeed, consequently, the rebuilding effort became the birthplace of great innovative architecture. Now, of all American cities, Chicago is perhaps the most vivid example of the Gilded Age. An epithet coined by Mark Twain, you know?" Roy patted Rolla on the shoulder in a fatherly manner. "Maybe you'd care to see the Home Insurance Building? It's the first of its kind to use a steel skeleton instead of cast iron and stone construction. When it is complete, it will stand ten stories high."

"Please, lead the way," said Rolla, following cheerfully.

Roy cocked his head in accord. "The Chicago Water Tower is also worth seeing. It is one of the few surviving buildings from the fire."

The two of them matched each other step for step while heading up the brushed concrete sidewalks. When they reached Jackson and Quincy Streets, a fellow wearing a stovepipe hat, red satin shirt, and opera tails handed them a flyer.

"I've seen this show. Quite a spectacle and the food is wholly good."

Rolla caught his expression and carefully looked over the handbill: a drawing of a dancehall girl in one corner and a food critic's review of the menu in the other. "If you're sure it's worthwhile," said Rolla. A glint of doubt telegraphed across his face.

"I'm sure. And if you enjoy this show, I have another venue you're sure to worship," winked Roy.

"Aren't I the fortunate one to have a guide who knows the town so well?" said Rolla.

Roy raised his brows and grinned thinly as he stirred Rolla in the direction of the dancehall.

"Before we head in the direction, I have heard there is a Brentano's book store in Chicago. I really must pick up some additional reading material," said Rolla.

"I am not aware of such a store, but you could ask at the drug store on the corner up," pointed Roy.

Rolla smiled and dashed up to the drug store. Once inside, the clerk told him Brentano's, the New York Bookseller, would not open until next year but that they had a nice selection of popular books he could look through. Though the choice was limited, Rolla found two books with good reviews, The Prince and the Pauper by Mark Twain and Portrait of a Lady by Henry James. Now satisfied he had found good stories to keep him occupied, he headed toward the restaurant with a spring in his step.

When they arrived, they found that the man in the street had staged himself at the entrance and exhibited a toothy smile. "Glad you could make it, boys. You won't be disappointed."

They entered a dark corridor, where another man wearing a waiter's apron escorted them to a table. Rolla looked about and noticed all of the dinner guests were men, not a woman in sight. "Is this a proper club?"

Roy roared with laughter. "Let it be a surprise."

Rolla picked up the menu and wearily scanned the room, pushing aside his concerns.

The same waiter from the corridor stopped by the table to collect their food order. Roy leaned over, patted Rolla's hand with a knowing look, and said, "We'll have two New York steaks cooked rare, a baked potato, sautéed mushrooms in butter and wine, and a bottle of Bordeaux." He then opened his cloth napkin and scrubbed his front teeth without a trace of inappropriateness.

Although appalled by his table manners, Rolla was somewhat amused by his audacity. He nodded in agreement, then wondered who would be paying for this rather extravagant experience. Rolla had vowed to use his money with the most outstanding frugality. Asking his father for more money was not a scenario he cared to visit. Yet, he couldn't help from being suspicious.

Halfway through their meal, the red velvet stage curtain parted. A man as round as a jack-o'-lantern sauntered out, holding one side of the curtain as it lay draped over his shoulder like a vaudevillian cape. "Welcome to the Bull Street Theatre and Dinner Show. Tonight we have a captivating lineup of Chicago's most coquettish dancers who anxiously wait to tantalize your most secret fantasies." A clamoring of foot stomps, hand slapping, and whistles burst forth.

Rolla glanced over at Roy, who was grinning from ear to ear.

"Please, put your hands together for Miss Dalia and her Nymphs."

The man walked off, pulling the curtain open. The wooden stage floor revealed a tattered surface streaked with black heel marks. Two overhead lights out of the five, casted dark shadows mid-floor and at either flank. Nevertheless, the girls romped onto the floor, rustling their flounced petticoats knee-high. Their hair was bountiful, and parts of it hung over bare shoulders. Lips were painted bright red, and bosoms spilled over their Edwardian corsets like over-proofed dough. Rolla had seen a few dancehall shows before, but when they kicked their legs up, he caught a glimpse of their naked nether regions, and his jaw dropped.

Roy jabbed him in the ribs. "What did I tell you? Never seen anything like it before, have you?"

"Can't say I have," coughed Rolla, as pink-faced as anyone might be. After some time of impure staring, he returned to his meal, sneaking an eyeful every now and again. Meanwhile, Roy clapped and hollered when the dancers bent backward, skirts up over their heads. Finally, in an attempt to calm his schoolboy shyness, Rolla finished off the first bottle of wine himself.

"Ain't this the life!" shouted Roy. "Best show in town."

After the show, Rolla and Roy staggered out of the theatre more than a little tipsy. Rolla stuffed his thinner billfold securely into the breast pocket.

"Now, don't you worry about the money," said Roy. "I'll repay you just as soon as we return to the train. I was sure I had my wallet with me when we left."

"I am not worried," said Rolla, but of course, he was. It had begun to dawn on Rolla that Roy was not as he presented. He was likely down on his luck and skimming what he could from lonely widows and unsuspecting lads such as himself. Nevertheless, Rolla did not suspect him to be any real threat.

Down Van Buren Street and over two, Rolla, feeling rather gay, began singing one of his favorite tunes of the day: "*While strolling through the park one day. In the merry merry month of May,*"

Roy joined in, "*I was taken by surprise by a pair of roguish eyes.*" They stopped and crooned like two alley cats, their heads together in harmony, "*In a moment, my poor heart was stole away.*"

They stopped in front of an ornate Victorian with lights in the windows and shades drawn tight. A piano and a trumpet moaned inside the walls. Roy clapped his hands, bounded up the steps, and knocked three times.

The door opened. An older woman with deep facial lines, darkly lined eyes and strands of pearls emerged into the doorway. Roy turned and motioned Rolla over. "Ten dollars apiece boys, pay upfront," announced the madam with incredulity after recognizing Roy from previous visits.

Roy hurried up the steps and looked back. Rolla had not moved a muscle.

"Mr. Jones, the clock is ticking," said Roy.

Having just gotten engaged, Rolla had no intention of partaking in such lascivious behavior, pulled out his pocket watch, turned, and began running. "The train leaves in fifteen minutes."

Roy smacked his forehead and called out. "I know a shortcut. Follow me."

Rolla did not want to believe him, but realized he probably did know an alternate route, pivoted, and chased after Roy.

"Down the alley," commanded Roy.

"Better know where you're going," insisted Rolla, running shoulder to shoulder.

"This isn't my first close call," said Roy, his comb-over flapping in the wind like some sort of wing.

Rolla saw a shrewdness in his smile. "You're a scalawag, Mr. Thursdell."

"Now and again," admitted Roy. "Hurry, or we'll miss the train." They scaled a low fence and jumped onto the other side.

Rolla took out his watch again and glanced at it as he landed. "We've got four minutes." He sprinted ahead of Roy down a short set of steps, hurdled over the humming tracks, and hopped onto the platform just as the train moved forward. Rolla yelled, "Hurry, man."

Roy ran hard. Rolla was his chance at a fortune, and he wasn't going to let him escape. Rolla grabbed a handrail, leaped onto the train step, and turned back. Roy mashed his teeth, trying to catch up. The edge of the platform was on fast approach.

"Faster," yelled Rolla.

Suddenly, a muscle cramp seized Roy's leg, forcing him to limp, "I'm not going to make it."

Rolla inched further out onto the step, stretching further. The end of the deck was seconds away. Then, just as the train left the platform, Rolla commanded, "Jump for it."

Roy pushed off with his good leg and screamed, "God, save me!”

Chapter Five

The Chicago Northwestern train followed Lake Michigan into the Milwaukee station. Majestic white swans congregated along its shores in large numbers. By 1884, Milwaukee's population growth had facilitated the construction of the Chicago, Milwaukee, St. Paul, and Pacific Railroad's Everett Street Depot. The depot promised to bestow a grand entrance to Milwaukee when it was finished, unlike its current wood-sided station. It would feature a 140-foot-high clock tower and a combination of Gothic, Queen Anne, and Romanesque Revival styles of architecture. To the nineteenth century, lavish railway termini and hotels were what monasteries and cathedrals were to the thirteenth century. They became representative of the art, the people, and the spirit of the age.

After the Civil War, the northern railroad barons found themselves exceedingly wealthy and set about building shrines to themselves. The stations became a source of pride to the cities they adorned and the builders who made them. These massive edifices were confections of brick and stone, extravagantly ornamented, and studded with ells and clocks. Some of the great architects of the day had a hand in designing them: Louis Sullivan, H. H. Richardson, Stanford White, and the highly influential D. H. Burnham. The railroad development brought massive settlements and grew economies where none had existed before. Territories were admitted as state's under the U. S. Constitution. The railroad quite literally knitted the United States together as a republic.

Train stations in populated cities were palatial compositions. Yet, while the Northern Pacific railway had only opened a year ago, towns along the route had been anticipating its celebrated arrival for more than a decade and, as such, were in competition. Stations were built to reflect not the township's current economic health but its desired financial muscle to attract the many new settlers.

Unlike the industrial cities, the Wisconsin landscape tabled rolling green pastures, clusters of bushy trees no higher than a five-story building, and blankets of freshly harvested cornfields. Mounds of tree clusters, both gentle and charming, dotted the sloping countryside with feminine distinction. Other trees huddled beside modest rock formations, which reportedly contained significant amounts of iron ore. Single rows of blue spruce, guarded by an army of gangly locusts, scatterings of white birch, groves of northern red oaks, and smaller plantations of poplars and cottonwoods were standard. Patches of cattails and a consistent sprinkling of lupine filled the green terrain with blues and reddish browns. Wisconsin had become known for cheese production. As such, Rolla expected to see hundreds of grazing milk cows, the most viable alternative to wheat growing in those days, but he saw few. Even so, Dutch gambrel barn roofs with extra-wide midsections for drying and storage adorned by pointed tops and flared eaves were routine. All the while, Rolla wondered, would Spokane Falls be like this?

Tourists could never have imagined the horror lightning storms brought to a dark summer sky for all its ladylike beauty. One such night, hundreds of lighted sheets flashed across the sky, and electrified skewers pierced the earth's crust, making Rolla lean from the windows and cover his face. The clouds set off bombs so loud he plugged his ears and jumped in his skin. Rain drove down in such abundance the crew was on the lookout for flash floods. The cruel wind split and upended trees. Roofs were torn clean from supporting walls. A handful of tornados randomly touched down, terrorizing the countryside with a glaring disregard for life. Then like a torrential shower of artillery, hail pounced on the train—each thwack bruising its metal veneer and black painted skin.

As daylight arrived, the battered train crossed into Minnesota, making its way to the St. Paul Railway Station. Time zones had been established in November of '83. Crossing the Minnesota state line, the time changed from Eastern to Central time, an hour earlier. Rolla debarked and promptly boarded the Northern Pacific 1031 steam engine on platform 12.

Rolla was eager to see the mighty Mississippi. Mark Twain had written enthralling stories with *The Adventurous of Tom Sawyer*. Rolla had read the story of the boy missing school and getting into fights, and Tom's punishment: whitewashing a fence. Cleverly, he turns the punishment into play by tricking other boys into finishing his work. Another novel by Twain was due out next year revolving about the characters of Huckleberry Finn and a slave boy named Jim.

Witnessing the river provided him with ground-truthing and would make the written stories more illustrative. Rolla moved from his compartment to the dining car for a better look and to quench his welling thirst.

A seemingly unending stretch of brown water headed toward its southern destination. In most respects, it looked like any big river. Still, to its distinction, its headland source began way up north at Lake Itasca in northern Minnesota, not far from the Canadian border. It flowed over two thousand miles to the Gulf of Mexico and into the Atlantic Ocean. Thirty-two state tributaries fed this watercourse, including the Missouri and Yellowstone Rivers. It was a river, like all rivers, driven by currents, aware of the knowledge from whence it came and where it was headed. An understanding Rolla pined to know more of.

The gauntlet had been thrown down with the deaths of his three siblings when Rolla was only five. It had forever branded his heart to live his best life and subsequently launch this expedition. He was grown, educated, and ready in his bones. Primed in his heart. Fit in his body. Rolla in the secret recesses of his mind had transformed himself into a warrior. Each time he made headway—made a critical decision, built another brick, negotiated an agreement—adrenalin surged through him. The warrior in him felt its integrity and reverberated in its power. That self-assurance led him to believe that nothing could stop him if he worked hard and acted honorably.

When they crossed into North Dakota, Rolla began to understand the true meaning of the Great Plains. It was the flattest landscape he'd ever seen. Only an occasional nipple of a hill stood on the plains to interrupt its pancake appearance.

In Fargo, the air was crisp yet heavy like air off an ice block. The season was changing, and every animal sensed it. The station was modest in design, with six-foot double-hung windows on both sides: six windows on the top floor and six windows on the bottom floor. The same pattern existed for the station's front and back but with two fewer windows: no towers, no giant clocks, just a pitched roof, modest gable arches, and brick construction. The metamorphosis from East to West Coast architecture painted a vivid portrait of a changing nation.

When they trained over the great Missouri River between Bismarck and Mandan, the river was tame. Between Bismarck and Dickinson, more featureless countryside perfect for growing copious amounts of wheat, tobacco, and cotton whizzed past the windows. Rolla found it hard to stay awake during these parts until a few miles from Dickinson, a herd of grazing buffalo was seen up ahead on the tracks. These excessively disproportioned animals, with thick upper bodies, narrow hindquarters, and stocky half-moon horns, caused one to wonder why didn't they topple over.

The bison seemed oblivious to the approaching steel locomotive baring its wooden grates like teeth of a baboon or of its billows of spouting steam shooting above. The train slowed to a stop.

Once, hundreds of thousands of buffalos had fed on the abundant plains grass. Their thick coats and fatty, sweet meat became so desirable they were butchered to near extinction by white men. Less than six hundred were alive by 1884. The engineer banged the bell rope from side to side while the crew yelled at the animals to move along. But, the buffalo didn't seem to hear or care. Several pregnant females lay down on the tracks to rest.

The crew, a few cowboys, and Rolla climbed down from the train. The bulls did not cower. Instead, they lined up shoulder to shoulder; massive heads and shiny black snouts snorted and grunted. Their tongues slid up and drew off their constant snout dribble. Hooves scratched the ground in hostile retaliation. Several men hollered; others picked up rocks and pitched them. The buffalo did not flinch. Rolla found a log, waved it over his head, and roared like a grizzly, a trick his father taught him when frightening off animals bigger than himself. Still, the bulls did not back down. With their horns lowered and hooves squared, the buffalo readied themselves. A moment sat suspended as each man, and each beast stared its opposition down. No one knew if buffalo's bluffed. Suddenly the alpha signaled with a snort, and the bulls bunted forward. The men scrambled, crawling over each other to get back onto the train. The exasperated chief engineer got out his gun and pulled one off into the air. That did the trick.

When Rolla made it back to his seat, Roy stopped by. "Buffalo may be dumb, but bullets are brilliant."

Rolla nodded and chuckled pink faced.

At the western end of North Dakota, just outside of Dickinson not far from the Montana border, the landscape changed from impossibly monotonous to painted canyons. Scads of deer and antelope played on the hills while a swarm of twenty-five thousand cattle covered the grasslands like locust.

Nomadic groups of Indians camped in circle or horseshoe formations between Miles City and Billings. The tipis, covered in buffalo skins and painted with victorious tribal events, colonized the vista. Children played in the center while men rode on horseback guarding the perimeter. A family of badgers made a beeline through the tall grass, away from passing trains and men on horseback. The Indian's route followed the Yellowstone River that flowed from Glendive to Livingston, providing abundant freshwater and fish while they moved west to hunt buffalo and bear.

Rolla set down his book to take in the transformed landscape. He could not have imagined that many cows even existed. Their obvious need for water had him pinning for a cold glass of water. Still, he wondered: would Spokane Falls be like this?

He walked into the sitting room. The narrow car's left side was wholly occupied with white passengers. The other side was nearly vacant except for one Indian man sitting by himself. Without a second thought, Rolla sat down across from the man. His hair ran past his elbows in straight locks; his animal skin shirt had intricate beadwork. Not long after his arrival, a waiter approached.

"What can I get for you today?" said the waiter.

Rolla wasn't sure who he was speaking to, the Indian man or himself. The waiter pointed his order book at Rolla, who gestured to the Indian man. "Name's Rolla. Would you care for something to drink?"

The impassive-faced Indian turned, "Hau, me, Hecote Holt. I'll have a beer."

"And I'll have coffee," said Rolla.

The waiter left with a dubious expression. The two men sat without speaking until Rolla could no longer contain his curiosity. "Do you ride the train often?"

"No."

The waiter returned with their drinks and set them down.

Hecote picked up the glass and drank the entire beer in one go.

A few minutes went past, "How was your beer?"

"Good," motioned the Indian.

Rolla nodded, wishing he knew how to better talk to him. "Where are you headed?"

"My people are of Coeur d'Alene."

"I'm going to Spokane Falls."

Hecote hummed.

"We just crossed into Mountain Time and lost another hour," said Rolla. "Isn't that something?" He hoped that would spark a conversation, but it didn't. Instead, they sat together for the next hour in silence.

When the train stopped in Billings, Roy invited Rolla to stroll down Main Street to search for a dress and book shop. There wasn't a great deal of time, just long enough to stretch their legs and buy a gift or two.

"Do you know how many tribes occupy the region?" said Rolla, fitting his Boller hat snugly upon his head against the increasing chill.

Roy squinted down the street, "I think they are primarily Cheyenne, Crow, and Blackfoot tribes in this area."

"You don't say," said Rolla wondering about the differences.

"Ah, here we go," said Roy, opening the door and stepping into Miss Lily's Dress and Variety Shop. "Hello, name's Roy Thursdell. This here's Rolla Jones, we're hunting for gifts for our wives or, in his case, wife-to-be."

A middle-aged woman in her thirties with ringlets and a woolen neck wrap came out from behind the counter.

"Well, I'm sure we can find something they'd love," said the store Ms. Lily. "How about some perfumed stationery?"

Roy held his index finger to his nose and glanced around. "I was thinking about a neck scarf."

"Certainly," said the Ms. Lily, pointing. "Right this way."

Roy and Ms. Lily sauntered off while Rolla investigated a spinning rack of postcards at two cents apiece. Rolla filed through the cards and picked out one that showed the flat landscape he's been eyeing for days. It was a bleak and uninviting photograph. Sadie would find this most distressing. Another one was of a saloon scene with a crowd of men leaning against an ornate bar drinking whiskey with several painted ladies. Rolla chuckled, knowing this was a good card for Roy. He glanced over at Roy, who used the clerk to model several scarves. He spoke in a whisper. She blushed and giggled. Rolla pivoted away, remembering the fiasco in Chicago. Another card pictured a mass cattle drive. Mr. Wither's might find this interesting. There were several hand drawn pictures of Indians riding bareback that were quite artistic. Finally, a family of six standing beside a country cottage with their horse. Not a smile among them but the card presented the kind of image he thought would sit well with Sadie.

Stepping out of the shop, Miss Lily held the door and waved goodbye with a lace handkerchief playfully. I held a small paper bag of post cards. Roy decided not to buy anything. A group of cowboys on horseback took notice. Roy and Rolla proceeded down the wooden sidewalk, not giving them a second thought.

The cowboys followed with piqued curiosity. Clip-clop, clip-clop. A horsetail swished flies away. Clip-clop, clip-clop. Another horse shook its head, rattling its bridle and ill-fitting bit. Clip-clop, clip-clop. The cowboy nearest to the sidewalk wore a mud-brown shirt and had two missing front teeth. He spit a brown mess onto the ground. "Who do we have here?" he said.

Roy glanced back and whispered, "This could be trouble."

Rolla threw a sideways glance at the cowboys. Wide salt stains marked their straw hatbands, bandanas hung loosely under their scruffy beards, and flies circled in interest. "Perhaps," muttered Rolla.

"Where you boys headed?" asked the shorter man in the middle with a gallon-sized hat, its crown comically tall.

"Train station," said Rolla, politely tipping his hat.

"Where you from?" repeated the middle one.

"Bristol, New York," said Rolla.

"You're a long way out," said the brown-shirted cowboy, winking at his partners.

Roy rolled his eyes, grabbed at Rolla's sleeve, and tugged him forward.

Rolla pulled back. "Take it easy."

The cowboy furthest away lifted his concealed arm over his head and let sail a looped rope. The rope encircled Rolla's shoulders and cinched him up tightly in nothing flat.

Rolla dropped the postcards and grabbed the rope to brace himself. "We're not here to cause trouble."

"I saw the way you looked at Miss Lily," said the brown-shirted one with a smile that revealed yellow tobacco-stained teeth. "She's a married woman."

A man with silver spurs walked out on the opposite side of the street, the spurs clinking each time a heel struck ground. He took a wide stance and laid one hand on his holstered pistol. "Dale, I'm warning you—if you make trouble, I'll tell your daddy what kind of fool you are."

Dale pushed back his hat and raised one eyebrow high. "We're just getting to know each other."

"Fun's over, let 'em be," said the silver-spurred man who Roy and Rolla assumed was the sheriff.

Rolla stepped back.

Dale laughed. "Look at him wriggle, like a calf crying for his momma."

"Dale," said the sheriff, "you want to spend the night in jail?"

Dale starred blankly ahead and sighed. "Can't have any fun anymore." Swinging a leg over the saddle, he slid off his horse. Dale strutted over and pulled off the rope. When free, Rolla shoved Dale back two steps. Dale pushed Rolla back. Rolla and Dale broke into an all-out shoving contest. The two were well matched. They jostled and grunted against the other for a spell, but no matter how hard either tried, neither could throw the other off.

Dale stepped back huffing, wiped his brow with his sleeve and smiled." You outta buy me a beer,"

An unconvinced expression dashed across Rolla's face. "Why should I buy you a beer?"

"Give me one reason not to?" said Dale, grinning wide.

Rolla thought about it and couldn't come up with a good reason, "You're on, but only one."

Rolla and the boys walked off, revisiting the pushing game's hilarity as if they had once been high school chums. Again, Rolla wondered, is this what Spokane Falls would be like?

Traversing east to west in this virgin country revealed a nation's clumsy effort toward progress. Rolla hoped his crossing would follow a less clumsy path in the direction of his dreams and liberation. Where this road ultimately ended, no one could say for sure. Still, the journey, like water's innate drive forward, led his mind into unchartered places of adventure.

****

The train whipped through Butte Montana without slowing down and revealed the start of the Continental Divide. Its ridge was the boundary that separates the continent's river systems. In America, all rivers on the east side of it, including the Mississippi and Yellowstone Rivers, flow into the Atlantic Ocean. All the rivers on the west side of it flow into the Pacific Ocean. Waters flow into the oceans without filling them: waters flow from it without ever draining them. Fresh rivers and streams mysteriously drive toward saline waters to be repurposed just as rain and fish swim upstream to spawn and die. The newly hatched float downstream on both sides of the divide until once again it's time to return.

****

The last stop in Montana was Missoula. A spectacular landscape. A sky so vast you could see for miles in any direction. The beauty of it made it seem like Missoula's opportunities were better than any other.

It had steep sloping mountains with conifers climbing up it like hairs on the back of a neck. There was a deep valley floor where three rivers moved through the Missoula cleavage: the Blackfoot, the Bitterroot, and the Clark Fork, all en route to the Pacific.

Rolla set out to discover Missoula on his own. As he hiked along a foot trail, he noticed the trees were bushy, like in Michigan, Wisconsin, and Minnesota. But Missoula's trees towered over them at one hundred and fifty feet. Grasshoppers peppered the road, and monarch mobs flitted from flower to milkweed, enjoying the few weeks of life granted them. He walked several miles, appreciating the exercise after sitting for many days. As the afternoon light began to wane and dusk blanketed the mountain's shoulders, Rolla came upon a bar with music and dancing. Crickets chattering on the porch shattered when he walked up the stairs. Rolla pushed through the swinging doors and strolled up to the bar. A minute later, he was knocking back a cold beer.

A saloon girl no taller than his sister cozied up, "Howdy. Want to dance? Only a nickel?"

Before he could answer, two cowboys at the other end of the bar started yapping loud enough for everyone to hear. "What kind of a job does a man dress like that for?" said the boyish-faced man with muscular arms who was pulling off strips of pemmican and stuffing them in his mouth.

The other cowboy, awkward and lanky, laughed through his overgrown mustache. "Bet he's one of those fancy city boys who couldn't ride a horse if his life depended on it."

The bartender, bald on top with long stringy hair on the sides, stood polishing a whiskey glass. "Pay them no mind. They're drunk," he said with a smirk on his face.

"I can ride any horse you got," said Rolla.

"Oh yeah?" said the lanky one. "You think you can ride Dirty Boy Diggins?"

Rolla swallowed the beer in his mouth. "As long as he's broke, not lame or swayback."

"Well, why don't we just see what you can do with D.B. Diggins," said the boyish-faced cowboy.

"Maybe some other time," said Rolla.

"You afraid?" challenged the lanky one.

"Nope, don't have the time."

"You know your handle is a bit long. I think you need a little trimming. Smith, over there's a damn fine barber. He could get you fixed up in a jiffy," said the lanky one.

Rolla waved a hand, indicating no.

The boy-faced cowboy or "arms" as Rolla had decided to nickname him, came around the corner of the bar." Where you headed, pretty boy?"

"Spokane, Washington," said Rolla, stepping back from the bar.

"You don't say. I heard some of them boys are a little light in the drawers. You one of them?" said Arms.

Rolla finished his beer and moved with calculated coolness." I'll be on my way."

"You one of them," shouted Lanky.

Rolla turned back and dropped his arms. "Not that it's any of your business but I am engaged to be married this spring. Now, if you'll excuse me."

"Maybe I don't believe you," said Arms.

"Makes no difference to me," said Rolla.

"Quit your ribbing and let him be," said the bartender.

Rolla made his way to the doorway. Arms and Lanky, unwilling to drop their intimidation, rushed him. Lanky grabbed a shoulder, spun him around, and pinned Rolla's arms behind him. Arms slugged him twice in the gut. Rolla doubled over. Arms, powerfully strong, left him gasping for air. Lanky released his grip, sure he was done for, but Rolla rose with an uppercut to Arm's jaw, forcing him to bite his tongue and spit blood. Rolla threw his head back, butting into Lanky as hard as he could, bloodying his nose and loosening a tooth. Lanky stumbled back, holding his mouth, and slammed into an empty chair. Arms came at Rolla again. Rolla, knowing he was no match for him, planted a foot between his legs, not a gentlemanly tactic but sometimes necessary in dire situations. Arms keeled over. Rolla scooted out of the saloon.

On the other side of the door waited Hecote, the Indian he had talked to on the train, "Follow me."

Rolla was startled but followed without hesitation. Hecote ran soundlessly with his arms hanging loose. His moccasined feet glided over the ground without so much as a patter. Rolla was awed. Down a dark alley, over a hedge, and around a wagon, they took cover.

“They will come to the other side," whispered Hecote, pointing. "We'll double back. Who taught you to fight?"

"Middleweight champion in college," said Rolla guardedly.

"Good skill out here," said Hecote.

Rolla turned to him." Why are you helping me?"

Hecote looked at Rolla with dignified confidence. "You treated me as a friend."

Rolla paused and acknowledged his words with a tip of his head. "Ready when you are."

Hecote's whispered, "We run now."

Hecote and Rolla made it back to the train undetected with ten minutes to spare before departure. On the landing, Rolla extended his hand for a shake. Hecote balled his hands into fists, crossed his wrists, and thumped his chest. Rolla understood it to be a sign of friendship and returned the gesture. Both had made a friend that day. The gap in their culture was of little consequence, and making friends across lines made them proud.

Rolla made his way up the dark train corridor. Most of the travelers had settled down for the night. As he approached his designated sleeping compartment, the legs of a man in pajamas stood behind the half curtain, rifling through Rolla's belongings. Rolla stopped and listened until he recognized the pajamaed man's slippers. It was none other than Roy. He yanked the curtain aside.

Roy nearly screamed at the fright of getting caught and immediately started to justify his actions. "This is not how it seems," mewled Roy.

Rolla glanced down and saw the deed to his property in Roy's robe pocket, "You're stealing from me?"

"Oh no, not I. I was merely,"... said Roy, putting his hands together in a praying position.

"All that we've shared, now this. I knew you were a hobo, but I didn't take you for a thief."

"Please don't hit me. I am desperate," pleaded Roy." You don't have any idea what it's been like for me."

Rolla plucked the deed from his pocket and grabbed him by the neck. "I don't believe a word you say."

"Please, I beg of you. I'll never bother you again. You have my word," said Roy.

"I am not going to hurt you. On the contrary, I am going to turn you into the authorities," insisted Rolla.

Roy's throat clenched. "You're right. I am nothing more than a weasel. A broken sniveling weasel. I am ashamed of myself. Go ahead, do what you must." Roy dropped his head and whimpered, a dishonest gaze cast to the floor.

"Who else have you stolen from?" said Rolla.

"Oh, please don't ask such a thing," said Roy.

"I'll tell you what—if you return everything you've stolen with a letter of apology, I will not turn you in."

“But some items have already been traded. I can't return what I no longer have."

"Return everything you still possess," demanded Rolla.

Roy winced and mewled again. "All right, that's the right thing to do. I shall gather them up and begin composing tomorrow at breakfast," said Roy.

"No, you will bring me everything you've stolen, write out your letters of apology, and return the items this very night. If you do not, I shall turn you over this minute. It's your choice."

"But it's nearly ten," whined Roy.

Rolla pulled out his pocket watch, which contained his only family photo, and flipped it open. It was a watch Roy had secretly eyed many times before, "This offer ends in one minute— sixty... fifty-nine...fifty-eight...fifty-seven.”

"All right, all right, I'll run, get my valise, and return immediately," promised Roy.

"Fifty-six...fifty-five...fifty-four," said Rolla.

"I'm going, I'm going," said Roy, scampering down the shadowed passageway, grumbling in dissension.

When Roy returned, he unpacked his valise of eleven items. Three pocket watches, one ladies' ring with six semi-precious stones set in gold, a bundle of cash, one hand-carved smoking pipe, an embossed leather wallet, and three silver spoons from the kitchen.

"Not only are you a thief, but you're a petty one at that. My deed would have been quite the haul for you," said Rolla.

Roy remained chastened as he pulled out a handful of sheet paper with the railroad insignia.

"Write your first one to me, and read it back when you've finished."

Roy sighed like a punished schoolboy.

Rolla sat and watched Roy write. A few minutes later, Roy handed over the letter written in beautiful old English script:

Dear Mr. Jones, Please accept my sincere apology for taking what was not mine. You have treated me as a friend, and I have betrayed you. I have crossed so many, and I am ashamed. I vow to cease this disgraceful lifestyle and find honest work.

Roy Thursdell

"Keep writing," said Rolla, wedging the letter between the window glass and the frame.

When Roy finished writing all the letters, Rolla escorted him to each victims sleeping accommodations. He kept his distance so as not to be implicated but listened in. Nonetheless, most victims after being awakened fumbled about trying to understand what Roy was declaring. Two passengers had been up reading and were most incensed. Time would tell if his apologies would be enough to compensate his victims. Either way, Rolla's friendship with Roy Thursdell ended that night.

****

The Northern Pacific made its way, slow and steady, around a pile of mountains from Lookout Pass in the Rocky Mountains of Montana, the highest peak being more than 7, 300 feet. Into the Bitterroot Range, its highest peak over 11, 000 feet, and plummeted into the Coeur d'Alene and Sandpoint, Idaho Territory. The trees crowded together tighter than matches in a box and taller than any trees he'd seen before. Rolla was astonished as the train crossed the massive span of an 8, 400-foot wood trestle over Lake Pend Oreille. The last leg of the journey was close at hand; his excitement was no longer suppressible. With a tremble in his hand and less than an hour's ride left, Rolla would finally set eyes on the land of Spokane Falls.

"Nestled among the pine-crowned hills on the banks of the Spokane River
whose water power is the marvel of the West, at the western extremity of a picturesque valley, rises the young City of Spokane Falls"
—The Rainbow Seekers, A KXLY Publication

Chapter Six

Late September 1884

Rolla's heartbeat sped up as the train rounded the bend into Spokane. His eyes darted to and fro, grabbing images and comparing each to previously seen drawings. The city looked colorless in the drizzling rain and dumpling sky. The streets were narrow and covered in mud, manure, and urine. All manner of traffic—wagons, carriages, horses, and foot traffic—all shared the same rutty byways. Buildings were built at street level with little or no separation from the dirt. Some of the mud was more than a foot deep. If people weren't careful, the clay would suck the shoe from the foot. Some retail stores had false fronts to provide space for signage. Most did not. Many shops were unpainted square boxes with little or no adornment. Although it was more developed than some of the towns they trained through his first impression left him crestfallen. Sadie would despise this place. Hell, he wouldn't blame her if she refused to get off the train. He closed his eyes and prayed for a measure of his mother's stoicism. When faced with disappointment, his mother was fond of saying, "Find a new vantage point." Rolla wanted desperately to rejoice at the very sight of this muddy western town, but his joy was woefully absent.

Filing out of the cabin single file, Rolla found himself holding his breath, releasing it with force, and grabbing onto the next one. Stepping off the train onto the freshly swept platform, he drew in the scent of the land. To his surprise, it smelled fresh, as mountain air is known to be: crisp and filled with pine pitch, fresh-cut cedar, campfire smoke, and soil aromas of herb and spice. A small amount of hope moved in as a tightening in his throat. A hustle of people spun around him, mostly as a blur, others in sharp contrast: women in demure bonnets and men in wide-brimmed hats on the threshold of a new life. A slight grin lifted his mouth on one side.

The ornate street lights and scrolled benches that bedecked the newly constructed station of carved arches and brackets appeared to be a quirk compared to the rest of the town. As a bear might wait at the edge of town, pondering whether he should risk going forward or turning back before being spotted. He shook his arms loose and let go of his last captured breath. A single-window telegraph office stood on one side of the lap-sided depot. A sign outside said open, and a clerk in a green visor was hard at work within. He would take a moment to send a note to Sadie and his parents. Rolla noticed a slight tremble in his hand as he wrote.

Dear Father and Mother, I have arrived safely.

Time will tell if this is an adventurer's dream.

Yours truly, Rolla

To Sadie, he wrote:

Dearest Sadie arrived safely.
Spring can't get here soon enough.
With all my love, Rolla

He collected his bags and headed uptown for the Sprague Hotel, where he had secured a month's reservation. The streets were filled with deep puddles and decaying leaves. On his very first step into the street, he slipped into a pool of mud that covered his shoe. He stomped off what he could while managing to splatter a few liquid droplets back onto his wool trousers.

Wagons and buggies slogged past, flinging more bits of muck onto his hat and face. Blotches of chimney smoke hung low in the cool afternoon air like potato soup. The moist air had a definite chill. As he approached the middle of the street, an older couple slowed their wagon and stared at him as if they'd never seen anyone like him before.

Directly behind the couple, two men on horseback called out, "What's on your head?" His tailored suit, brown cashmere Boller hat, and trained mustache were apparently out of place in Spokane. He surmised that if these locals got off the train in New York, they would have felt out of place too. Proceeding with care through the street stew, he reached the other side where a wood sidewalks had been constructed. An older man with his feet propped up and a corncob pipe in his mouth tipped his hat, "Get off at the wrong stop?" More proof his appearance presented as odd as a modern bicycle. There were all sorts of people on the street: cowboys, Chinese merchants, miners, fur traders, shop keepers, and a sizable contingent of saloon girls. A drunkard down in the mud struggled to get to his feet. Rolla helped him to his feet. The man thanked and headed back into the saloon.

A painted lady with red hair and freckles called out. "Well, howdy stranger! Name's Lady Colleen. You new in town?"

He tipped his hat. "Ma'am."

She leaned forward, exposing her cleavage. "Welcome to our fair city." She batted her eyes and smiled. "You know where you can find me," said Lady Colleen pointing to the sign above that read Jake's Saloon.

"Yes, ma'am," his face flushed hotly as it had in Chicago.

Making his way up the sidewalk, he took stock of the many storefronts: the Charles McNab Drug Store, Louis Ziegler Hardware, J. J. Blaylock Shoes, a book and notion store, a candy and peanut shop, and the Poodle Dog restaurant. Most buildings typified the daguerreotypes he'd seen of the West over the years in books and newspapers. Simple structures by New York standards. Simple Victorian facades, arched trusses, and token ginger breading. Street-side, he passed a slew of ragtag hitching posts, horse troughs, livery stables, a land office, a fur trading post, and a doctor's office with laborers lined up outside. Spokane Falls was more developed than he'd first thought, but booming would not be how he would have described it.

When he came upon Stuart's General Store, he stepped in for a look-see. A little bell chimed as he entered. The store smelled like the back end of a mink, of lanolin and neats-foot oil jumbled together with cherry pipe tobacco.

A fastidious clerk with silver-dollar-shaped spectacles approached, "What can I do you for?" he said, pushing his spectacles up the bridge of his nose.

"Pemmican and directions, if you please."

The clerk looked down at Rolla's shoes, "You're new in town?"

"Just arrived from New York," said Rolla.

"Kindly go back and brush your shoes off in the scraper," said the clerk.

Rolla took stock of his once-polished shoes now coated in mud, winced, and dashed out the bell-chiming door. Three women dressed in everyday cotton dresses walked past, talking under their bonnets. People looked dowdy and spoke plainly. A pang for the abrasive New York accent came and went. Maybe James Withers was right after all. This decision could well be a mistake.

He returned to the general store counter as clean as possible given the crusty boot scraper outside the door.

The clerk, straightening a stack of ladies mittens, lowered his gaze again. "Will you be staying awhile?"

"I'm not sure yet," said Rolla without thinking.

"If you do, you're gonna need boots," said the clerk. "I have some in the back. By the way, name's Stuart. And you are?"

"Rolla Jones, I'm here to build the water system."

"You don't say," muttered Stuart, looking over Rolla's fine woolen suit. "Let me show you what I have."

The shelves were stocked floor to ceiling with boxes of boots, guns, and hats. By the time Rolla left the store, he had a pair of leather work gloves, a heavy woolen coat with elbow patches, a six-inch knife with a holster, and an odorous pair of mink-oiled boots. Moreover, he had replaced his felt Boller hat for a wide-brimmed hat. He walked to his hotel while scarfing down chucks of jerky without notice from those on the street.

The door to the Sprague Hotel sagged in the middle and required lifting to pry it open. The foyer was dim and the floor crackled like stale bread crust. A small bell sat at the front desk. He tapped it and waited. No one came. He tapped again. Still, no one came. Finally, when he struck it a third time, a thin blond woman, who looked like she'd just pulled on her clothes, stumbled out. Her eyes were gray, and her smooth face reflected loss.

"Pardon me, I must have fallen asleep," she said. "You need a room?"

Rolla set his bags down and smiled, "Reservation for Jones."

She shuffled through a few loose sheets of paper on the desk until she found the letter he had sent confirming the reservation.

"Here we are." She curtsied. "By the way, I'm Mrs. Sarah Franjic. I own the place."

Rolla tipped his hat. "Pleased to meet you, Rolla Jones."

She tilted her head sadly and placed a registration card before him. "Payment is required in advance."

"Six dollars a week as agreed?" said Rolla, handing her a twenty-dollar bill and four silver dollars.

She nodded with hungry eyes, snatched the money, handed over the key, and relished the feel of the cash in her hands. "You'll be in room nine, at the top of the stairs on the left. There's a bathroom in the back of the house," she said, pointing, "and a cookhouse through the double doors. Do you think you'll stay longer than a month?"

Rolla looked around the foyer and attempted to be positive, "That's the plan."

She tucked a strand of hair behind one ear, trying to look put together. "Let me know if you need anything else."

"Yes, ma'am," he said, catching a glimpse of suggestiveness in her tone.

The staircase creaked and popped as he made his way up. The railing wobbled. He opened the door and peered in: a single mattress on a spring platform, a couple of candles on a wooden desk, a bentwood chair. The oak wardrobe had a single drawer at its base, and an old shoe brush lay on the floor next to it. Set in the far corner were a chipped pitcher and washbasin, a hand towel, and a soap bar with cracks running through it.

Rolla set his bags down beside the armoire. In place of its handle, a bit of string hung from the hole where the knob would have been. He unfastened his suitcase buckles. The window nearest the bed was half-opened and looked over the street. An incoming waft of air smelled of machine oil, wood shavings, and manure. On the road, a stream of people and horses bustled through. New York felt as far away as China. One more piece of jerky from its cloth bag and out, he headed, leaving the armoire door ajar and his luggage unpacked.

His boots got muddy walking across the street, but it no longer concerned to him. He nearly walked past City Hall, mistaking it for a schoolhouse. He caught sight of a bulletin board posting events and council agendas: The topic of the day: saloon violence and alcohol consumption.

When he entered the hall, an older woman wearing a Margery blouse with a rounded collar, pleats and lace trim held a tickled expression. Her eyes sparkled and her nose scrunched up making her look like a pixie. Her nameplate said Mrs. Smithey.

"Is the meeting still in session?" asked Rolla.

"It is. Please sign in," said Mrs. Smithey.

Mrs. Smithey ushered Rolla into the chambers, tugged down on his sleeve so she could whisper in his ear. "The meeting is presided over by Mayor Fred Nicholls. On roll call, the councilmen present are Bender, Thomas, Krakenberg, Smith, and Follet, and Council Chair F. A. Rossiter. Absent is Councilman Franzen. Last week's minutes have been read and approved."

The hall's interior was a converted church with a hodgepodge of tables and chairs set at its flanks for bake sales or other such activities. Two clusters of pews occupied either side of the aisle in front of the half-circle of council tables. A craved-wood podium stood between the benches for those who wanted to address the council. Six gaslights, two on each sidewall and two positioned over the council table, would light the room.

Rolla sat back to observe the dynamics between those in attendance with the town meeting already underway. Getting a first-hand look at the mayor and council members in action seemed an intelligent first step. His impression of his correspondence with Mayor Nicholls led him to believe this was an educated, astute man.

Jeb Thomas, as it said on his nameplate, had the floor. "I have three formal complaints from respectable families." He held a stack of papers in one hand and set it on the table. "These families contend the cause of most of the West's poor reputation can be traced to alcohol. Furthermore, they concluded, shootouts, gambling, thievery, and vagrancy are all tied to drinking."

F. A. Rossiter snorted, "As it is in all cities ... around the country." His nostrils flared, accentuating a relatively flat proboscis.

Thomas leaned in and peered at Rossiter with a stern expression. "So, what, should we just surrender?"

Rossiter picked up a pencil and perched it over a sheet of paper. "Let me make a note of your solutions."

Thomas groaned. "Today's task is presenting issues."

"This is not going to be an easy fix," said Mayor Nicholls, a dignified man with neatly combed facial hair. "Most of the issues occur at night."

A rumble of voices sprung up among the townspeople in attendance.

Rossiter blurted, "I am of the opinion that women and children should be off the streets at night."

Two women booed. "Your solution is a curfew for women?" said one of the women, throwing one hand up in disgust.

"The problem is getting worse. A woman was defiled behind Jake's," said the other.

The mayor hit the gavel on the tabletop. "Thomas, find out what other cities are doing about this issue," said Nicholls.

The woman standing was of Sadie's age and ilk, "The Woman's Christian Temperance Union could be quite helpful. They deal with this issue across the whole country. It is a growing problem."

Rossiter shook his head. "Giving women a platform is not a good idea."

The woman was aghast and let it be known.

Rolla knew right then and there that Sadie and Rossiter would surely come to odds. Rossiter reminded him of his thermodynamics professor, an irascible possum. The only way to get good marks from a man like that was to go along with whatever he said. On the other hand, Thomas came off as even-keeled although quick to self-justification. Either way, this was a lively group.

The mayor stood. "I make a motion to form a committee to study the issue and devise a plan to combat the problem."

Thomas leaned forward in his chair. "I second the motion."

"All those in favor say yea," said Rossiter. "All those not in favor say nay. The yeas rang out above the nays.

"The yeas have it," announced Rossiter with an irritated expression.

The rift between Rossiter and Thomas was both comical and so small town.

"Those interested in joining the committee, raise your hands," said the mayor. "Thomas, please take down their names and provide a meeting schedule by next week. Will four weeks be enough time to put a plan together?"

Thomas opened his calendar and ran his finger down the page. "We'll do our best."

Mrs. Smithey reentered the hall and handed out copies of the ledger to the council and audience members. Standing stood erect she clasped her hands, and proclaimed, "Several new claims against the city were referred to the finance committee," she said. "The finance committee, chaired by Councilman Bender, reported upon the following bills."

A man in the back pews stood. "I was supposed to get paid last week but haven't received a nickel."

Mayor Nicholls turned to Councilman Bender. "See to it, if you please."

"I will," said Councilman Bender, a skinny man with an Adam's-apple that bumped up and down his throat like a float ball on a boat.

At half-past four, Mayor Nicholls adjourned the meeting. The townspeople shuffled out as Rolla made his way to the front.

"Excuse me, Mayor, I am Rolla Jones."

A vacant look came upon his the mayor face.

"Your new water superintendent," he added and held out his hand.

Mayor Nicholls's face brightened. "Mr. Jones, we've been expecting you. Good to meet you," said the mayor pumping his hand with zeal. "How was your passage?"

"Long, and quite illuminating," said Rolla.

Before he could continue, the mayor called over the councilmen. "Come meet Rolla Jones, our new water superintendent." The men surrounded him, shook hands, and slapped him on the back a few too many times, reminding him of a gathering of his father's generation.

Rossiter moved in. "We've been in dire need of someone with your skills. I hope you're ready to work."

"I am," said Rolla.

Rossiter nodded, "Good man. Come, let me show you a map of our city." He waited for the mayor to move in the same direction before following Rossiter to the wall where a four-foot-by-four-foot map hung.

"We're here," pointed Rossiter.

Rolla pulled out his reading glasses and moved in for a closer look. He had studied many maps of the area, but none as detailed as this one. "How large is the central business district?"

The mayor interjected, "We have thirty-two blocks under various stages of development."

"With residential development on three sides," added Thomas gleefully.

Rolla touched a spot on the map. "And this must be Crystal Island where the pump house should probably be built."

Rossiter looked at him with a surprised expression. "Correct. How did you know?"

"Stands to reason. The pump house needs to be where the river runs strongest," said Rolla.

Mayor Nicholls stuck a ruby-colored pipe in his mouth. "Boys, I think we got ourselves a ringer." The band of them chuckled and shook hands as proud fathers do. That felt good to Rolla.

"What do you say, fellas? Let's show Mr. Jones some Spokane hospitality," said the mayor. The men grinned widely behind their disobedient mustaches. The fashion trend had made its way out West, but the finer details of trimming and waxing seemed to evade them.

"A beer sounds mighty good," said Rolla.

The mayor headed for the door. "Follow me." Everyone filed in behind him except Rossiter, who walked shoulder to shoulder. Rolla watched the two of them squeeze through the door like some vaudeville act as neither would give leave to the other.

They walked into the saloon, a dusty wood-floored place with few gas lamps, and took over four empty tables. A rough-hewn bar made three feet thick, and ten feet long made from a slab tree sat against the back wall with whiskey bottles and beer on its shelves.

"Jones, have a seat," said Nicholls, pointing to the chair beside him at the table nearest the window.

Rossiter balked as he passed. "He could sit here if he chooses sitting one table over."

The competition between Nicholls and Rossiter seemed like poker players bidding for the pot. Rolla figured careful navigation would be necessary to work with the two of them. Rossiter wanted to be in charge, but Nicholls had the community's trust and the council.

As soon as Rolla sat down, the councilmen started firing questions, where he went to school, what his father did, and if he had a family of his own.

Rossiter leaned over the table past Thomas at Rolla. "What do you think of our town?"

"Well, I— ," said Rolla, feeling backed into a corner.

"First impression," said Rossiter wryly.

The men stopped and turned their attention to him.

He stammered. "I've only just arrived," he said, trying to sound convincing.

"Everything rather small compared to New York?" said Rossiter.

He needed a diplomatic answer. "Size isn't the only criteria, is it?" said Rolla smiling.

Thomas was the only one to get the double entendre.

Nicholls chimed in, "Where are you staying?"

Grateful for the diversion, he said, "I've checked into the Sprague Hotel for a month."

Thomas winced. "A bit lacking in the finer points, but you should find the accommodations acceptable."

"Watching your dollars, that's sensible," said the mayor.

The councilmen, who looked prosperous in their own right with gold-chained pocket-watches and silk shirts from China, nodded.

"Just make sure Miss Sarah has changed the sheets and towels," added Thomas. "I've heard she can be a bit forgetful."

Rossiter became empathetic. "One can't blame her. Her husband and child died of scarlet fever last winter. Left her to run the place on her own."

"It will be fine for a month," said Rolla. What he wanted to say was how Miss Sarah's situation saddened him. Clearly she was still in mourning.

Rossiter lighted a match. "Do I note a bit of disappointment in our town?" said Rossiter.

"Heavens no," said Rolla, wishing Rossiter would drop the subject. "It's been a long trip, and I haven't had a moment to appreciate my surroundings."

With a thin green cigar between his teeth and a flame at its tip, Rossiter added, "If you change your mind, let me know. I have a nephew who might be able to fill your shoes." He puffed on his cigar and smirked at Nicholls. "You remember, I've told you about him."

Rolla flinched as he realized Rossiter played under the table.

The mayor grunted and turned toward the bar. "Whiskey!"

Thomas, who had come to sit beside Rolla, leaned in. "Ignore him. He's just trying to goad you."

Rolla laughed, vowing not to let Rossiter catch him off guard. He had committed to this place and job. He'd be damned to give up without a fight. If he left, it would be on his terms.

The bartender put down a tray of shot glasses and mugs, two whiskey bottles, and three pitchers of beer. He pulled out the cork with his teeth and poured each glass full.

Mayor Nicholls raised his glass and called out, "A toast to our new water supervisor and running water."

The men in the bar raised their glasses and shouted endorsements. By the time they left, Rolla was seeing double. Thomas and one of the other councilmen walked Rolla to the door of his hotel. They staggered away, singing,' *Tis the last rose of summer left blooming alone*" —a favorite Irish jig.

Thomas called back. "See you bright and early Monday morning."

Rolla waved and tried to open the front door. He scanned the darkened streets and tried the door once more. It wasn't long before he discovered he was pulling instead of pushing. He crawled up the staircase humming another favorite, "*While Strolling through the Park One Day.*" Once inside his room, he landed on the bed, face down without checking the sheets.

"Love this river, stay by it, learn from it,"
—Herman Hesse, Siddhartha

Chapter Seven

Sunlight streamed in at an angle and spotlighted the floor before the armoire. Rolla rose with a churning stomach and a head that felt as if he'd run into a low-hanging branch. He dressed slowly and quietly with a mouth full of sour paste and gingerly made his way down to the hotel's cookhouse for a breakfast of eggs, fried cornbread, and pork back. It went down easy enough but threatened to come right back. He should have never agreed to six shots of whiskey. Drinking hard liquor was not a regular thing for him, and as such, he had little tolerance. After breakfast, feeling a bit steadier, he filled a canteen with water and walked to the nearest livery stable, talking down his rumbling stomach.

At the livery stable he heard a man shoveling and walked toward the sound. With a mess of hair spreading out from his hat like twisted wires, a man of twenty-nine was hard at work mucking out a stall. Rolla watched him work until the hand stood up, set the shovel against the wall, and turned. "Sorry I didn't see you there. Can I help you?"

Rolla's stomach gurgled loud enough for both of them to hear. "I'm looking to rent a horse for the day," he said, holding his stomach.

"Right, follow me," said the hand picking up the two brimming buckets of manure and clomping out of the stall. At the back was a group of sleepy nags huddled together. In New York, the stablehand would have fetched the horse on their own and brought it around.

"I've got some property to see a few miles out of town," said Rolla.

The stable hand dumped the buckets into a heap, removed a rag from his pocket, and wiped the back of his neck. "Gonna stay awhile?"

Rolla extended his hand. "Name's Rolla, Rolla Jones, I'm here to build a water system."

The stable hand tipped his hat. "You don't say? What happened to the Holley Water System? I thought they were going do it."

"Don't know the story," said Rolla.

"So you're gonna bring us running water. That'll be dandy," said the stablehand, "I look forward to the day I won't have to slog water from the tower."

"I didn't catch your name," said Rolla.

The stablehand turned to the horses. "Names Francis, Francis Clark. Any of these horses look good?"

Rolla pointed to a tan horse with a blaze on its forehead. "How about that one?"

"Naw, she threw a shoe," said Francis.

Rolla took another look at the languid horses. "Okay, how about two over?"

"You won't care for her. She's cranky and stubborn. Let me fix you up with the one in the back with her head down," said Francis. "She's old but reliable."

A belch escaped from both ends. "Excuse me," said Rolla. "Whatever you think."

Francis smiled and turned back toward the horses. "Okay, I'll saddle her up."

Rolla watched as Francis systematically brushed out the horse, cleaned its hooves, saddled and bridled the horse in less than five minutes. His movement was as streamlined as any he'd ever seen. "You're fast," said Rolla.

Francis tipped his hat up and smiled. "Done it a few times is all."

"I'll say," said Rolla.

Rolla and Francis shook before departing.

"Maybe I could buy you a beer sometime?" said Rolla.

Francis nodded, "Maybe so."

Rolla pressed his fist into his bloated stomach, took the reins, and began walking out.

"You know you can ride her out," said Francis.

"Got it," said Rolla, gritting his teeth as his body involuntarily broadcasted more outbreaks.

****

At the land office, Rolla met Jeremy Lavigne, a man in his thirties, a right, pleasant fellow who spoke with confidence. "It's fertile land out there. You won't be disappointed."

Rolla didn't know if he was trying to sell him or speak the truth. Either way, he was encouraged. Both Francis and Jeremy were of similar age.

Rolla walked toward the river, still burdened with a bruising headache and sour stomach. The dense sky began shedding clumps of wool. The sketches he'd seen of the river were quite spectacular. Still, he could neither hear nor see it even from this close. Were the pictures made more impressive to get saps like him to move out west? How could a river of its reported size be this inconspicuous? Rolla primed himself for another letdown and doubted Sadie would stomach this benighted little town. Neither Sadie nor Rolla were accustomed to anything this rural. Aside from the reception he got from the council, Spokane Falls was turning out to be lackluster. Yet, returning to New York as a quitter was not an option he would consider.

The last hundred feet sloped sharply as the emerald river came into view. Rolla held his breath. The rushing water had cut a deep passage through the canyon—a half-mile wide, as strong as a flash flood, yet as slippery as a serpent over smoothed boulders. Its fast-moving water was capable of sucking down anything passing overhead. Anyone in a boat crazy enough to venture down this river would surely be in pieces before calm waters prevailed.

A drop of drool leaked from his mouth. The drenching, rapid river made him frightfully thirsty. Yet with all its fury, it possessed a quietness like no other river he had encountered—a murmuring like the shushing of a baby, a secret beckoning if one listened well. Its voice sank in—quieting some of his worries—it was the river that held the promise he sought.

Jeremy at the land office had given him detailed instructions on locating the 160 acres he had purchased, sight unseen. Said there were a handful of farms along the northern wagon road. Samuel Clifton's farm was closest to the road just west of his property.

Reaching the Post Street Bridge and determined to view the property that day, he cast his sour stomach aside and mounted the rented horse. The bridge wobbled high as a stilt walker above the canyon river. It creaked, swayed to the right, and shuddered in the wind. It didn't take more than two steps before his stomach forced

Rolla to dismount. He leaned over the rail, panting, trying to calm his stomach and clear his bulging brain.

Once on the other side, Rolla left his breakfast in a bush.

He made his way eastward. A few distant farms although hidden among tall trees revealed themselves with weathervanes atop pitched roofs. A trail of chimney smoke lay floating softly on the air current. The landscape stirred him as an invisible whisk tossed needles and leaves about. The pulse of his breath and the clop of the horse's hooves marched in his ears. If Jeremy was correct, it would take another twenty-five minutes to reach the acreage.

The territory was populated with ponderosa pine, towering Douglas fir, and western larch trees. Various leafy trees nestled in clusters on both sides of the road— mountain ash, paper birch, and quaking aspen, all dressed in fall hues. The trees smelled of yams and brown sugar. Bunchgrass scattered about like pepper on eggs; browning spears overtook the few remaining green ones. A few unwed sage bushes mussed the sloping landscape, casting a sharp sting in the air. The clouds began disrobing a small corner of the ice-blue sky looking southwest.

He retrieved his father's pocket watch from his vest, and with a flick of his wrist, flipped it open. A small photograph captured the seven of them: Mother, Father, Renaldo, Clara, Cora, Alice, and Rolla. The picture was fuzzy, but their faces were clear to him. Alice and Rolla were now the only surviving children. He hated that truth.

He spotted what seemed to be the last farmhouse closest to the road and decided this could be the Clifton farm. Trotting up the rocky path on the old mare, two hounds ran up barking and wagging their tails. One was a blue tick, the other a hound with a gray muzzle. He'd get a dog one day. A man in overalls and seemingly in his forties stepped out of the house, his hands in his pockets.

"Who goes there?" called the man when Rolla's rented horse began snorting and shaking her head and shortly cropped mane into a rattling barrage of ticks and clanks from bridle to rein.

Rolla was forced to wait for the horse to finish its jouncing. "Are you Samuel Clifton?"

"Who wants to know?" replied the farmer.

"Name's Jones. I've bought the property next to yours. At the land office, Jeremy said I should stop in and introduce myself."

Clifton said, "Do I hear an East Coast accent?"

"Yes, sir," said Rolla.

"Go to one of those fancy schools out there, did you?" said Clifton.

Rolla shifted in the saddle. "I completed my studies in engineering."

Clifton stepped to the edge of his porch and doffed his hat. Rolla got down from his rented horse and extended his hand. Clifton's knuckles were as big as flower bulbs. The skin on the back of his hand was like tanned leather, a fate Rolla figured he would one day have to welcome. A doughy woman carrying a laundry basket stacked full of folded clothes followed by two teenage boys came from around the back. Her chestnut hair sat on her head like a round basket. Her eyes were kind, but she held her mouth in a most unfriendly manner.

"This here's our new neighbor," announced Clifton to his Mrs. and teenagers.

The boys tipped their hats.

The Mrs. waved.

"What can I do you for?" said Clifton.

"I am here to get the lay of the land and to stake out its boundaries."

Clifton ran one hand through a long swag of hanging hair. "I'll show the boundaries if you want."

Rolla stood taller." If it's not too much trouble, that would be most helpful."

"I'll saddle up. Mary, can you spare a piece of your fresh-baked bread for Mr. Jones? He looks a bit off."

Mary set her basket down and retreated into the house, returning minutes later with a thick slice of fresh-baked bread smothered in freshly churned butter and honey. His first bite transported him back to his mother's kitchen as the melted butter, blackberry honey, and warm, stretchy bread filled his mouth. A memory of Renaldo and him licking their fingers came flooding back. Now, as the butter and honey ran down his chin, the decision to come out West started to feel pretty good. He wanted to lick his fingers clean but decided to retrieve his handkerchief and clean up as best he could.

"Thank you, Mrs. Clifton. That was superior," said Rolla, still wiping his mouth and fingers clean. It was hard to tell by their wooden expressions, but he later found out they were happy to have a neighbor.

A few minutes later, the men road onto the property through a break in the bank of cottonwoods that skirted the road. The pale grass was long and leaned up toward the sloping ground ahead, indicating the wind mostly came from the south. Out of the corner of Rolla's eye, a shadowy figure crept out from beside a canvas tent. He couldn't have been more than twenty years old and appeared as a drifter.

"Do you know him?" muttered Rolla to Clifton under his breath.

Clifton shook his head and called out, "This is private property."

"Sorry, mister, I got no place to go," said the squatter.

"Where are you from?" asked Rolla.

"From town, my father threw me out without so much as a dime," said the young man turning his hat in his hands.

"Who's your papa?" said Clifton.

"Only the meanest man in these parts."

"What's your name?" asked Rolla.

"You can call me Benny."

He was suspicious until he realized there was nothing to gain from being on the land except fewer rabbits and pheasants. Everyone has a story. Rolla hoped Benny would not be detrimental to his.

Benny, a bit thick around the middle and flat-footed, approached. "I'd be happy to watch the place and help out as need be."

Rolla gave him the once over and noticed his clothes were machine-made. His shirt buttons were mother of pearl, and his shoes had once been polished. "Okay, Benny, you can stay, but when I say you gotta go, you go." He hoped not to regret the decision.

"Thank you, sir. I'll do right by you. You have my word," said Benny.

Clifton threw a glance of skepticism. Then, clucking his horse, he moved ahead without another word.

Benny stepped back and waved.

Some ways forward, Clifton craned his neck back and said, "The road we came in on is your southern border."

Rolla looked back through trees toward town and the mighty Spokane Falls River. "Some of these trees will have to go if I am to have any view."

"I figured," said Clifton, rocking forward with the motion of his horse, "you gonna farm it?"

"Most certainly, my fiancé will be here in a few months," he said. "Just enough time to get the house foundation built and start framing."

Clifton ducked under a branch and navigated his horse through a narrow path of rotund rhododendron bushes. "Whatcha gonna plant?"

"We're talking about planting fruit trees:—apples and pears, berries—plus nuts, and seedling trees for sale."

"Hmm," said Clifton nodding his head.

"How about you?" said Rolla.

"Only the most profitable crop in these parts barley," said Clifton.

"You don't say," said Rolla, surprised by his answer.

"Yup," said Clifton. "Over there about sixty feet is your western border. I suggest you pace it off, adding a few inches to each step."

Rolla had purchased two bundles of wood stakes, a ball of blue yarn, and an oil pencil from Jeremy at the land office. Down from his horse, he walked through the crisp leaves and decaying grass. He penciled SW on the stake and pushed it into the ground. The sound of the stake sliding into the earth tickled him.

Back on his rented horse, Rolla asked, "How long have you been here?"

"Since before the boys were born," said Clifton, advancing his horse toward a steeper hill. "I've seen much change."

"Do tell?" said Rolla, nudging the horse to follow along.

"Biggest change, the population. Swole up like a boil on a hog's ass ever since silver got discovered in the hills around Coeur d'Alene —and since the railroad reached us." Clifton looped the reins around the saddle horn, removed his grubby straw hat, and pushed his graying-brown hair back under. "Yup, lots of folks moving here, but not so many like you with an education and such. Naw, most of them are mudsills frittering away their money on whores and hooch. They'll move out when the cold sets in."

Rolla chuckled, remembering last night at the saloon when a throng of laborers erupted, throwing chairs across the room. Now, as he staked out his boundaries with his new neighbor, he caught a glimpse of what it would be like to belong to Spokane Falls.

"I'll have to hire lumberjacks to clear some of these trees," said Rolla. "One hundred and sixty acres is a decent amount of land."

"Yup," said Clifton, "that it is. "He Leaned down to spit a mess of brown through his teeth. "This here's the half-mile mark. I'd put a flag by that big old pine tree if I were you."

Rolla got down off the horse, wrote NW on a stick, tied a piece of blue yarn around it, and pushed it into the ground with the heel of his hand. To spare the old horse some wear, he walked a good part of the way up the steep pass. Between his compass and Clifton's navigation, it took less than two hours to mark the boundaries. There was room for a sizable homestead, thought Rolla. Room for orchards. Room for crops and berry patches. Space for children to run. A place for dreams to grow.

Rolla drew in the land's bouquet of smells. It couldn't be denied. The property possessed something magical. A sudden desire to weep passed through him. Could this be it? The more they walked the boundary—the more he saw of it—the more his confidence rose. They finished the tour with an assured handshake.

"It was kind of you to help me," said Rolla, tipping his hat. "I'll be around at the end of the week if you need help or need something from town."

Without ceremony said Clifton,"Will do," then clucked his horse to a trot before disappearing through the trees.

Alone at last. A chance to feel the pulse of the land. He closed his eyes. On first listening, it was as quiet and still as his favorite time of day, that small window of time known as the blue hour just before the sun peeks over the horizon. A brand-new day when possibilities seem endless. Then he heard the hum of the wind like the sound Mom made when she removed a roast from the oven. A cluster of juncos scratched and chirped as they fluttered in their dirt bath. A deep creak from the mighty oak echoed. Several conifers that had grown too close rubbed against each other in a low hum. Leaves fell. One settled on his foot. A bee whizzed past his cheek and moved to avoid it. The sun dappled the bleached grass and dark forest floor beneath his shoes. He moved into the sunlight and felt its friendly warmth.

If Monet could have painted this landscape, a kaleidoscope of greens from apple to juniper would lay on the canvas. Of yellows from straw to Meyer lemon and driftwood gray to bonfire black — and spiraling magentas. A dance of vivid colors on a canvas to show its changing light. Rolla leaned down, grabbed a handful of soil, and rubbed it between his fingers. The earth smelled of pine needles and mushrooms and Christmas spice. He wasn't going to taste it, but somehow a tiny bit less than a button lay on the tip of his tongue. He pulled his tongue into his mouth and savored the soil. A peek of its vital force vibrated through. He'd never tasted dirt intentionally, but this earth was without a doubt a fertile stew. A place where one could plant their best life. It was a place where children and their children and their children would always be welcome. A stretch of soil where they would always and forever belong.

A few hundred feet from the road, the land leveled off. Leaves tumbled like ill-shaped wheels across it. At the northeast corner, an Englemann spruce stood two hundred feet tall, if not more. A mess of Rocky Mountain junipers skirted a patch of basalt rock erupting out of the ground like a fallowed field to the west. Picking up a rock the size of a small anvil, he heaved it into the air and listened to it bounce on the earth with the thump of a ripe watermelon. The land felt familiar yet altogether novel the way his courtship had with Sadie. Pursuing her was like blueprinting an intricate multi-level house. Long periods of thought were spent discovering where each line, each angle, must intersect. He learned how to wait for her intention to unfurl and her heart to enliven. And he was happy to wait for Sadie, who possessed that essential element, goodness. Not many twenty-year-olds would have agreed to such an adventure with a dreamer like Rolla, but she saw his truth, and he saw hers.

Somehow Rolla knew this plat of land was plumb. The way a sailor knows when a vessel headed for open seas is seaworthy. The sky was bluer, the thrill of adventure tingled at his fingertips, and the hope of good fortune expanded his heart. He missed New York. He missed his city life, but he wasn't going back. He would live a life worth remembering here, an undeniable life. That knowing bolstered him and gave assurance. He had lost three of his siblings before they were able to make their mark in life. A fact that haunted him daily, yet grateful for his one remaining sister Alice. Standing on the land with the valley before him, he resolved then and there: the homestead would be as much for them and Alice as it would be for him and Sadie.

The afternoon light began drawing long shadows on the forest floor. Chattering birds foraged for their last meal of the day. A cooling breeze urged Rolla to return to town. He had staked out the homestead and discovered the house footprint could be more extensive than first calculated. Maybe there was even room for another bedroom or a library.

That night in his hotel room with the two candles perched on the window sill, he reworked the design for an additional four hundred and fifty square feet. That made him grin. A good many things had made him smile that day. Most of all, and maybe for the first time, he felt comfortable in his skin. He would accept the challenge and stay in Spokane. Even so, his decision didn't stop him from tossing throughout the night.

Chapter Eight

As sunlight uncovered the slumbering valley, a fog of air floated from it. Dawn was the best time of day —body rested, mind clear, the world quiet. Rolla walked through the streets, taking notes, sketching, and pacing off distances between future fire hydrants. The solitary sound of his footsteps on the dirt was peaceful. A myriad of ideas that had been ruminating since his arrival demanded to be on paper.

Spokane seemed different at dawn. Everything was tucked away like the dishes in a china cabinet, but it didn't feel tidy and composed. It felt unsupervised. It felt insubordinate, showing little restraint and heedless thinking. That energy excited him, even delighted, and its restlessness was coolly unnerving. Was it the unknown or the fear of not measuring up that kept him alert? Had his schooling and training adequately prepared him to lead this pivotal voyage? With a clenched jaw, the hair at the back of his neck pointed like thistle pins.

The doors to City Hall were locked. He walked across the street for coffee at the Big River Cafe and found a bench outside to work calculations. At 8:08 a.m., Rossiter showed up.

Rolla grabbed his things and bolted across the street. "Good morning."

"Good, you're early," said Rossiter, unlocking the door. "Follow me."

Down the short corridor, Rolla tracked Rossiter, looming behind him like some sort of Sasquatch. Their footsteps echoed against the windows and bare wood floors as they crossed the Hall to a closed door at the far end of the room. Behind the door, a staircase led to an upper story with four offices. He climbed the stairs and found all but one office door had a name painted on it. Rossiter's office was first. He charged in, pointing to the other chair in the room.

Rolla stepped inside pacing about. "I got a chance to see the river yesterday."

"Impressive, isn't she?" said Rossiter, sitting with a thud. He reached for his pipe, dug through the bowls ash, tapped out the contents, and refilled it with fragrant tobacco.

"A true marvel of water power," said Rolla. "A resource of this magnitude could solve a good many problems, not only water distribution."

Rossiter tamped down the soft tobacco and lit his pipe. "Go on." He flamed the fire with several strong pulls. "Nothing better than a bowl of cherry tobacco to start the day."

"I can't help but fantasize about the power and opportunity the river presents," said Rolla.

Rossiter dragged on his pipe and released a mass of smoke in the air. "There's time for that later," he said, taking the hookah from his mouth. "Place the founder's first on the list for water."

Rolla arched his neck and lowered his chin, "Ah,—well, fire pumps must be the priority. That task in itself will take a year."

"A year?" said Rossiter with a bewildered look. "I've been telling the founders of this city who are also the project sponsors six months."

A wave of panic zinged across Rolla's shoulders. "I don't see how. There's an entire underground infrastructure to build." In the founders' eyes, he was already six months behind on a project he had yet to start.

Rossiter looked indignant. "They're funding a major portion of the system. So the sooner they get water, the better. Wouldn't you agree?"

Footsteps on the stairway echoed, and soon after, Jeb Thomas appeared at Rossiter's doorway. Rolla's jaw stiffened. After witnessing Rossiter and Thomas's contentiousness, he didn't want to appear to have already allied up. Too much was at stake to start on the wrong side.

"Good morning," said Rolla, sounding grateful.

Rossiter pointed his pipe at Rolla. "We'll talk later."

"I look forward to it," said Rolla in earnest, yet wondering how he would maintain his neutrality.

Thomas stepped into Rossiter's office. "Recovered from Saturday night?" said Thomas, with a flicker in his eye.

"Yes, thank you," said Rolla, grinning.

Thomas removed his coat and confidently swung it over one shoulder. "I see Rossiter has already had a go at you. Let me guess, he advocated for the founders."

"Oh, never you mind," said Rossiter, brushing ashes from his desktop onto the floor.

"So predictable," said Thomas, turning to Rolla. "If you'll follow me, I've put some information together for you."

"Very good," said Rolla, moving out the door.

The next office on the right side of the hallway was Thomas's. He turned the doorknob, hung up his coat on the wall hook, and sat down at his desk. "Watch out for him," said Thomas in a whisper.

Rolla nodded in relief. "Will do."

Thomas's rectangular frames contrasted his round hazel eyes and sharp chin. He pulled a file from a lower drawer and passed it over the meticulously kept desktop. "These documents will give you answers to population density, projected growth, experts in the area, resources at your disposal, and city maps to aid in logistical decisions."

"Exactly what I hoped for," said Rolla, throwing an appreciative glance at him.

A clatter of footsteps boomed up the stairway. Mayor Nicholls was first to appear at Thomas's door, holding a stack of mail.

"Good morning, sir," said Rolla.

The mayor proceeded down the short hallway and called back, "Give me ten minutes, then we'll talk."

"Sure thing," said Rolla, glancing back over the papers Thomas had given him. Three councilmen then swarmed in the doorway like yellow jackets on mud.

Councilman Bender stepped in. "We tipped a few on Saturday, remember?"

"Right, you're the pig farmer." Rolla was pleased he had recalled him from such an inebriated state.

"Correct, we talked about getting the water lines to ranches and farms. Got to have water to feed the beasts and irrigate the crops," said Bender.

"I already have that on my list," said Rolla.

Bender cocked his head with an impressed nod.

A clean-faced man with black hair and a boxed-shaped nose pushed in. "Well, there he is, the man of the hour. I don't know if I told you how pleased we are that you're here. Your impact on Spokane

Falls is going to be tremendous. One day we'll probably commission a statue in your honor."

Rolla waffled at the comment.

"Harold Smith, am I right?" said Rolla, reaching over and shaking his hand.

Smith smiled and rocked back on his heels. "Don't forget—the mills are first priority. They generate a great deal of commerce, and their need for running water is significant."

Rolla opened his notebook and wrote it down. "Got it."

"And don't forget we talked," said Councilman Krakenberg, a narrow-faced man wearing a tailored sack suit with a wingtip collar and a coach tie. "What do steam engines run on? Water, of course, and coal but the need for running water should come before all other demands. Our livelihood depends on the railroad."

Rolla's tongue went dry. Rossiter wasn't the only one maneuvering for the top position. Managing expectations would quite obviously consume as much of his time as designing and building the system. Could he persuade the mayor to consider his designs before all these other expectations land on his charge? Thoughts caromed about until he remembered the words of Sadie's father: "This is going to take some real sand to pull off." He was right.

"Mr. Jones," bellowed the mayor, "you can come in now."

Moving to the door, the other councilmen grabbed and shook Rolla's hand, peering at him intently for confirmation. Rolla nodded in a conciliatory manner.

"Mr. Jones, I haven't got all day," called the mayor.

Rolla hurried into his office, eyes wide with alarm. "I apologize. A few of the councilmen were—"

"Close the door," interrupted the mayor. "I was trying to save you from them. Go ahead, have a seat."

Rolla exhaled and sat down. "Thank you."

"You must have questions," said the mayor, still shuffling through the mail on his desk and setting the envelopes in neat piles.

"I do. However, may I have your permission to begin designing the pump house and a preliminary subterranean schematic for the pipe system as I see fit?"

"Preliminary subterranean schematic," smiled the mayor. "You're going to have to talk plainer than that around here."

Rolla's face warmed in recognition of his meaning.

"I'll schedule forums so the council and townspeople can share their concerns," the mayor continued. "Meanwhile, by all means, begin designing your ideal system. But know you'll be making changes—lots of changes. I'm certain hordes of citizens will pester you." He threw a few circulars into the trash. "Let me know if things get out of hand."

"I can handle it," said Rolla.

The mayor looked up and, in a fatherly tone said, "Good man." Then, leaning down to pick up one dropped piece, he added, "We'll publish the approved plan in both newspapers and post it on the community board."

Rolla looked out the window to the waking street below. "Maybe leave a notebook on the community board for those who want to write down individual perspectives."

"There you go again using fancy-schmancy words. Let us say, 'concerns.' You see, not many are schooled in your East Coast language," said the mayor. "A good many will want you to explain it to them. They'll interrupt when you're in the middle of dinner with your mouth full."

They laughed.

On the notepad, Rolla wrote SIMPLIFY in one-inch letters. Nicholls finished sorting the mail and stood up. "The morning meeting begins in ten minutes. I'll show you to your office, where you can leave your things. It used to be the storage room, but it has a window."

"I'll make it work," said Rolla confidently.

Chapter Nine

On his fifth day in town, William Blythe, founder of Spokane Falls, invited Rolla to dinner. Located in town behind two ten-stall livery stables sat the Blythe House. A steep cedar shingle roof and a six-column porch made a stately impression. The manicured flower beds and maple trees on either side garnished its appearance. The virescent hues of summer were being replaced by autumn oranges and pinks. In just a few weeks, the trees would stand naked in the cold air, stripped of their merriment, but for now, they were dressed and quite glorious.

Rolla dismounted the rented horse and handed the reins to the stableman. Every last one of the horses he leased was sway-backed and worn. He hoped to buy himself a gelding broken, not busted on Saturday.

Greeted at the front door by the majordomo, Rolla followed him into the inspiring home of stone floors and Oriental rugs, of oil-buffed wood-paneled walls, and crystal chandeliers. There were grand oil paintings of sprawling European landscapes, marble busts of historical people, and high-polished solid-brass door hardware. Man alive, what a house, thought Rolla. The Wild West, its lawlessness and savagery were as far away as New York was. He could have been anywhere. The attention to details, the finery, and the elegance brought homesickness. He lifted his head and squared his shoulders as a brewing sense of importance rose in him.

One set of footsteps echoed as a man, he knew to be William Blythe by the portrait hanging in City Hall, marched into the foyer.

He was stocky, wore his hair long, and kept his face clean-shaven. "William Blythe. Good to meet you. Any trouble finding the place?"

"No, sir," said Rolla.

Blythe motioned to follow him down a long corridor. The air was musty with the smell of cigar smoke and aged wine barrels. "Everyone's here and eager to hear your plans."

Rolla stammered. "You know the plans are in their infancy. I cannot speak of them with any certainty."

"Oh, no need to worry. Tell us what you do know," said Blythe, continuing down the hallway. "We've been waiting a long time to get this project underway. We are all quite enlivened."

Rolla hurried to match him step for step as uneasiness coiled in his jaw. The idea of being cornered by the people financing the project—and possibly his salary—was intimidating. It seemed strange for someone in his position to be invited to the founder's house. Even so, Sadie and their parents would be pleased to hear of the hospitality extended by Spokane's upper echelon.

As they entered the dining room, adorned by gaslights with crystal droplets, it immediately brought him back to the many gentlemen's clubs out east. Above the sconces, deer, elk, black bear, and cougar heads hung on the walls. A large portrait of a half-clothed woman occupied the wall behind him. Another wall had a collection of musketoons from the Civil War. Below the guns were rows of French wine set out on an ornate Italian buffet.

Blythe rested a hand on Rolla's shoulder and cleared his throat. "Gentlemen, let me introduce Rolla Alan Jones, our newest convert from New York. He's here to bring what we've been yearning for: water at the tap."

The men cheered and pounded the tabletop.

Rolla straightened and bowed. Another whoosh of excitement rushed through him. He proceeded to shake hands with each of them, a small collection of wealthy, influential men here to determine if the candidate was up to the job: trailblazers such as Horace Rasmussen, a prominent banker; James Mueller, a leading lawyer; G. Blankinship, a wealthy businessman with diverse holdings; and S. A. Johnson, known to be the chief stakeholder in the silver mines of Idaho. These men were regularly written about and referred to in the business section of the Spokane Review.

To Rolla's surprise, Frank Rossiter sat at the end of the oval table. How did he fit in with these men? Rossiter possessed a successful law practice but did not begin to emulate their wealth and influence. There must be another reasons he was included. Being the center of attention, manipulated by the best operators in Spokane and perhaps the whole Wild West, was in Rolla's mind comparable to sparring with Duncan Cross, a world-class champion boxer.

Once seated, the majordomo held the service door open. Maids filed in, one by one delivering ladles of caramelized onion, yellow potatoes and velvety soup with dollops of creme spooned into the center. Then they brought a generous steak with a wide ribbon of sizzling fat and a spoon of steaming au jus sauce poured over the juicy meat. It was the best meal Rolla had had in a long time—maybe ever.

He relaxed and listened to the dinnertime conversation. Truth told, it was rather mundane and reminded him of his father's friends who met regularly on Sundays at their home. The gentlemen discussed new projects and the positive influence these works had on the city. They argued about the number of saloons opening in town and the transient workers disrupting the townspeople's serenity.

Rossiter interjected. "I told the city council, we need a curfew for women and children to manage the growing labor problem."

Blythe snickered. "I'll bet that went over well."

Johnson and Mueller agreed.

Blankinship covered his glass with his hand as a server leaned in to pour more wine. "And what was their response?"

Rossiter threw up his hands. "A new committee was established to study the problem."

"If I had a dime for every time I've heard, 'form a committee and study it,' said Blythe stroking his chin. "Maybe the simplest solution is to stop issuing liquor licenses and close the bars early."

Rossiter stared at his wine glass and swirled its remains. "I'll bring it to them, but I doubt the council will go for it either, let alone the townsmen."

"Use your powers of persuasion," winked Mueller. "After all, isn't that why we made you the chairman?"

Rossiter was their boy. He was the mole at City Hall. Having their ear gave him a trumped-up sense of power—a power he could work against anyone who opposed him. Now the constant blustering and the total disregard of what others thought made sense. He would have to watch himself around Rossiter or surely pay the price.

One of the maids poured Rolla a second glass of dry French red wine when Horace Rasmussen turned his attention on him. "We understand from Frank that getting water on the hill could take as long as two years. Surely there's a way to expedite the timeline?"

Rolla wiped his mouth with the linen napkin, set it back on his knee, and tried to relax. "The pump house has got to be built first. Then the pumps have to be delivered. I estimate it'll take three to six months, depending on product availability and transportation from the distributors who are out east."

"Go on," said Rasmussen.

"In the meantime," said Rolla, "we will dig trenches to lay down the water and drain lines."

"Don't we have connections to some of those fellas out East?" said Rasmussen, a fit man in his fifties with a mustache that joined his sideburns.

Johnson, who had more than a few wooden teeth, set down his fork. "We do, and I think they would respond to incentives."

Blythe leaned over the table. "You may have something there. Let's see what we can do."

Johnson sucked at his teeth. "What other issues affect the timeline?"

Rolla took another sip of wine. "I have a small team of diggers and can't spare one of them. If one gets hurt or sick, it will slow progress."

The six of them fell silent tapping their fingers on the dining table.

"You need more diggers," said Blankinship.

Blythe swooshed a mouthful of wine and swallowed. "What if we had our own crew of diggers?"

Mueller's eyes widened in agreement. "Mr. Jones, you could supervise them through an onsite foreman."

Blythe turned to Rolla. "And there could be a bonus in it for you."

Rolla hated to throw water on the fire. "I would have to get approval from the mayor and the council. I suspect several will object. Furthermore, I could never accept a bonus for fear it would be seen as bribery."

"Don't worry about the mayor or the other council members," said Rossiter, with a dismissive wave of his hand. "I'll handle them."

Rasmussen leaned back in his chair and tapped his hairy fingers on the tabletop, "Did you say this is your first position out of college?" Rasmussen was letting Rolla know his inexperience was showing. Rolla, in turn, longed for the day when people would stop bringing that up.

"Yes, sir, but I worked every summer with John Smeaton, considered by many to be the Father of Civil engineering. I worked with him on complex construction projects of Nash Construction, a giant in the field."

The men nodded their heads and looked persuaded.

Rolla had seen high rollers in action before and knew not to underestimate them or get on their wrong side. But, it had always been someone else's problem. Now it was him on the line. "I'm designing the pipeline schematic now. As soon as I get approval, which is proving difficult, I'll be ready to dig."

Blythe set down his fork and knife. "We'll pull together a team of laborers and talk later. Until then, I think we have the beginnings of a workable plan to get water to our homes sooner rather than later." Blythe picked up his glass. "To Rolla Jones!"

A hint of discord clenched his jaw as they congratulated each other. What would the mayor say? Had Rolla already jeopardized his position? After dinner, the men retired to the smoking room, but Rolla stayed as long as politeness required. He left, knowing he had somehow lost control of the project and wondered he'd get it back. Political maneuverings and private deal-making was not part of his education. It wasn't even part of his character. Rolla's approach had always been candidacy and straightforwardness. That night Rolla realized, like it or not, things were done differently in Spokane.

The ride home was tedious. The rented horse stopped and turned back repeatedly. She wanted nothing more than to stay in Blythe's barn. With insistence, Rolla pushed onward; either the tree bends or it breaks. Either he conformed and gave them what they wanted, or he risked being seen as someone unwilling to negotiate. He wanted to build the system—that much he knew.

That night a fitful sleep ensued. At one point, he threw a pillow from the bed in a burst of frustration. Finally, when the morning sun peeked over the Rockies, he was ready to make concessions.

Chapter Ten

Rolla bounced out of bed each morning. Four hours of sleep was all he needed to work sixteen-hour days. It was a thrilling time in his life. He was unbeatable, the hero, the prince of Spokane Falls. He fed on it like a hungry cub. His crew was ahead of schedule, and everyone was pleased. Everywhere he turned, people greeted Rolla with smiles and waves. It was as if he had been there all his life.

He purchased a four-year-old bay with a black mane and tail and white socks on all four legs. He named him Cyrus after his favorite uncle. He was a beautiful horse, and they hit it off from the start. Each weekday he rode Cyrus from one job site to another. After work on Fridays, Rolla often met up with his friends Francis and Jeremy for a beer at Jake's. No sooner did he put down two bits for a beer did the bartender slide it back and point. "Already paid for."

The general manager from the Pacific Hotel, Bart Flower, raised his mug.

Rolla excused himself and went to thank him. "Mr. Flower," he said, touching mugs. "How are you, sir?"

Mr. Flower was a tall skinny man, as bald as a baseball. "Fine, fine. How's it going—the water system, I mean to say?" Flowers had a nervous habit of licking his lips incessantly.

"I've got six teams digging trenches around the city," said Rolla, taking a healthy gulp, "If I had any more, I'd need two of me."

Flower chuckled. "I've employed a crew of plumbers to install the inside lines. We'll be ready when you are."

"Excellent," said Rolla. "Won't it be a grand day when everyone can turn a faucet and out comes water?"

Flower leaned in and whispered. "Maybe you could check their work before the big day? I'd hate to spring a leak."

Rolla raised his mug. "Don't worry, I'll check everyone's work."

Flower raised his cup and declared, "A toast to Rolla Jones." Everyone in the bar raised their glasses and shouted, "Here, here!"

All except Francis and Jeremy, who had grown weary of the attention. So many wanted a word with Rolla or just to shake his hand. He'd be lying if he said he didn't enjoy the celebrity his position afforded him. However, there were aspects of his status he found bothersome.

One of the worst was Mrs. Florence Rossiter who made a habit of showing up at dig sites with her society friends to deliver salmon jerky, hot coffee, and freshly baked muffins. She'd call Rolla over with a few flaps of her handkerchief and introduce him; her gloved hand clutching his arm and pivoting him around as if he was a pet on display. Rolla found it an exhausting dog and pony show and more than a little embarrassing. His crews got a big charge out of it and ribbed him every chance they got. He needed to find a way to prohibit her from visiting the sites. Yet getting on her bad side could be as dangerous as getting on Rossiter's.

When Frank Rossiter did turn up, he would shoo her off with a glint of suspicion held in his eye. "Thank you. It's hard to get my work done with an audience," said Rolla, hoping Rossiter would tell her to stop coming around. Either nothing got said, or she ignored him. When Rossiter discovered his son, Benny, was working for Rolla and boarding on his property, it further exasperated an already tumultuous working relationship. Rolla didn't tell Benny he knew who his father was. He preferred the young man to reveal it himself.

On several occasions, when Rossiter became frustrated by Rolla's insistence on following the plan, he'd blurt out on several occasions. "He's a good-for-nothing. You'll come to regret having him around. Just ask my wife next time she drops in on you." Rossiter then lobbed a menacing glance letting Rolla know sabotage was close by.

Nothing in Benny's behavior corresponded with Rossiter's claims. Fathers are sometimes the last to recognize the true nature of their sons. Rolla decided to follow his instincts. If Sadie had any reservations about the boy when she got here, he'd do something then. Right now, he enjoyed Benny's company, possibly because Benny had no association with work or Spokane's socialites. Either way, he was a darn good worker.

Soirees were held regularly, and Rolla was expected to attend. This week's gathering was at Rossiter's residence on the South Hill, where most aristocrats resided. The parlor was large. A forest-green marble hearth surrounded a roaring fire along the far wall. Scattered around the candlelit room were chair settings and settees where people gathered and talked. The center of the room was open for those who preferred to stand or, on occasion, dance. The walls held fine oil paintings, hand-painted plates of iconic Civil War scenes, and tapestries from foreign lands. Several waiters walked around with trays of champagne and single malt Scotch. A small crowd fawned over Mayor Nicholls, who was busy telling war stories.

Rolla paired up with Jeb Thomas, who introduced him to everyone he hadn't yet met.

They approached a grand-looking woman in her seventies, with silver-spun hair and a smile that never left her luminous face. "You must be who everyone is talking about."

Rolla held her satin gloved hand, bowed, and kissed it. "Rolla Jones, at your service."

Thomas interjected, "Mrs. Van der Berg lives a few streets over and is the proprietor of the Bank of Spokane."

"We have high hopes for you and the modern conveniences you are bringing to Spokane Falls," said Mrs. Van der Berg. "Why it wasn't but twenty-five years ago Spokane Falls was just a trading post for animal pelts. Now, look at us."

"I am pleased to be part of its development," said Rolla.

"They're not working you too hard, are they?" said Mrs. Van der Berg.

He smiled and shook his head. "No, ma'am." But truthfully, he was tired and eager for a good night's rest. Tomorrow was Sunday, his only day off and the only day he had to work on the house. Too much of his time required socializing to make people feel good about the wait and the money. He developed a kind of pitch after having to repeat it a myriad of times. When he began, Mrs. Van der Berg and her family brows sat low.

"Each day, progress is made," said Rolla. "We are, assuming no major hiccups occur, on schedule." They blinked and lifted a brow. When he said, "The majority will have running water by the end of next summer. We're working as fast as we can."

He delivered the last statement. "If you know a faster way, submit it in writing to the city council. We'd be glad to consider all ideas and suggestions." That left them smiling and shaking hands.

Oh how, he wished Sadie could be at his side. She had a way of making him feel at ease. If work weren't all-engrossing and time-demanding, these months apart would have been so much worse.

Thomas, who stood beside Rolla, nursing his third glass of Scotch, pulled him over to a group of men sitting off to one side. "These men are the big players in town. You'll want to get to know them and stay on their good side if you know what I mean."

"I've met with a few of them already," said Rolla.

Thomas' eyes widened. "Have you now? Do tell."

"Not much to say," said Rolla, having realized he nearly revealed his personal connection to them. "It was a while back when I first arrived in town."

Thomas watched Rolla's expression and body language for a clue to their connection, but Rolla remained as an effective chameleon. The attorney, George Blankinship, who had his hand in most everything, spoke out, "Jones, you planning other projects when this one is complete?"

Rolla had many dreams, to be sure, not just of the fruit and tree nursery. He was keen to run a steamboat tour on Lake Coeur d'Alene and possibly invest in retail. But he wouldn't reveal his plans until Sadie and he had worked them out. Several other men within the group indicated they, too, would be happy to consider investing. He was grateful for their partiality toward him. But, independence was what he wanted, not associates. With respect, he raised his glass, "When I decide to start my own business, you'll be the first to know."

Blankinship, a man of poise, pursed his bottom lip and nodded contemplatively.

"Get a business plan together," said another. "I'll tell you if it has any bones." The circle of men got a kick out of the suggestion and broke out into a volley of conversations.

Outside, the night air was cold and clear. People lingered longer than usual, talking at length about their summer travel plans. Rolla knew his summer would consist of work and house building. His most extended trip would be picnics beside a swimming pond. When he saw two couples leave the party, he seized his chance to leave as well. He said his goodbyes and excused himself.

Bundling up against the chilly night air, Rolla didn't hear Florence Rossiter creep up behind him, but he felt her hands slide into his coat pockets and reach for his groin. He spun around and found her standing there in wanting, her delicate features filled with longing and desperation. She was an attractive woman with green eyes and golden hair. Although her need to be desired and cherished made her vulnerable, Rolla found it repellent. He looked away, removed her remaining hand from his pocket, and held it briefly before releasing it.

She stared up at him, her eyes pleading. "Come upstairs. There's something I want to show you."

Her proposition startled him. He backed away with a lighthearted chuckle, trying not to insult her. Was this typical of the upper echelon? He glanced through the cut-glass window in the heavy front door. It broke the moonlight into a rainbow of geometric shapes. What could he respectfully say to escape? He had to be careful not to damage her dignity. Rolla returned his eyes to her lustful face. "Thank you for the most lovely evening, Mrs. Rossiter. Work begins at dawn and I must be getting along."

Florence purred against him just as her husband walked into the foyer, his mouth agape. "What's going on here?"

Rolla jerked and stepped back. "I was just on my way out the door."

"No, you weren't. I dare say you were seducing my wife," said Rossiter.

Florence smiled widely, thrilled at the attention and jealousy stirring in her husband. "Don't be ridiculous, Frank. I was merely saying goodbye to our guest. It is customary."

“And just so you know, I was doing no such thing," said Rolla putting on his cossack hat.

Florence moved toward her husband and turned back so he could not see her wink and seductive lip bite.

Rossiter expelled his breath curtly. "Get back to the guests Florence." All the while, his gaze remained fixated on Rolla.

"Thank you for the lovely gathering," said Rolla who grabbed the front door cold brass knob, turned it, and slipped out the door. The crisp winter air rushed in. He glanced back and seeing no was watching, sprinted to the barn.

Cyrus trotted down the road in the direction of downtown, needing little guidance. He knew the way. In the biting air, Rolla's breath sent flurries of fog around him, forming crystals on his mustache and hat. Rolla stewed through the dark ride home. Was Rossiter aware of her indiscretions? Was this a typical upper society game to abate the boredom of their lives? Florence had the power to destroy his reputation before Sadie arrived and long before the system was complete. He was warier of her then of Rossiter and the bigwigs in town. Her power would not discredit his work but would slander his good name. The most dangerous feature of the West for him was turning out to be the Rossiter family. He wrapped his neck scarf tighter and shivered at the thought.

Chapter Eleven

Spring 1885

Eight months had passed, and finally, the long-awaited day was here: Sadie would arrive on the two o'clock train. There was much to do. On the weekends, Rolla slept under the lean-to he'd built for Cyrus while building the foundation and framing the house. Today he needed a proper bath and clean shirt to look the part of a desirable future son-in-law and husband.

The mayor offered his horses and carriage after Rolla informed him of his impending guests and the gravity of their visit. A strong bond of respect had grown between them, so much so that Nicholls further offered his coachman. A private coachman would impress the Withers, and Rolla could ride inside. A proper introduction to the city was crucial in creating a favorable first impression. His earliest image of Spokane almost had turned him back—a predicament he couldn't risk with Sadie and her parents.

A hot bath and shave were first on his list, but not before purchasing a new cotton button-down shirt, undergarments, and a tie.

After wiping his boots squeaky clean at Stuart's General Store doorway he stepped it.

“Is today the day?" asked Stuart from behind the counter.

"Yes, sir," he beamed. “and I require some finery."

Stuart came around from the corner and put out his hand. They shook hardly. "You've come a long way," said Stuart and he should know. He was the first one he met, and from the start, he'd steered him right.

Rolla squared his shoulders. "Thank you."

Stuart smiled with distinct pleasure at the effect his compliment had on him. "Well, let's see what we can do to make a gentleman of you."

"I used to be one," chuckled Rolla.

Rolla paid a dollar twenty-five for a white starched cotton shirt, a dollar fifteen for the undergarments, and thirty-five cents for a burgundy tie. Stuart threw in a small bottle of bay rum aftershave lotion and off he went to the bathhouse.

He whistled and scrubbed himself clean in a tin tub filled with steaming hot water. Rolla closely shaved his grinning face, being careful not to nick his face. He applied a good dose of hair oil, a splash or two of the after shave lotion, a twist of mustache wax, and he was ready.

****

On the street, Lady Colleen waved with a feather fan from her bordello window on his way to the station. A pair of ladies strolling down the sidewalk nodded as he promenaded past. He was a show horse on parade. Francis and Jeremy were also out on the street and saw his prance.

"You're looking right, dapper," called Francis.

"Big day for Romeo," said Jeremy.

Rolla laughed without restraint.

Francis and Jeremy clapped and hollered.

****

Jared, the mayor's coachman, pulled in front of the train station just as Rolla reached it. A middle-aged man who had served in the Union army wore an undertaker's hat and held a cordial expression on his face.

When Rolla spotted the train chugging down the tracks into town, its mighty plumage inky against the blue sky, a smile spread across his face. He flipped open his pocket watch; 2:00 p.m. "Right on time," said Rolla loudly. He got to whistling as his heart pumped vehemently. Finally, the Northern Pacific pulled alongside the station and released its final blow of smoky steam. He ran up the platform dodging small groups of townspeople nearly colliding with two Chinese men. The smoke from the train floated to a group of raggedy ponderosa pines standing at the end of the track. It stuck to the branches like the silky threads of a caterpillar nest but soon evaporated into the air.

Searching every window for a glimpse of Sadie, he jogged back and forth on the platform until he spotted her, then she, he. His heart boomed in his ears.

Sadie rushed to an open window and called out. "Rolla, here I am."

He lunged forward. "Welcome, darling."

She bent down to look through the lowered window.

Their eyes were on each other and shining with animation. "I'll be right there," said Sadie.

"Hurry," said Rolla. He watched her move through the train car to the exit.

She hurried past her parents and several children in the aisle then came to a complete stop behind an elderly gentleman making a slow exit. "Excuse me, may I pass?" Rolla heard her say, but the man ignored her. Sadie glanced back at Rolla, bit her lip, and to his surprise, climbed over several seats and jumped into the aisle in front of the man.

"How unbecoming," said the old man.

Sadie was unfazed. Moments later, she appeared at the top of the car steps. He rushed to the steps and Sadie jumped into his arms. They squealed and twirled and kissed wildly. She smelled good, like mint and Castile soap, and looked more beautiful than he remembered all these months apart.

"Hello, Mr. Jones," said Sadie, looking demure and glancing up at him with a coy expression that left him weak.

"Hello, Miss Withers," he said. They stared at each other with an abundance of fertility.

Rolla spotted James and Harriet Withers stepping out and broke from Sadie's embrace. He tugged her toward them, but she held back in playful resistance. Oh, how Rolla prized her humor. He wore a welcoming smile to greet her parents, grateful they had made the long, arduous journey on Sadie's behalf.

James Withers, who looked about the crowd of travelers, spoke from the side of his mouth. "You're drawing a crowd."

Sadie rolled her eyes toward her mother.

"Really, boy, you must be more discreet?" scolded Mr. Withers.

Mrs. Harriet elbowed her husband. "Oh, let them be. There was a time when we weren't so different."

James Withers pulled on his coat lapels and rendered a stiff smile.

Rolla cleared his throat." Good to see you, sir." He grabbed his hand and pumped it. "How was your trip?"

James Withers chuckled. "Well, no gang of train robbers came to pillage. I am fairly certain we weren't carrying any loot."

Rolla smiled. "Excellent!" He turned to Mrs. Harriet. "Train travel appears to agree with you. Thank you for coming all this way."

Mrs. Harriet let fly her honking laughter. "Pay no attention to my husband; he's just overprotective." She was a likable sort.

Rolla was all fired up to show them a bit of the town. He turned to Mr. Withers. "I'll see to your luggage."

"They'll be with the attendant," he said, pointing to a Black man in a blue uniform arranging suitcases into neat groups.

Rolla hopped over. "The Withers Family?" The attendant searched through groups of valises, his murky black eyes like bean soup. "Here they are."

Rolla tipped him and gathered up the four suitcases. "I'll return for the trunks," he said, heading for the carriage parked in front of the train station.

Sadie called out, "Do you need help?"

Rolla shook his head even though the weight of the luggage pulled hard on his frame.

"You sure you can handle them?" Mr. Withers called out.

"Yes, sir." Rolla was elated. He could have carried the whole train on his back. He hoisted one suitcase up to Jared. "Two trunks to come," said Rolla.

"The trunks go up first. After that, whatever doesn't fit, I'll put in the boot," said Jared.

"Right," said Rolla, setting them down on the platform and bounding off for the trunks.

He nearly yanked his shoulder from its socket, trying to pull the first steamer trunk alone. The attendant noticed and soon picked up the other end.

"Thank you," said Rolla with relief.

James Withers stepped in, stuffed a bill in the attendant's vest pocket, and said, "I'm afraid even you'll need help with these."

Together the Jared and Rolla hoisted the first trunk onto the wrought-iron roof rack. By the time the luggage was loaded, the station had cleared out. Sweat beaded up on Rolla's forehead and ran down the sides of his face.

Sadie and her parents ambled toward the carriage admiring the station's western charm. Spokanites were proud of their new station with its ornate ginger-breading in the eaves, gables and its wide overhangs. The clapboard, painted in a cinnamon brown with sashes trimmed in brick red, may never compare to Grand Central station, but it was handsome nonetheless.

The attractive blue carriage, detailed in black trim and white wheels, had isinglass windows and lace curtains. Rolla unlatched the carriage door and folded down the footstep as they approached.

James Withers looked the carriage over with raised his eyebrows. "Nice! Yours?"

"An arrangement made for my honored guests," said Rolla as he assisted Mrs. Harriet into the carriage.

Sadie came to wait beside him. Her sheer nearness made his face grow hot. When it was her turn, he took her hand and touched her waistline as she stepped into the carriage. Heat radiated onto his hand. An intoxicating sensation dashed up him. For a blissful moment, he was light-headed like a dandelion seed blowing in the wind.

With the luggage tied down and Jared confident of the route, Rolla had laid out, off they went. Sadie sat close. He ached to touch her, but her father's forbidding eyes told him to keep his hands to himself. Nevertheless, he was content to sit next to Sadie on this glorious day bubbling like French champagne waiting to be let out. On the west side of downtown, a grove of sugar maples, Hungarian lindens, and white willows skirted the town's perimeter. A warm wind moved through the trees. Its playful current ruffled each leaf in a shimmer of spring greens. It was a perfect day to see Spokane for the first time.

The carriage bumped down the muddy, wheel-rutted streets toward the Grand Hotel.

"Oh my," said Mrs. Harriet, holding on to her hat as the carriage rocked through a washboard patch of road. Along the way, Rolla pointed out Spokane's first skyscraper, the new all-brick Spokane-*Review* newspaper building, three stories high, located on the corner of Riverside and Post just a few blocks from the train station. The Falls City Opera House, catty-corner to the *Review*, came next. The four of them couldn't help laughing at what Spokanites considered skyscrapers.

"The opera house is also new," said Rolla. "Spokane is determined to be known as a show town and already enjoys an active scene with plays, concerts, and operas."

Mrs. Harriet leaned out the window to get a better look. "You don't say?"

He held back from speaking about the salacious variety, and vaudeville shows well seeded and thriving in town. The genteel Spokanites were certain the risqué shows were single-handedly ruining its reputation. He was sure the Withers would have shared that opinion had they been aware.

"Over there," he said, "are three mills occupying the entire block of Howard Street. The oldest is the Spokane Wood Mill, with the Echo Roller Mills and Spokane Oat Meal Mills in its shadow."

James and Mrs. Harriet sat up when the carriage rolled past St. Aloysius Catholic Church and its school on the northern end of town. Two substantial brick buildings which sat amongst a sea of wooden hotels, boarding houses, storefronts, and businesses.

"Queer as it may seem," said Rolla, "we exceed San Francisco in electric street lights."

James Withers leaned out the window with a contemptuous expression. "Yet your streets are unpaved."

"It's on the docket. Priority number one is finishing the water system and a higher learning institution called Gonzaga University, due to be completed next year."

James Withers crossed his arms and continued scrutinizing.

Sadie smirked and turned from her father.

Before the long journey could catch up with the weary travelers, they trundled down to the river's edge to Rolla's favorite spot. A place where trees, sweet with spring, hung over the water, stretching over the rocks that looked like green glass. A stillness overcame them. The Withers leaned out to get a better look. Evident by their awed expression, they found the river as compelling as he first had.

"It's not Niagara," said James Withers, making an obvious comparison for an East Coasters.

Rolla sat back. "Nor is it the Great Mississippi, but it is quite remarkable, don't you agree? You can see why a city would prosper here."

James Withers nodded.

"The color of the water reminds me of one of my emeralds," said Mrs. Harriet.

Sadie turned and smiled at Rolla with intoxicated eyes. "It's everything you said it was, darling."

Rolla began to feel the worry that had weighed on him lift. One day he would tell her how important her words were to him.

As they made their way back to the hotel, a band of women picketed with signs that read: Join the Women's Christian Temperance Union. Jared slowed the carriage.

Sadie perked up. "So it's true." She clasped her hands and peered out the window. "A decent size group."

"Sadie Elizabeth," said Mrs. Harriet, "do not get involved with those rebels."

Sadie looked perplexed. "Why not? I agree with much of what they stand for."

"Do you think there's a way to stop men from drinking?" said Mrs. Harriet.

Sadie waved at the picketers. "They're not just about prohibition, Mother. The movement will shape our culture away from male dominance, gun violence, and the destructive effects of alcohol." As the picketers moved closer, their voices grew louder. Two women hoisted signs against the window and sang,

It's a Long Way To Tipperary,

It's a long way to go.

But my heart's right there.

Goodbye, Piccadilly! Goodbye, Leicester Square!

It's a long long way to Tipperary,

But my hearts' right there.

Mrs. Harriet backed away from the window.

James Withers swiped the air with his top hat in annoyance. "Aren't you well cared for?" His eyes were surly. "Why would you join? You've been handed everything you ever needed. Haven't you?"

Sadie became emboldened. "Is it the prohibition you're against or the pro-feminist spirit of the WCTU?" Sadie grabbed on to Rolla's hand and turned from her parents. "Either way, I will be part of the movement."

"Pure Poppycock if you ask me," grumbled Withers. He glared at Rolla. "I hope you're prepared to deal with Sadie, the revolutionist." Harriet stroked his arm.

With a blank stare, Sadie said. "Do you know who's in charge of the union?"

Rolla wanted to avoid more discussion on the matter but felt compelled to answer. "Not sure. It should be easy enough to find out."

The Withers may not have been aware that many women of her age shared Sadie's perspective. They two had numerous discussions on the issue, and Rolla supported her views. She'd participated in rallies and marches on campus. Still, in the face of her parent's disdain, the protest didn't improve their impression of Spokane.

Mrs. Harriet clutched an inside handle. "I'm afraid the train ride has taken its toll on me. I need to rest a spell before dinner."

"Good idea," said James Withers.

Wishing they could have avoided the unpleasantness of the picketers, Rolla said. "The hotel is just in the next block."

With a Mona Lisa smile, Sadie looked at Rolla. He arched his back, knowing they would finally have a moment alone.

They pulled in front of the hotel, and Rolla jumped out. Stepping down from the carriage, Mrs. Harriet had become unsteady. He walked her into the hotel reception area and helped her into one of the upholstered chairs.

Back outside to assist Mr. Withers, he suggested, "Shall we meet at six for dinner in the hotel lobby?"

Mr. Withers nodded in weary agreement and made his way inside alone.

****

Rolla stepped onto the mounting step to ask Jared, "Will you take us on a tour of the grand homes on South Hill?"

Jared cocked his head. "My pleasure."

Then like a bird gliding into its nest, Rolla opened the door, slid next to Sadie, drawing his first relaxed breath of the day. With itching restraint, they waited. They passed through the downtown and under the railroad bridge until they reached the road that led up to the South Hill. He nuzzled against her forehead, felt her breath on his mouth, and whispered, "Finally."

Sadie murmured back, "Finally."

He took her hand and kissed the palm. "I missed you so much." They laced their fingers together, and soon their palms were as close as two hands could be. They exchanged hypnotic glances, and before kissing fully, she said, "I want you desperately." He responded, "And I you, my darling." An unstoppable fever came over them. They couldn't get enough of each other. An outpouring of desire boiled up. They pulled at each other's clothes. He imagined them in bed, tasting her naked skin, running his hands through her hair and over her body. He wasn't sure he could control the build-up any longer when the carriage came to a rolling stop. They parted panting, giggling—euphoric.

Chapter Twelve

He listened to Sadie breathe, soft as wind through tree tops. Her warm body beside his, still as a fawn. Her dark hair —a mink coat sprawled over the pillow —caressed her shoulder and flowed down along her slender neck. Her dark hair was in contrast to her skin, white as the cabbage butterfly common in these parts but with a luminous pink tinge. He wanted to make love again, to stay hidden in their cocoon, but it was Monday, and he had to go to work. He had to force himself out of their wedding bed and leave the rousing swaddle. To leave the warmth of his bride, his lover, was more difficult than kowtowing to Rossiter's arrogance. He promised himself one more kiss, one more sweet nuzzle of her roundness, one more breath of her scent would have to get him through the workday.

Behind the paper decoupage dressing screen—he administered himself a good washing, shaved, applied hair oil, brushed his teeth, and waxed his mustache. Then he tossed the gray water out the window, rinsed, and wiped the bowl clean for Sadie. The small mirror attached to the dresser wasn't much, but he saw himself, beaming, charged for the day.

Rolla tiptoed to the door to find Sadie waiting with a thrice-used paper bag containing a Washington apple, a chunk of hard cheese, and a roll bought yesterday from their favorite bakery. Her hair cascaded in ringlets, half-covering her slumberous blue eyes. "I tried not to wake you," he said with a fervent kiss and a severe reluctance to leave their boarding house oasis. “You’re going to have to push me out the door."

Sadie giggled softly, kissed him, turned the knob with one hand trembling, and pushed him out.

With their heads resting on either side of the door, they moaned.

Softly she turned the knob and locked the door.

Sadie bounded into her new life with the appetite of a bobcat. Each morning she began by organizing the many tasks necessary to expedite the construction of their home. She contacted vendors, combed through catalogs, sourced deals on doors, windows, paint, sinks—everything needed for the home. It took weeks to get supplies by train. But, with Sadie at the telegraph office several times a day, things started arriving daily. Procuring was a big job—a job Rolla had fallen behind on. Nevertheless, her savvy nature was the critical component to getting the house done before winter's entrance a mere seven months away, maybe less. She was more tenacious than he had realized, and he heard about it from several in town. Over dinner, Sadie shared her escapades.

“I was at the lumber yard selecting two by fours when the workman suggested I send in my husband in my place. I told him that it won't be necessary you trusted me to handle this job and many others," said Sadie, "he got in an awful huff. Still, he loaded the timbers I selected without further comment."

Stuart commented, "Your Mrs. has become a regular customer. Every time she walks through my door, I grab a pad and pencil. She's on a mission, that one." That put a bounce in Rolla's step. His happiness became audible to him and others as he whistled throughout the day.

She began exercising her newfound freedom away from her parents by devoting a few hours a week to hand out pamphlets and recruit women to join the WCTU. He'd see her on the street below his office window, standing on a soapbox. She was fearless and stood up to everyone. He would be lying if he said it didn't make him nervous to see her out there waving those handbills at every passerby. She kept a tally of the number of women she had signed up at home. It was her badge of honor.

However, her involvement in the women's crusade presented Rolla with challenges. One day, Mayor Nicholls, Rossiter, Thomas, and he discussed the project. Rossiter leaned in,
"So, how's the little woman? I'll bet your inability to control her makes for a wild time under the sheets?" He laughed and winked with slimy disrespect.

His suggestion launched Rolla into a rage. Bolting up, he yanked off his coat, tossed it to the floor, and raised his fists. Suddenly hate made sense to him. He had never felt it before, its gritty disregard for life. Never felt the free pass it hands over to the primal urge to kill. The desire to hate enough to kill someone was rattling.

"How dare you say such a thing," said Rolla, growling.

"Don't be so sensitive. I meant it as a compliment," said Rossiter with a shit grin.

Thomas threw up his hands and rolled his eyes, "More schoolyard antics from our illustrious chairman."

Rolla didn't back off. "Good God, man, where are your manners?"

Nicholls lowered his head, screwed up his eyes, and through clenched teeth said, "You're lucky he has restraint. Most would have already decked you."

"Come on now, boys," said Rossiter looking sheepish, "I was just having a bit of fun."

Every muscle in Rolla's body tensed. "You leave me no choice. I challenge you to dual tomorrow morning at the break of dawn. Name the place."

Rossiter laughed loudly.

Thomas and Nicholls stared at each other amazed by Rossiter's gall and Rolla's impetuousness.

Rolla moved toward Rossiter. His fists were tight. Nicholls and Thomas cut him off. The satisfaction of fighting him would have been worth it, but the fatal outcome would have been disastrous. Rossiter knew it. Rolla knew it.

"Apologize, Rossiter, or I'll fire you," said Nicholls.

"You wouldn't dare," snarled Rossiter. "Besides, you can't. I'm irreplaceable."

"Ha, I can and I will," shouted Nicholls, the veins in his neck bulging blue.

"Say it, Rossiter," demanded Thomas with his lips pulled back from his teeth.

Rossiter smirked. "I apologize. Are you happy?"

Rolla stared down Rossiter until he blinked and moved back. "If there's ever a next time, I won't hold back."

“After all I've done for you," said Rossiter turning around retreating to his office.

Now it was Rolla's turn to laugh but laughter was the furthest thing from his mind.

"Jones, take a walk," commanded Nicholls.

Rolla charged through the front door and marched down the street, away from where the WCTU and Sadie were congregated. It felt wrong to walk away. He wasn't the offender. Yet, it was he who had to get a hold of himself. He had to find a way to work with the son-of-a-bitch. One day Rossiter was going to wish he hadn't messed with him.

Chapter Thirteen

Coming home to Sadie was a refuge. Nothing else mattered but her touch, her scent, her eyes on him. They made love before saying hello. Her passion helped him forget the earlier incident. Even over dinner, he couldn't take his eyes off her.

With glee, Sadie reviewed the progress she had made on the house. She went through the list, ticking off each item, most notably the ones she had completed. "Did you know there are several quilting clubs in town? What are your favorite colors? I love navy blue and yellow together." She dabbed her mouth of the excess cream from the fish stew. "Of course, I will have to make many quilts." Sadie stopped to chew then continued without an answer from him. "Oh, since I joined the WCTU, I have become their best recruiter." She raised her hand in a fist, the sign of solidarity. "It's all so rousing," said Sadie with a wink that made Rolla blush. "Mind you. We still can't vote," she said, rolling her eyes. "Women in this day and age, not being able to vote?" Without so much as a breath, she pointed her fork at him. "New York is where trends originate. However, at this rate, women's rights will happen far sooner here than there. Now that I am here, that's fine, but man alive, let's make some progress people."

He laughed at her exasperation and tried to replicate it by sighing and placing a hand on his hip. "People."

She squealed at his pantomime, and they clinked their water glasses together.

After taking several large bites of food, and it leaking from the corners of her mouth Sadie said, "I am famished. Aren't you?"

Rolla stuck his food-covered tongue out. A whoosh of silliness dashed through them. Covering their mouths, they inaudibly laughed red-faced.

The following day was Saturday. They got up early and loaded the wagon with supplies. Sadie grabbed an old shirt of Rolla's, then donned her walking boots and an everyday cotton skirt she could wash out easily. The sun already sizzled on the skin; hats and water would be essential today. Cyrus and the mare Rolla had purchased for Sadie lifted their hooves high and pranced up the roadway, happy to be out of the stables. Halfway across the bridge, Rolla and Sadie paused to marvel at the waterway and listen for its wisdom. They had made a pact always to give the river proper homage whenever crossing it.

When they reached the land, Benny greeted them with a smile. "Good morning." His hair had grown beyond his hat and he was twenty pounds lighter than the first time Rolla had met him. Living in a tent and cooking for himself proved an effective diet method. "Mrs. Jones, I received delivery of the cedar siding and a load of bricks," said Benny, "this is going to be a good day."

After unpacking the wagon, Sadie rolled out the house plans and studied them. "I think the kitchen is too narrow, and there isn't enough counter space to put out my cooling racks."

Rolla studied the drawing. "I will have to take space from the dining room. Can you live with that?"

Sadie looked back and forth between the kitchen and the dining room sections. "Yes, I can live with a smaller dining room, oh, and the parlor needs a window on the east side to let in the morning sun. Imagine how lovely it will be to feel the warmth of the sun on a cold winter's morn?" Although her changes required more money and time, Rolla agreed to every request. Her specificity made the home better, more practical—with a higher aesthetic appeal. When it was complete, they'd be happier because it represented both of their visions.

Benny and Rolla got cutting the stringers for an exterior three-step stairway. Sadie took over once they had nailed the stringers in place, humming while she worked, rarely asking for assistance. As soon as she finished fixing the risers and treads in place, she tested them by tromping up and down. "Look at that—my first set of steps." She jumped down one step and back up another. "Sturdy too." Minutes later, she was digging out the front walkway to lay a brick path in a chevron pattern. A hand shovel and a hand hoe were not the perfect tools for such a job. A steel rake would have helped. It was hard work: the ground needed to be level before laying down sand and bricks. Her fingernails, caked in dirt and jagged from scratching the earth, were raw by the end of the job. Nevertheless, as Benny and Rolla noticed, she persisted.

Benny nudged Rolla's arm and spoke in a low voice. "She's something."

Rolla looked back at her. A flush of pride welled within. "She sure is."

"Whew," sighed Sadie as she stood up and let her arms hang loosely by her sides.

"Everything all right?" asked Rolla.

"Just needed to stretch my legs." Minutes later, she was back on her knees, toiling in the soil.

At lunchtime they ate eight chicken sandwiches between them, a bag of apples, and three pieces of coconut cake.

Gulping half a canteen of water and spilling the rest down his shirt, Rolla stopped for a breath and looked over to Sadie. "Why don't you rest awhile? We've got time to finish the walkway tomorrow."

Sadie batted the air. "Don't be silly. I am going to lay down all the bricks I can. Some need cutting; we'll do that tomorrow, and then I'll pick up the yard."

"Suit yourself," he said, "I just don't want you to overdo it." He'd noticed she was more tired than usual and slept in longer.

Picking up the yard included gathering the wood scraps and bent nails, separating the pieces according to size, and setting them into neat stacks. It was a tidy construction site, thanks to Sadie. Even so, there wasn't an hour they let slip past without the two of them stopping and gazing at each other, drifting into each other's arms for a tender smooch. Her heart inspired him; the life they were building felt more robust, more righteous, more abundant every day.

"Back to work, woman," he said in jest.

"Yes, sir Mr. Boss Man," said Sadie with a grin.

Benny was proving to be an able farmhand and trusted friend. He still hadn't confessed to being Rossiter's son, but Rolla didn't care. To him, Benny was just a young man trying to figure things out for himself. They were an amenable pair. He admired Benny's for his new independence and thought little of his secret.

Rolla looked at Benny. "Why don't you sleep in the house? It's better than a tent by a long shot."

"If you don't mind, that would be a big improvement," said Benny with a humble nod.

"Absolutely," Sadie said. "We should have thought of it weeks ago."

Before day's end, they trekked to the upper eighty. Their legs were heavy with fatigue, backs stiff and aching.

"I have an idea for the seedlings," said Benny, rolling his sleeves above his elbows and pointing east. "If you look yonder, that hillside's got room for hundreds of seedlings. The fir trees are far enough back to let in plenty of sunshine. That'll leave the flat land for berries and fruit trees."

Rolla was interested in grafting apple trees to create new apple varieties. He wanted to invent a red apple that baked like Gravensteins. He had begun ordering and stockpiling hard to come by seeds through catalogs and newspaper ads.

"I don't think we should plant hazelnut trees," said Sadie, yawning. "I read that a single hazelnut tree can occupy a space of twenty feet and produce only fifteen to twenty pounds of nuts."

Benny and Rolla signaled their agreement. Together the three of them were a darn good team. The property was a choice piece of land. Regular rainfall, pooling water under ground and running down the creek was an omen that would serve them well for the years to come.

Chapter Fourteen

By the spring of '88, Rolla and Sadie's lives were jammed from sun up to sundown. Each day began as the sun opened over the eastern horizon like a great gray wolf yawning. Sunlight streamed through the windows. The house stretched softly as they woke enfolded in each other's arms. In that instant, the sun turned on the lights over the valley, and clouds began retreating. The clock on the dresser ticked-off the seconds before Daniel would crawl into bed with them. He had just turned three. Sadie was pregnant with their second child but was not feeling herself. Rolla worried it was twins. When he heard Daniel pad into their room, he stretched out an arm and pulled him into bed. Daniel slid between them and burrowed down with his thumb in his mouth. Though Rolla dreaded touching the cold floor in bare feet, the powerful pull of duty hailed. Though they were overworked their dreams were manifesting. Sadie and Daniel snuggled while he readied himself for the day.

Residents in and around the city had running water. Each fire hydrant was operational. Water lines to farms and ranches were underway. There wasn't a day when people didn't thank him, claiming that running water had made their lives better. One little girl hugged his legs, saying her mother smiles every time she turns the faucet. He had become one of them and was proud to be called a Spokanite.

Their small fruit business began to take shape. But the apple, pear, and berry orchards required a great deal of time: winter pruning and clean up; bee pollination in the spring, and harvesting summer and fall. Before the start of his supervisory job each day, Rolla delivered orders most mornings year-round. Their catalog offered jarred peaches, pears, honey, and seedling trees wrapped in addition to the fresh fruit. He and Benny built a roadside fruit stand at the end of the driveway, which Benny stocked daily. Sadie tended the customers, managed the jewelry store, Daniel, and her regular chores. Rolla worried it was too much for her. She assured him everything was under control. He half believed her.

He hoped to start paddleboat tours at the beginning of the summer of eighty-nine. That was dependent on getting to Lake Coeur d'Alene twice a month to make necessary repairs. The boat he purchased had been poorly maintained and required many fixes. Rolla worried how Sadie would deal with him being gone at least two days a month.

Thankfully, there wasn't a day he didn't feel Renaldo's spirit watching over him. As a little boy, he had relied on Renaldo. He was both his protector and best friend. It would have been so much better to have an older, wiser brother to help with the many chores and decisions he regularly faced. Sadie was more than he could ask for in a wife and business partner. She worked tirelessly alongside him. Rolla promised her, "If things keep going as they are, we could retire in twenty years."

Yet on this particular morning, with Cyrus waiting, that goal felt a long way off. Sadie dashed out the front door and vomited over the edge of the porch railing.

Rolla dropped what he was doing and rushed over. "You all right?"

Sadie clutched the post, wiped her mouth with a corner of her apron, and turned back. "Need some toast is all," she said, bracing her growing belly. "Come on, breakfast is ready."

Rolla helped her inside, his brow furrowed tight.

Her morning sickness seemed worse this time, so much so that an unlit fear lurked continually in the recesses of his mind. "Why don't you take it easy today? I could ask Mrs. Clifton to watch Daniel for the morning while you catch up on sleep."

With her face drained of color, she said, "There's too much to do."

"Whatever you've got to do can wait a day," he pleaded, "right?"

The morning light probed at the dark circles under her eyes. "Rolla, I'm fine. It's just a little morning sickness. It goes with the territory."

Daniel scampered in with his mint-green blanket wrapped around his hand. "Come, little one," said Rolla, removing his work gloves and setting them aside. He picked him up, placed him in the feeding chair, and swung a leg over a dining chair. That move always made Daniel laugh. Rolla dove into his breakfast of eggs, bacon, toast, and coffee with fresh cow's milk. The eggs were good and runny. Sadie knew just how to make them.

Daniel yawned deeply.

"Wake up, sleepyhead. It's almost noon," said Rolla, smiling at him. Daniel's thumb was posed in front of his mouth, and his bed hair sprouted up on one side. He looked through the front window and saw to the natural morning sunlight. "Nuh-uh," he said, smiling around his thumb.

Rolla kissed his forehead and caught a whiff of his honey-scented breath. "Can't fool you."

Sadie set down a plate of scrambled eggs and oatmeal with sugar sprinkles for Daniel and handed over Rolla's lunch bucket.

Suddenly she shut her eyes, pressed one side of her belly with the heel of her hand, and moaned.

Rolla leaned close to her belly. "Dear baby, go easy on your mom, please."

Sadie cast her gaze to the floor and smiled faintly, a look that always made him feel inadequate. Could a man ever know what a woman endures to grow a child in their body?

"Oh, I left two baskets of fruit on the porch," said Rolla." Will you see Benny stocks the stand?"

Sadie poured herself some coffee and set the pot back on the table trivet. "Of course," she said, then sat down beside Daniel to help with his food, who was making his usual mess. "Do you have time to stop by the jewelry store and review the books?"

“I should have about twenty minutes."

"That should be enough. And bring back last month's receipts. And ask Wiggins if a shipment from the Foreigner in Attleboro came in," said Sadie, "and tell him I'll be in by the end of the week."

Rolla stood up, stuck the last forkful of food in his mouth, and grabbed his pail. "Maybe you should write this down?"

"Bye, dada," said Daniel with too much food in his mouth.

She sighed. "All you've got to do is remember three little things: receipts, Attleboro, and the end of the week."

Rolla snatched two more pieces of toast and looked at Daniel and Sadie wholeheartedly. "I'll remember, sweetheart. Will you take it easy today?"

She smiled and looked as if she was holding back tears. So many mornings, Rolla didn't want to leave their cozy home, not while Daniel's chubby little hands reached for him in such earnest, not while she looked so weary. "If I could stay home, I would," he said, tousling

Daniel's hair and kissing Sadie. He propped open the door with his foot. "Please find some time to rest."

A look of annoyance came over her face. "Rolla, you'll be late."

He retracted his foot and left. Again, guilt seized him until he reminded himself he was doing this for all of them. She's strong; we're strong. We'll get through it.

Rolla stepped back and pushed the door open. "We have to carry on; it's what successful people do."

Sadie took a deep breath. "I love you too."

He trundled down the long driveway when a southwestern wind blew past. The handmade rockers sat on the curved porch seesawing in the wind. Branches from the ancient large-leaf linden scratched at the upstairs window. Although not grand by Victorian standards, his homestead design had been inspired by European designs where homes grew from the landscape as naturally as trees and shrubs. Ornate hand-fluted fascia boards adorned both gables over the windows on the second floor. It had taken him weeks to get them just right. Four slender columns stood on either side of the front door.

He designed the interior to meet today's modern ideas; the kitchen and dining room shared a common space. Windows on every side of the house invited streams of natural light. The upstairs bedrooms were spacious and decorated by Sadie with pragmatic elegance. She selected scrolled brass Victorian hardware for each door handle and window lock. Beveled glass, cut in diamond shapes, sat below a half-moon transom window at the front. An oversized river rock fireplace dominated the main room. The kitchen's main feature was an iron-clad wood and coal stove, in perpetual motion.

The painted roadside sign lay in the ditch as he reached the road. He had set the brake and gotten down from the wagon when a massive gust of wind blew past. His hat blew off and tumbled under a bush. Rolla righted the sign on the embankment above the road. Leaves clung to the sign that read "Riverside Nursery - R. A. Jones" until another flurry of wind rushed them off. He pulled out his hat from under the bush, brushed it off, and securely pulled it over his head.

The very next driveway was Sam Clifton's. He had helped Rolla stake out the property's boundary that first day. Clifton's narrow roadway was edged with rhododendron and Oregon grape bushes. Clifton's dogs rushed up, their tails wagging. Rolla set the brake and unloaded crates onto the front porch.

Sam sauntered up, stuck his well-worn pitchfork in the ground, and leaned on it. "Mornin."

Rolla set half a crate of berries down. "Mornin."

Sam left his perch and looked over the berries. "Raspberries look good."

"I'm off to a banner year," said Rolla.

"So soon after planting," said Sam.

"I got lucky." Rolla placed the last crate down and pulled out the order book.

Rubbing the back of his neck, Sam said, "Say, can I settle up with you at the end of the month?"

"Well," said Rolla, rolling his eyes, hoping he'd realize he was having a bit of fun with him.

Sam broadened his shoulders. "You know I'm good for it."

"I'm just joshing with you. That'll be fine," said Rolla.

Sam's demeanor changed. "You pulling my leg, were you?"

Snickering, he said. "Had you going there, didn't I." Then, another gust of wind raced between them. They squinted against the dust and held onto their hats.

Sam grinned, "Yeah."

"Say, is your Mrs. nearby?"

Sam turned and yelled, "Mary."

Mary ambled out, wiping her hands on an apron, her nose and cheek dusted with flour. "Mornin, Rolla."

Rolla rubbed his hands together in hopes he wasn't overstepping their friendship. "Do you think you could drop by and relieve Sadie for an hour or so? She's exhausted and needs more sleep. This pregnancy has been really hard on her."

Mary pondered. "After lunch, I'll have some time," she said with her regular deadpan expression.

He sighed in relief. "Thanks, and you may have to convince Sadie. She can be stubborn."

"As we all can," said Mary.

Rolla stepped up into the wagon, pulled on the reins, and said, "Back," to Cyrus. A bat or two of the reins, and they were on their way to town.

Sam waved and called out, "You're gettin' the hang of things."

"Thanks to you," he said, waving back.

One more delivery, and it would be time to put his superintendent hat on. The pace, although vigorous, was grand. Alone on the road, he flexed his chest and swiped the air with a hand. He was young and healthy and believed he had the world by its tail.

****

As he crossed the bridge, the jade-colored waterway of the Spokane River came into view. He laid a hand over his heart in reverence. Each time he observed this magnificent river, an awed sensation flushed through him, and the burdens he wrangled receded. Out of respect, Rolla tipped his hat for the river's relentless determination and grace—the grace of knowing when to yield, when to surge, when to wait. A reminder of how to conduct oneself in all matters of life. The expanse of the Inland Empire Valley—its fat sky and ghostly lavender hills held strength. As the river moved toward its purpose he drove toward his.

The pump house was a one-story wood structure built for the water pumps on Crystal Island. The river split and navigated around its perimeter in great agitation. When he arrived at the stroke of seven, Andrew Akin, his assistant, greeted him. A man twenty-years his senior, bald and trollish, held a clipboard and pencil, ready to work.

"Good morning Mr. Akin," said Rolla. "How are you this fine morning?"

"Could be better," said Akin, "but what's the point in complaining."

Rolla tilted his head in concern." Anything I can help with," said Rolla, afraid his wife was ill again.

"We'll be fine," he said with a faraway look in his eyes.

He patted his shoulder. "Will you let me know if there is?" said Rolla pausing for his response. Akins nodded and repositioned the clipboard to indicate he was ready to begin.

Rolla rolled up his sleeves and laid his hand on the bladder of the first thousand-gallon pump. Direct contact with the cold wrought iron and the water within told him something inexpressible about the machinery. Crouching down to read the gauges and test the fittings, Rolla called out. "Pump one, sixty-five psi. Fittings secure."

Akin pushed back his glasses, ticked pump one on the printed form, and wrote down "65 psi."

"Pump two, sixty-two psi, fitting's loose. Hand me the monkey wrench, will you?"

Akin grabbed the wrench from the nearby tool bucket and handed it over.

Rolla tightened each bolt one-quarter inch. "That should do it. Check the pressure in an hour, will you?"

"Will do," said Akin, his chin puckered in earnest.

"Now for our troublemaker," said Rolla, stepping over to it and squatting down. "Damn, only forty-seven. Check the basket strainer and flow rate. I'll check the Zerk. It probably just needs more grease."

"Let's hope you're right," said Akin.

Once the systems checks were complete, Rolla sat down at his desk. A minute later, Akin approached with hands in his trouser pockets looking bashful.

He looked up from the desk. "Something else?"

"When's the last time you stopped by the firehouse?" said Akin, scratching his chin.

Rolla set his pen down and leaned back in his chair. "Mm, not for a while."

Akin jingled his pocket coins. "I did, just the other day, and I was not impressed. If a four-alarm fire broke out, I doubt they'd be up to the job."

He had his attention. "Please elaborate," said Rolla.

Akin sat down in the chair on the other side of the desk. "All the work we've done won't matter if the fire department isn't on its toes."

"How do you know it's not?" said Rolla.

Akin lowered his head and sighed. "I got in the habit, while at my last post, of stopping in regularly and checking on fire stations. I never said anything for fear it would come back on me. That was a mistake." He retrieved his handkerchief and blew his pug nose.

Rolla sat forward. "And what have you seen to indicate the same situation exists here?"

"The volunteers are rarely at their post. There's supposed to be a skeleton crew at all times. When they're not fighting fires or running drills—equipment maintenance is essential— every day," said Akin.

"So you're saying our system is dependent on firefighters, over whom we have no control, and they are not ready for a major fire?"

Akin lowered his head. "Yep, but it didn't come from me."

Rolla crossed his arms and stared out the small window. "That is most concerning."

"Once you see it, you can't unsee it," said Akin resting his hands on his knees.

An image of firefighters running frantically through flames as the fire crawled up sides of buildings flashed across his mind. "I'll swing by the station and take a look for myself," said Rolla.

"The council should at least be made aware," said Akin.

"If warranted, they will be," he said, scanning the bookcase for fire department regulations. "You're aware this kind of information will not be welcomed."

Akin raised his eyebrows and cocked his head. "I'm glad not to be in your shoes."

It occurred to Rolla that Akin might be over-reacting. But if he was right, ignoring it could result in a loss of life. That possibility was unacceptable.

When the clock chimed at noon, Akin, who was still working the pumps, looked up. "Back in forty-five minutes?"

He knew Rolla's lunch routine. "Thank you for your concerns and observations regarding the fire department. It must be unsettling to possess information of this nature when it could harm your position."

Akin nodded. "Yes, sir."

****

The river ran along the north side of town. The railroad tracks came in from the northeast corner of the city. From there, the tracks skirted the eastern side to the south before arriving at the southwest corner. Sadie's tiny shop sat at the intersection of Mill and Riverside Streets. An excellent location for foot traffic. The streets of Spokane were steadily losing their ramshackle western appearance. In just four years the downtown had added two drug stores, a handful of churches, four hardware stores, three men's furnishings, one photo gallery, two paint shops, one soda water factory, two millinery stores, three livery stables, one shoe store, three blacksmiths, eight saloons, one gun and locksmith, and five hotels. The thirty-two blocks under development when he arrived were now complete.

As he walked through town, folks waved, and he waved back. He tipped his hat at two women crossing the street. Laborers who worked for him called out. Stan, the corner bakery shop owner, leaned out his door. "Will I see you tomorrow?"

"I'll be by before the cinnamon rolls are out." They had taken to buying bread weekly in exchange for baking apples and berries. It lessened Sadie's workload. She felt guilty about it, he didn't.

At the end of the block, R. A. JONES JEWELRY SHOPPE was open for business. Legally they could not put Sadie's name on the storefront. A fact that irked her every time she thought of it. When he stepped across the front door threshold, a few shoppers browsed quietly.

Thomas Wiggins, Sadie's store manager, was there to greet him.

"Good afternoon, sir," said Wiggins.

Rolla stopped and whispered, "How are things going?"

Wiggins nodded enthusiastically. "Good, I think they're ready to buy."

"Good man. I'll be in the back office if you need me," said Rolla.

Rolla broke into the fried chicken, potato salad, and cornbread Sadie had packed for him while he reviewed the ledger. He was hungry, and the food tasted perfect. Minutes later, Wiggins opened the door and stuck his head in. "Sorry to disturb you, but your favorite customer would have a word with you."

Rolla was suspicious and hope it wasn't Mrs. Rossiter. "Give me five minutes to finish my lunch."

"Very good," he said, closing the door.

Rolla gobbled down his remaining food, wiped his mouth clean, and brushed his clothes for food bits. Readying himself for the pending encounter, he made sure his teeth were clean in the small mirror on the wall. He pasted a smile on his face and approached two women. "How may I be of assistance?"

The women pivoted toward him.

"Ah, Mrs. Rossiter, nice to see you," hoping his false sincerity was undetectable.

She smiled flirtatiously, her chin low, her eyes coy. "Mr. Jones, do you remember Mrs. James Follet, the councilman's wife?"

Mrs. Follet curtsied.

Rolla bowed. "Yes, of course, how are you this fine day?"

Florence Rossiter extended her gloved hand. "You're a man of impeccable taste. So tell me, which earrings do you prefer?"

He took the earrings, placed one near her face, tried the second, and leaned back for a thorough assessment. "On you, both are lovely, but I think the ruby stones are the more fetching."

Florence gazed at them for a moment, "Oh, I don't know. Isn't red too bold. What do you think, Annabelle?" Both women were of similar ilk. Attractive, yet too embellished for his taste: High collars made of lace, plumes of feathers in their hats, heavily perfumed, powdered skin, and striking lip paint.

"The earrings are a match for your lipstick color," said Rolla.

"How true," said Mrs. James Follet.

Florence handed the earrings back and squeezed his hand. "All right, I'll take them."

"Every woman deserves a set of ruby earrings, don't you agree, Mr. Wiggins?" He stood but a few feet away.

"At least the modern ones do," said Wiggins.

"Please wrap these up for Mrs. Rossiter," said Rolla.

"My pleasure. May I put these on your account?" said Wiggins.

Florence rolled her eyes. "Of course. Is there any other way?"

Wiggins motioned politely. "Very fine. I'll just need a signature. Please, step this way."

Bowing politely, Rolla said, "I must take my leave. Please give my regards to your husbands."

Florence tipped her head, "Must I?" She paused and feigned a laugh for effect. "Say, you're coming to the soirée on Saturday, aren't you?" Her hat feather pecked the air.

. "You can come alone. Others are."

Rolla nodded reluctantly. "I believe we have it on our calendar and intend on being there." He straightened his lapels to establish assuredness.

"Wonderful! It's going to be a big affair," said Florence. "You wouldn't want to miss this one."

Annabelle leaned toward Rolla. "All of Spokane's best will be there."

"Well, of course, you'll be there," said Rolla with a sly smile.

"I would never miss one of her grand parties," beamed Mrs. Follet.

The women batted their eyes.

"Oh, Mr. Jones, you are a charmer," said Florence.

"Isn't he though," cooed Mrs. Follet.

"If you'll excuse me, ladies. I must get back to my duties while I'm still on lunch break."

As he turned to leave, he overheard Mrs. Follet whisper to Florence, "Too bad. He's so married."

Chapter Fifteen

Rolla packed up his lunch scraps and dashed to the fire station with eleven minutes left on the clock. The double doors, held together with hand-pounded iron mounts, were open. A boy of fifteen pushing dirt around with a broom was the only person on site.

"Excuse me, young man, is the chief here?" said Rolla.

The boy stopped his pathetic sweeping. "He's at lunch."

"All of them?" asked Rolla.

"Of course, all of them," said the boy with a snigger. "It's the lunch hour."

Rolla recoiled. "I'm Rolla Jones, from the water department. Mind if I have a look around?"

"Suit yourself," said the indifferent boy.

The station was tidy. Hoses coiled on the wall hooks. Fire wagon ready for hitching a team of horses. Helmets lined up along the back wall to military exactness. Everything looked in order until he walked around to the captain's office. Rolla came upon the posted training and maintenance schedules outside his door on the wall. According to the timetable, they were weeks behind on equipment checks, emergency protocols, and ready preparedness training. Rolla found it unnerving, considering how hot and dry the summer was last year. Rolla knew it wasn't wise to leave the responsibility of an entire station to a kid. If there was a four-alarm fire precious minutes would be lost getting back to the station. Akin was right to be concerned. Rolla will make mention of it at tomorrow's meeting. He'd have to tread lightly. The fire department was the council's responsibility, not his. They were to meet at Rossiter's home due to an abscessed toenail. Rolla didn't anticipate a fight, but then every conversation with Rossiter was more difficult than need be, and doubted this would be any different.

Chapter Sixteen

In Rossiter's den there were leather chairs, an oak roll-top desk, green velvet curtains, and paned glass cabinets handsomely appointed. The books, held preciously within the cabinets, were legal books that spoke pretense. Rolla sat in the chair closest to the west window to enjoy the floating breeze. Thomas sat to his left, making notes in his journal as he so often did. Mayor Nicholls brushed his clothing and smoothed down the tails of his suit coat. Rossiter hadn't arrived but could be heard struggling down the staircase.

"I'll see if he needs help," said Rolla, getting up and making his way to the bottom of the stairs. Mrs. Rossiter was assisting him down the long staircase. Her arms trembled against the strain he placed on her demure shoulders.

"Come to help, have you?" said Rossiter with a wince. Florence smiled at him the way she always did with—libidinous intent. A smile that made Rolla feel they'd committed adultery. That thought made him uncomfortable.

"Please, allow me," said Rolla, placing Rossiter's other arm over his shoulder and lifting him down the last few steps. With each step, Rossiter sucked air and followed it with a groan. Once seated he rested foot on a pillow. A foul stench permeated the room.

Everyone but Rossiter seemed to notice.

"Just the four of us today?" said Rossiter.

"It still gives us a quorum," said Thomas.

"Either way, there's not much on the docket this week except for the volunteer fire department," said the Mayor. "Jones, it's your initiative. What's the story?"

Rolla shifted in his chair and gulped. He didn't want to be there. He didn't want to be the messenger of this issue, but he couldn't undo what he had set in motion. "A concerned citizen alerted me to problems with the fire department. I took it upon myself to stop by the firehouse and discovered a few issues worthy of your consideration." Rolla looked to each of them to ascertain if this topic had already hit a sore spot. No raised eyebrows or clenched fists were apparent.

"Why have you paused?" said Thomas, his countenance quizzical.

Rolla gathered his nerve. "The station appears inadequately staffed and grievously behind on their training. My fear is that if we were to have a major fire, they wouldn't be up to the demands of the situation." So there he had said it.

Thomas leaned back in the soft chair. "What do you mean?"

Moving to the edge of his chair, Rolla spoke. "The other day, I stopped in to find a kid sweeping out the station and no one else."

"Maybe they were at lunch. Everybody's got to eat," said Thomas.

"Policy requires lunchtime rotations," he said. "A skeleton crew should always be present."

"They're volunteers," said Rossiter.

"That doesn't mean they aren't required to follow protocol. And it's not the only issue," said Rolla. "The firefighters appear to be behind in training, at least if their posted schedule is accurate and who knows what other problems exist."

"Could you be overstating the situation?" said Nicholls.

Rossiter nodded." My thought exactly."

Rolla took an earnest expression. "If the firefighters aren't ready in an emergency, the system I've built will be next to worthless. A disciplined and poised fire department is an integral part of fire prevention."

Splaying his hands over his knees, Nicholls said, "What would you have us do? Hire an outsider to sort out the department?" He crossed his arms over his chest.

"I am not suggesting hiring anyone, but given the potential for disaster, I do think it warrants an investigation—a thorough investigation."

"Oh, poppycock," said Rossiter. "Do you know how much money your water project cost the city?"

"I have a pretty good idea, but it wasn't my project. It's your project," said Rolla.

Thomas stood up and walked to the window. "Mr. Jones, we've had no issues so far with the fire department. Furthermore, it'll cost money to ramp up any department. Have you thought where the money will come from?"

Rolla shrugged. "No, I have not. It's not my job."

Rossiter threw up his hands. “Well, it seems to be your job to tell us how to run the city."

"Now, don't get all fired up," said Nicholls. "Objectivity has its merits."

Must Rossiter constantly stir the pot? Throw everything and everyone off-center? Rolla held back and considered the question. "If additional funds are deemed necessary, why not borrow from Valkenburg?" he said. "I have it on good authority. His investors are eager to lend money."

"Their conditions are said to be steep," said Nicholls.

Rossiter leaned down to adjust his foot pillow. "Hear tell, they're fixin' to buy the whole town. Is that what you'd have us do, sell the town?" said Rossiter wincing as he lifted his foot.

Rolla crossed a leg over the other, trying to look conciliatory. "I no way have I suggested that, but this can't be ignored or put in some file for later. If people die, you'll regret shelving this."

"I think Jones has a point. It at least warrants follow-up," said Thomas standing nearby.

Rolla clapped. "A voice of reason," he said with relief.

Rossiter snickered. "I suppose it wouldn't hurt to bring in an expert," he said, shaking his head ever so slightly, "and have him assess the readiness of the fire department."

"Fine, do it your way," said Rolla. If he could have taken back those words, he would have.

Rossiter cleared his throat. "I don't care for your tone, Jones."

The two of them stare each other down. "Don't blame me if everything fails at a critical moment," said Rolla.

"Don't worry—the town won't blame you. It's the city counsel they will blame," said Rossiter pointing to himself.

Rolla slid a fist into his pocket and stared at the floor. "I don't know what more I can say. I've invested a great deal of myself in this town. I care about Spokane. It's my home too. I'd hate to have a fixable problem destroy everything."

"How's the harvest this year?" asked Thomas.

Rolla turned back, somewhat awkward yet thankful for Thomas' attempt to ease the tension in the room. Conversations about harvest were as commonplace as the weather. "Best year so far," he said, pushing back one side of the library's pocket doors. "Now, if you'll excuse me, I've got to get on site. We're fusing lines today."

At the door, Florence waited, smiling in her kittenish way.

He hurried to the door and tipped his hat. "Mrs. Rossiter."

Seductively, Florence tilted her torso. "Good day, Mr. Jones."

Rossiter overheard his wife's meow and yelled. "Don't you have something better to do?"

Florence walked briskly up the hallway, annoyed and most likely embarrassed.

Rolla exited the mansion and hopped on Cyrus. He had done what he could. It was now up to them.

Fire

Its smoke blinds and stifles, and the fires of love, punishment and war burn, devour and destroy.

Paul Diel, Symbolism in Greek Mythology

Chapter Seventeen

A man barges through a crowd of people at the steps of a boarding house hotel. "You can't go up there," the crowd yells. He ignores their censure and bounds up the staircase. The front door swings shut behind him. His room is on the second floor, where all he has in the world sits behind a thin wooden door — a photograph of his children, cash under the mattress, his father's silver gun. Fire snaps at his clothing. Smoke thickens. A black-and-gray storm cloud descending above him undulates as evilness. Each breath the man takes is more suffocating than the next. His hands shake while fumbling to get the skeleton key in the hole. Terror pierces his gut. Finally, he bursts through the door. A backdraft implodes, slamming him to the floor. His hair catches fire. Frantically he bats at the flames. The room is now a cave of twisting tongues. He backs up, but another roar of fire slams the door shut. There's no way out. He knows he's going to die. Through the fire, he sees a window. Everything in him says, don't do it, but there's no other way. He runs and dives through the melting glass window, falling to his death in a blaze of frying skin.

"Rolla, wake up, wake up," shouted Sadie shaking my shoulder.

My eyes open. "What!" The bedroom was quiet and serene. My pounding heart and gasping lungs were ill-suited to such a calm room.

Sadie kneeled beside me and petted my head. "It was just a bad dream. You're safe now."

I clutched her shoulder. "A man jumped out of a burning building. I think he died."

Sadie took my hand and caressed it. "Take a deep breath. Everything is fine."

Her face appeared calm as a mother comforting a child.

"But it was so real. I knew the people on the street," I pleaded, "they told him not to go in, but he wouldn't listen."

"Deep breaths," said Sadie, her face lined with worry. "Shhh, there's no fire."

I looked up into her eyes and saw the confidence of her words, and quickly my breathing started to settle. My heart stopped thrashing about.

Sadie rose from the bed. "This is further proof that you need a day off. Hell, I need a day off. We'll get Daniel and go to the lake. A nice cool swim in this horrible heat will wash away those pesky nightmares."

I rubbed my eyes. "It wasn't real," I said, wiping the sweat from my brow onto my nightshirt.

Sadie stopped at the door and turned back with a smile. "Come on now, get up, the day's running away from us."

I shook my head and rubbed my scalp wishing I could pull the dream out of my head. But, the thought continued to pester analogous to an itch out of reach. No matter how I looked at it, the fire destroyed a hotel, and a man died. When I dressed and went outside, the smoky air from the Idaho forest fires stoked the realness of my dream. Every so often, I'd catch myself grinding my teeth and have to massage my jaw to get it to release its tension. I had never had a dream like this before and prayed it wasn't some kind of a premonition.

On our way through town to the electric train transporting us to Lake Coeur d'Alene, thicker smoke hung in the air like a fur blanket. Some of the smoke was residue from the Seattle and Ellensburg fires, which had burned down sizable portions of those cities just weeks prior. Everyone we saw on the streets held bandanas over their noses and mouths to filter the taxing air.

Daniel squirmed between us on the wagon bench, the back of his hair soaked in sweat and in an irritated manner, he blurted. "Are we there yet?"

Sadie pulled out a jar of water and unscrewed the top. "Drink some water," she said as she dabbed the beads of sweat from his neck and forehead. Vapors of hot fumes waved off the many wooden buildings. Ninety-degree temperatures had forced most residents to the river's edge. Others hid in dark houses, trying to lessen the impact of the harsh weather. Sweat foamed and bubbled wherever tackle rested against Cyrus' thick hide. I left him at the livery stable with Francis to be watered and sheltered.

We boarded the train. Everything I touched was sticky and hot. We stayed quiet to keep our energy output to a minimum. Even fanning created more heat than just sitting still in the stifling heat. By the time we arrived in Coeur d'Alene, my head was dizzy, my stomach nauseated. This was a lot of effort just to cool down. It would have been easier to stay home, stand in a tub, and pour cool well-water over our heads. Instead, we got in line to debark the train. Perspiration ran down my back, down my legs, into my shoes. I kept pulling my shirt away from my skin for airflow. My handlebar mustache had long since lost its arch. Daniel brushed his mother's leading hand from his shoulder, saying, "Too hot, Mommy." When we stepped out of the train onto the platform, the shoreline was fifty feet away. A slight but much-needed breeze swept past. We closed our eyes and savored its cooling effects.

Akin to penguins, we tottered to the edge of the water, pushed off our shoes, pulled off socks, rolled up pant legs and skirts, and walked into the icy water. Instantly, my body's mercury decreased. Sadie stopped knee-deep in the lake. With her long cotton skirt tied up above her knees, she splashed her face, her neck, her hair until she was soaked to her waistline. When Daniel sat down in six inches of the snowmelt, icy squeals of delight erupted and didn't stop for a good long spell. I expelled the hot air from my lungs like a fireplace below. I couldn't remember the last time I appreciated the feeling of cooler air and cold water. The cold liquid ran over my head, tiny wet fingers snaking down my neck and over my shoulders. Renewed blood flow ran from all directions bringing back vital energy. One swallow, one splash, one water-filled hat over my head was restorative, like a barren landscape after rain that sprouts green tendrils and spring flowers.

Once we recovered, we walked to the dock where our steamboat was moored. It was nine-fifteen in the morning. I hoped to get some painting done on the boat after lunch. Five weeks had passed since the last time I was on the ship. The rains would be here in a few months. I wanted to take advantage of the weather before winter rolled in. Sadie wasn't sure about my little venture, but I knew it would pay off. She said, "You have more dreams than sense."

When we got on board, I went down to start up the engine. After a quick check, I fired up the boiler and waited for the steam to build. Then, I pulled paint cans out of the storage closet just as Sadie poked her head below. "What's that?" said Sadie.

"Marine paint," I said timidly.

She cocked her head and put one hand on her hip. "You're not planning on painting today, are you?"

I flinched and set down the cans. "Maybe once we've had our lunch and a swim?"

She walked down a few more steps, one hand on the bent rail the other holding Daniel's hand. "I thought we agreed on no work today, remember it's my birthday." Her lower lip protruded slightly as she glared at me.

I picked up a large screwdriver. "One hour while Daniel has his afternoon nap. We've got to use the time while we have it."

"That's our one hour of private time." Her blue eyes turned fiery.

A battle inside ensued the way two bears might fight over a beehive. I couldn't give her all I'd promised without the time and opportunity to make it so. My workdays were already splintered in a hundred different directions, my free time rarer than a harmonious meeting with Rossiter. I risked another question. "How about when we get back before the train departs?"

Sadie relaxed her stare. "I guess that would be all right," she said, sighing and turning back to climb the steps with heavy deliberate strikes.

My heart sank. I had become used to negotiating with everyone on every tiny thing. Clearly, it was wearing Sadie down.

After paddling around the river for an hour, we found a lovely secluded spot and downed the anchor about thirty feet from shore. I lowered the canoe into the water and tied it to the boat ladder. Once the picnic basket and Sadie were safely on board, I pushed off and paddled quickly toward shore. Dipping one oar into the glossy water, I pulled it back behind us. The canoe glided softly along while tiny ripples of water ruffled alongside. Daniel dragged his fingers in the water. Sadie held onto him by his bum.

She pointed to the water. "Look, a baby fish."

"Catch him, Daddy."

"No, I said, he's too small. He needs to grow much bigger."

Sunlight danced off the water as Daniel watched for more fish. Sadie gazed at him with a mother's tenderness, a tenderness that would melt any heart. Her dark curls tied loosely upon her head let go a tendril or two tendrils that clung closely to her moistened skin. That day with her azure eyes gazing at her baby boy, seeing the wonder on his face and their reflection on the lake was an image I will never forget.

Once we got to shore, Sadie went to work setting up the picnic area while Daniel and I stood ankle-deep in the water. I tried to show him how to skip rocks over the water's surface. "Look for a small flat rock, hold it in your hand like so, and with a sideways toss, let it fly." Daniel tried several times, but his muscle coordination was too immature to do anything but throw them down with a kerplunk.

"Well, done, Daniel, that a boy," I said, trying to encourage him.

He looked up with questioning eyes and a pouting mouth.

I squeezed his shoulder. "Don't worry. These things take time."

The sky over the west was murky brown as mud in a river. I couldn't take my eyes off of it. It just didn't look right.

"Lunch in twenty minutes," hollered Sadie. "Better get to the swim lesson."

Daniel yelled back. "I want some cake!"

"Not until we've eaten, and you've had your lesson," said Sadie. Then, in the same breath, she asked, "Rolla, what are you looking at?"

I tossed a flat rock with a sideways spin and watched it skip four or five times upon the surface of the water. I didn't want to reveal that this morning's dream continued to pester me like a gnawing, badgering fear. To mention, it would try her patience. If I could, I would have told her, "I should be at my post." Something in me told me so. But I knew what reaction that would bring.

She asked again, "What are you looking at?"

I should have said, "Oh nothing, dear," but I went ahead and told the truth. "The smoke, I'm looking at the smoke." I heard an exasperated sigh, took Daniel's hand, and walked to the shore. "Come on, let's get our bathing costumes on."

In several feet of lake water, I crouched beside Daniel and held his center up. "Paddle your legs up and down—that's it. Now cup your hands and pull the water back toward your feet."

"Like this?" said Daniel.

"Good," I said. "Keep paddling." I walked along with him, often circling back to talk to Sadie, all the while trying to push away the dream. But my mind wouldn't succumb.

"Mommy, look at me, look at me," squealed Daniel. "Look at me, Mommy."

Sadie lounged onshore with her feet up, her head resting on the basket. "I see you, well done."

By the time Daniel grew tired and hungry for lunch, he was swimming by himself in the shallow water. He trudged up the graveled shoreline panting and sat with a thud in the middle of the blanket. "Did you see me swimming all by myself?"

"Of course I did. I couldn't take my eyes off you," said Sadie smiling widely. "Congratulations, my love, you did it."

Sadie dished up potato salad, a ham sandwich, and lemonade for lunch. We gobbled up the food and sang happy birthday before eating the white cake with buttercream frosting. Sadie was now twenty-four years old, a mature woman.

After lunch, Daniel laid on a corner of the blanket in the shade and drifted off to sleep. Sadie drew a sigh of relief and rested against me. "What do you want to name the new baby?"

That question was pitched high. We had lost our second child, a boy. He was born still and gray and cold. It was a shocking image that never fades, especially for Sadie, who struggled through the pregnancy and the long delivery. We buried him on the ridge and put flowers on his grave almost every day. We included him in our prayers at night, knowing his spirit was with the Lord. Three months later, Sadie was pregnant again. We were hopeful for the forthcoming life and fearful such a misfortune could happen again.

"If it's a boy, how about Renaldo, and if it's a girl, how about Clara?"

Sadie sat up and crossed her arms. "We're not going to name our children after your deceased siblings. That would be morbid."

"I hadn't thought of it that way." I pulled her back to me. My hand slid over her slight belly. "Stop talking and kiss me."

With a coy smile, Sadie whispered, "I love you, Mr. Jones."

I whispered back the same, and we kissed. We rarely got a chance to kiss as we used to, always busy with obligations —building our dream. I pulled her closer. My blood rose. I wanted to make love but didn't think she would consider it.

Then she whispered, "Let's go over there," she pointed to a large tree, "and, well, you know."

We kissed long. Sadie paused, leaned back to check on Daniel. Then quietly, we stood up and snuck off for a bit of mom and dad time.

It was seven p.m. when we made it back to the docks of Coeur d' Alene. The heat had subsided, but not enough to stop from perspiring. Sadie and Daniel sat on the deck and read Black Beauty—his favorite story. Meanwhile, I hurried to paint the inner starboard side white. It had been a most agreeable day. Daniel got his swim lesson. Sadie and I got some time alone. And I found a few minutes to work on the steamboat. The thought of last night's nightmare was all but forgotten.

When the train left Coeur d'Alene at 8:15 p.m., I had gotten most of one side of the inner starboard painted with the first coat. Sadie sat motionless beside me while Daniel drifted off to sleep, his head on his mother's lap. A murmur of voices and the train's thrum lulled me to sleep. Drifting in and out, my chin dropping to my chest until last night's dream terrors barged in like the bugle call of an elk.

I looked around the train car as it rattled along. The air was getting hotter and thicker at every click. I repositioned Daniel's bandana making sure it covered his mouth and nose. Sweat dripped off the ends of my hair and down my neck, drop after drop, a leaky faucet. A patch of perspiration puddled at Sadie's cleavage. Occasionally, she'd cough or shift positions, and the pooled water would drain into her corset. The replenishing effects of the cold lake water had vanished, discomfort returned. I would be glad when the heatwave passed.

Chapter Eighteen

Minutes before reaching the outskirts of town, smoke snapped my nose and stung my lungs. An intense light ripped across the sky, followed by a loud kaboom. Everyone screamed and grabbed their ears. The train brakes hollered and shuddered as it struggled to stop. For a few seconds, I feared it would derail. Daniel buried his face in his mother's breast and let go of a high-pitched cry, a sound as traumatic as at his first vaccination. The look of duplicity in his eyes made me feel I was the meanest father ever. I tried to calm him, but he just clutched his mother in a panic.

I had to know what had happened. I got to my feet and—stepped over fallen clothes and picnic baskets to make my way to a forward window. What I saw was worse than any nightmare I'd ever had. The entire downtown of Spokane Falls was on fire. Big blood-orange jaws devoured everything in their path like a horrible barbarian. Terror shot through me. I yelled back to Sadie, "The town's on fire!"

An expression of horror spread over her face as she struggled to see, but poor Daniel wouldn't settle." Your post, go to your post," she said.

Go to my post? Or stay and protect my family? Battles lines drew within me like a split in a rock. "I can't leave you."

"You must," Sadie said while soothing little Daniel's back and shushing him.

"No!" Was all I could think to say.

Daniel started to quiet. "We'll be okay. We'll wait for you. Go," she commanded.

I so admired her courage, but everything felt wrong about leaving. However, I knew she was right. I had to try and do what I could. I jerked free from my thoughts. "Stay on the train. I'll be back."

She waved me out. "Go."

I got to the caboose door and yanked it open. An intense wave of heat, hot as an iron, blew over me. I pulled out my handkerchief, tied it around my face, scanned the ground for a place to land, and jumped into the chamber of heat. Landing on my feet, I charged down the steep embankment. My footsteps increased in speed. Halfway down, my foot slipped into a hole. Down I plunged, hitting my right knee on a jagged rock. I heard the bone crack and felt a blade of pain pierce through it. As I slid to a stop alongside a tree, I lay there trying to catch my breath. With a mouth full of dirt and lungs full of smoke, I wished I had something to bite until the paralyzing pain lessened.

I rolled over onto my left side and scratched at the ground to get my left knee under me. I couldn't bend the right one. Clawing up the small tree an inch at a time. It was so painful that I couldn't stop moaning. My stomach retched. Once standing, I spread my arms out for balance and began hopping on my left leg as fast as I could across Bernard Street on my way to the Howard Street Bridge, about two blocks. The pain of the bouncing motion made me faint. When I woke rakes of pain coursed through me. Every muscle trembled. A long line of drool dribbled from my mouth. If I had allowed myself, I would have laid down and cried. The smoke, black and thick, was unavoidable. My throat burned as I hacked every step of the way. Turning several times toward the train, I worried for Sadie and

Daniel's safety. If anything happened to them, I'd never forgiven myself.

At the intersection of Main and Washington, a dining table and chairs stood in the middle of the road. A stranded woman burdened with an infant in one arm and a toddler in the other waited with the set. The sight of the children tore me. Hurriedly she made her way to me.

"Please, help us."

Their faces were covered in soot. Ashes and embers floated about, sometimes landing on their clothes, creating small puffs of smoke that rose from it. Tears streamed their faces, all of them coughing, crying.

I scoured the area. Red-hot flames bore down like a mass of stampeding cattle charged toward us. "You're not safe here."

"We're waiting for my husband," said the woman.

"You've got to get to the river," I said. "Give me the baby and come with me."

The woman stood her ground. "My husband will be back with a wagon."

I came face to face with her. "If you stay here, you'll die."

Just then, another explosion crashed through the night air, knocking her and her toddler to the ground. The conflagration drew out so much air, the flames around us died out. It left no air to breathe —then like a lightning strike —and the fire returned.

I cringed at the inferno above me. A flurry of sparks stung my face. The baby followed the lit particles as they floated around us. As I batted them away, I saw a taller building from the corner of my eye burning upwards like a torch. The windows were spewing merciless flames of evilness. The avenue trees and the telegraph poles, which connected the town blocks, spread fire on an efficient grid. I flashed back to the first time I saw Spokane. It was a cloudy September day. The town looked sleepy, dreary, and I wondered if I had lost my marbles by coming here. Today it was my town, my home viciously ablaze —a holocaust of coals —everything reduced to red rubble. All was lost.

I helped the woman up best I could. We hobbled toward Howard Street, wagons crammed with passengers rushed by. Family groups moved in tight clusters. Townspeople carried blanket sacks full of belongings. The closer we got to the river, the denser the mobs became.

For a moment, the smoke was as heavy as gravy. Adrift and disoriented, my eyes shut. I forced them open, determined to get this family to safety. My parched lips, as dry as a tin bucket, yearned for water. The river, not but a hundred yards away, seemed unreachable. Still, the baby held onto me with a viselike grip. Firebrands rained down. A coach with three well-dressed women jerked forward, narrowly evading an elderly couple on foot. The Grand Hotel was billowing smoke. People dropped bundles from its windows and exterior staircases. A ladder crew helped many trapped on upper floors get to safety. The rescued ran for the river like terrified children running to their mothers' arms.

An explosion went off a few blocks away. A fountain of sparks mushroomed in the sky. Another blast roared up the street, tearing awnings from buildings and leaves from trees.

I made out a crew of men pushing what resembled a dynamite cart in the smoky distance. Was the explosion I heard a bomb? Would Nicholls have ordered such a dangerous tactic? I turned to the stranded mother. "I'll get you to the bridge. Then I must go."

She stared at me with devastation in her eyes. "How will my husband find us?"

She looked so pitiful, her eyes red and swollen, her cheeks covered in black ash. Shame snatched at me. "Just stay by the bridge. He'll find you."

When we got to the Howard Street Bridge, it was backed up with hordes of frightened people jostling one another. Then a group charged forward in heedless terror, pushing friends and strangers. Many dropped and fell over their stuff. Others lifted the fallen from the baking ground. I hated to hand over the baby, but I had to find a way to get across the bridge. If I could get to the pump station, I could force the system to expel more water. "I'm sorry. I've got to go. You'll be safe here."

The woman kissed my hand. "Thank you, dear sir." Her face was as pitiful as an orphaned child.

I pushed off with my good leg and lurched around the backside of the bridge. A cracking strain sounded from the bridge's deck under the weight of so many. There were hundreds of people, horses, carts, and carriages crossing it. I didn't have time to wait for my turn. I inched down the river embankment, thinking I could somehow cross underneath it. My left leg was numb. I tried bending it, but a blade of torture shot through me. A pain so sharp, I lost control of my bladder. For the next few minutes, all I could do was pant until the agony subsided. I spotted a steel girder flanking the entire length of the bridge—this was my answer. I grabbed hold of the girder and swung out over the river, scaling hand over hand across the overpass as fast as I could. Below, a boom of oily logs had caught fire at the river bank. Hot coals shimmered on its slick surface. Moments later, a puff of smoke floated out from under the bridge. I turned away and held my breath until it passed. Halfway across, my right hand landed on a hot spot, and I lost my grip. Dangling there, I saw a section of the bridge's decking section was on fire.

I reached up only to have my hand slip again. I tried a third time. The steel had become too hot to touch. I looked down at the gushing falls, where thousands of gallons of cold water rushed below me. Its undaunted spirit raced toward its destination while my life flashed before my eyes.

Daniel stood beside me at the dinner table, imitating a frog he found that day.

"He hopped up to my arm and sat there," he said, pointing. We laughed.

We laughed. Then Sadie and I were in our wagon, admiring one of the many beautiful houses in Spokane. "One day, I'm going to build you a house like that."

She cooed.

Then we were in bed. The sound of her contentment filled my ears. Was this it? Was I to die tonight? Would I leave my family alone to fend for themselves? I glanced down at the perilous falls once more. My hand was tiring, slipping little by little. I clenched my teeth, and with one last burst of determination, I reached up and shouted, "Help me." Suddenly my hand was caught by another.

"I gotcha," said a man with a Slavic accent. I looked up to see a square-faced man with a flop of blond hair and kind eyes.

He pulled me up onto the bridge. His hands were meaty and robust.

On the deck, I lay there panting. Then, the bridge crackled and popped, even more smoke rose.

The Slavic man helped me stand and saw my knee." You're injured. Let me help you."

"No time. I've got to get to the pump house." I turned to leave and remembered the bridge. "The bridge," I said, "it's on fire. You've got to get these people off. Can you do it?"

"How much time do we have?" said the Slavic man.

"Thirty minutes, maybe less," I said.

"I doubt they'll listen, but I'll try," he said and turned back.

"Good man." I hobbled toward the pump house and heard the Slavic man yell. "The bridge is on fire! Get off! Get off the bridge. It's going down."

I reached the pump house, grabbed the door, and swung it open. Akin was there working feverishly. I yelled at him. "Jesus, man, what have you been doing? The town is burning down."

Akin came toe to toe with me, unaware of my injury. One fist clenched, the other held the monkey wrench. A look of betrayal swiped across his face. "I've been feeding the boiler as fast as it will take it. I increased the pressure to 100 psi. Our trouble maker has been temperamental, but it's functioning now."

A streak of guilt burst through me as I grabbed the pipe wrench from his hand and opened the valve. Steam poured out, boiling water gushed. We screamed as scalding water splashed over us. The pumps rumbled and ticked a threatening noise. I applied brute force to close the valve, but the trap was stuck. "Hold it while I open the other one. Ready?"

"Full bore," shouted Akin. "This could be the end."

"Gotta try," I said, cranking the valve and pulling out the trap.

Without warning, we heard a giant crash and instinctively took cover. I screamed as my injured leg bent.

"What the hell was that?" said Akin, his eyes wide, his lower lip quaking.

I didn't have to guess. I knew what it was. "The Howard just went down. Help me out." I leaned on Akin. We made it to the edge just in time to watch a giant chunk of the bridge tumble down the river. The burning timber sizzled and popped like a hot frying pan submerged underwater, a truly unbelievable sight.

Across the river, against the black night sky, the whole town was a torrent of scarlet. The heat had a depleting effect on energy, like bloodletting. Most of the townspeople had made their way down to the river's edge. I wiped the black goo from my nose and pushed my hair out of my eyes. "Looks like he got them off in time."

"Who?" Akin said.

"A man who saved my life and for whom I will always be thankful." I leaned harder against Akin. "Come on, let's see if we can get any more out of those pumps."

Akin pointed in the direction of his house. "I left my wife to fend for herself." His mouth quivered. His red-lined eyes spilled tears. "What's the use. There's nothing left to save."

Gazing at him in sympathy, I said. "It was an impossible choice. I, too, did the same. But, we can't give up."

Chapter Nineteen

Spokane Gazette

VOL…No. 266 © 1889 Spokane Gazette Company Monday, August 5, 1889

Appalling Fiend Destroys Spokane Falls

What has now become known as the Great Fire of Spokane Falls started, as near as this reporter has determined, at 6:15 p.m., Sunday, August 4, 1889, at the southwest corner of Railroad Avenue and Post Street.

Circumstances were prime for a catastrophic conflagration. Summer had served up drought-like conditions with temperature in the nineties with piercing sunlight and no rainfall since July 16.

"Wilbur almost didn't make it out alive."

The city had grown in an undisciplined manner due to the demand for laborers in the Idaho mines, lumber camps, and wheat farms. Homes were built next to mills, next to businesses, next to lumber yards, next to shanties and lean-tos, most of which were pine-built —an exceptionally dry fuel source.

The fire was thought to have started in two places within minutes of each other. The first is believed to have begun at Wilbur Johnson's Kitchen Cafe. An oily rag over the stove caught fire when pork chops plopped into a bubbling skillet of fat. Flames shot up, jumped onto an oily rag, then straight onto the greasy walls.

Try as they might, owner Wilbur Johnson said, "We watched in awful fascination at the speed in which a quilt of flames and black smoke engulfed the cafe ceiling." Matilda Johnson said, "Wilbur almost didn't make it out alive." Mr. Johnson was treated at Sacred Heart Hospital for third-degree burns to his left shoulder. Both were treated for smoke inhalation and are expected to make a full recovery.

The second fire began in Lady Colleen's boarding house in a room located on the second floor of the saloon adjacent to the cafe. She was getting dressed for work and heating up her curling iron in a kerosene lamp chimney when allegedly a customer barged in and knocked over the lamp. Flames crawled up the lace curtain and out the open window catching the exterior ablaze.

Mayor Nicholls, having just finished dinner at the Grand Hotel with Councilmen Jeb Thomas and Frank Rossiter heard the clanging fire bell as they stepped outside. "I spotted a cloud of smoke above the rooftops," said Nicholls. "Right then, I had a bad feeling. People on the street just stood around watching. Instinctively, I knew we needed everyone's help. I commanded them to get their buckets and follow me. One after another, people joined in. I drove the crowd forward into what seemed like hell's gate."

Police Captain Stanley Everett and two of his officers on patrol heard the ruckus from several blocks over. "People began flocking to the scene jostling each other to get a better look," said Captain Everett. "We formed a bucket line and got working." Brave men covered in wet blankets ran into the buildings trying to stop the sprawling fiend.

Although the firehouse was within blocks of the fire, firefighters didn't reach the conflagration until 6:37 p.m. —twenty-two minutes after it had begun. Six firemen pulled a two-thousand-pound hose cart to the hydrant at the corner of First and Post and hooked it up. A weak stream of water flushed out of the hose. One witness reported, "The pressure was no better than a garden hose." Another said, "One powerful blast of water would have stopped the whole thing."

"The water pressure was no better than a garden hose."

A strong wind prevailed from the southwest and increased at times to almost a full gale. The sky sparkled with what looked like waves of orange fireflies. Many said it was beautiful at first. In the meantime, other downtown residents and business owners watching the fire roar up the street rushed back to save what they could. Residents began stacking their prized possessions in the middle of the sawdust streets, making it difficult for wagons to pass.

Mayor Nicholls ordered Councilman Thomas to run to the pump house and tell Water Superintendent, Rolla Jones, to raise the pressure as far as it would go. By then, the whole block was on fire. A brisk wind relayed the flame one building after another.

Thomas told this reporter, "When I neared the Howard Street Bridge, a parade of people trampled in the same direction. My tongue fought to swallow the paste of dehydration. The need for water was like no other desire I'd ever experienced except the desire to breathe clean air. I pushed and shouted, let me through. I'm on official business! But when I reached the pump house, the door was locked, and no one was there."

The town's dry wooden skin ignited like match sticks. Everything wooden was sizzling; paint bubbled, and oil squirted to the surface like the squeezing of a lemon peel. Flames broke out in the neighboring houses, and shortly the whole block was a hive of fire. People abandoned their houses hastily. Household goods that had been brought out on the street burst into flames. The fire, which now had a terrible headway, soon came in contact with the Ross house, and in a few minutes, the building was one mass of red. The Grand Hotel was next to be seen smoking. It, too, was soon enveloped in a thick buildup of smoke, through which a horrifying conflagration burst. The stately buildings, of which all we were so justly proud of, was doomed.

At Post Street, the following places were ablaze and soon consumed: McCullough's Cigar Store, Post Street Barber Shop, Pacific Cigar Store, Comet Saloon, Bodega Saloon, Finklestein Clothing, Casino Saloon, cigar store of Bishop and Co., Hoods Restaurant, Abram's Fruit and Cigars, Opera House Saloon, Ed Watson's Barnum & Son, clothing, Al Heuer's Cigar Store, American second-hand store, Wm. Butterworth, Withers, Coey & Thomas, drugs, Johnston's Grocery, and Leffler's Saloon.

The fire on the west side of Post Street was quick to devour buildings. The Minneapolis Lunch House, Coeur d' Alene Saloon, Blue Front Lodging House, R. R. Lunch Counter, N. P. R. R. Depot's office of the Spokane and Palouse Railway were all in the fire's clutches.

Bedlam broke out. The shrieks of train engines moving in an attempt to push standing freight cars clear of the blaze sounded above the screams. Shouts of men and women rushing from the Ross House and Grand Hotel echoed as a wall of flames rolled upon them.

The crowds on their way out of the city ran, dodging burning missiles hurtling down from above. The scene on Riverside Avenue was indescribable. Merchants ran around offering large sums to draymen for their services. In some cases, they endeavored to make them stop by main force. People were continually dodging teams of horses running through the streets at break-neck speed.

When the flames reached the opera house, they jumped onto it like a predator in pursuit of a kill. A black mare used for theatre productions, blindfolded and barely able to contain its delirium, was led down the interior staircase of the opera house. Once outside and the blindfold removed, the horse bolted.

The firemen had been working manfully and could do nothing more. Every minute or so, another loud report of walls crashing and ceilings caving set residents running for cover. A great host of cinders flew high then fell promiscuously in all directions.

"The roar and crackle of the fire were heard for miles," as told by residents outside of the city. Those who had witnessed large fires before said, "We never saw anything to equal the fierceness and rapidity with which the flames swept across."

More burning embers carried by the high wind fell upon the fleeing crowds; a patter of the debris hit rooftops; horses stampeded; citizens ran for their very lives. Random explosions were of a nature to cause all to think that the world was coming to an end.

A heavyset woman with a ten-year-old hysterically ran by me as torrents of smoke rushed out windows. "We're all going to hell."

"We're all going to hell."

When this reporter caught up with the mayor, his face and clothes were covered in soot, his eyes blood-shot and incessantly weeping. "I saw the faces of screaming children and hysterical women. Of men negotiating the removal of their possessions to higher ground with only a few opportunistic wagoners circling the area." All the while, the fire bell wailed.

At 8:10 p.m., the mayor, Rossiter, Thomas, and Captain Everett had come to an agreement: no amount of water could stop the fire. To prevent it from consuming every last structure, they decided to create firewalls to contain it. Blowing up a line of buildings on the east and west sides of the town was the only way to stop the trajectory of the beastly fire.

Everything as far as the eye could see was either burning or smoking: railings, trees, telegraph poles. The sky was an orange dome against a backdrop of billowing black clouds. The town of Spokane Falls was doomed.

With the assistance of Captain Everett, the mayor ordered giant powder to bring down the buildings. The danger of carrying powder kegs amid fire was not just risky. It was suicidal.

Behind the burning opera house on Monroe Street, at the corner of the Northern Pacific Right of Way and Lincoln, the first charges were set by four brave men. This reporter witnessed two men in their twenties light a fuse, turn and run. Seconds later, a deafening explosion sucked the air into a vacuum. For a moment, everything was still and noiseless, only to have the explosion return with a vengeance as the backdraft barreled down. It spread dust, razor-sharp wood splinters, bricks, and glass as far as one could see. One runner was pitched by the force into a storefront window. Another man was hit in the head by a brick and is said to be in grave condition.

The pressure of the bomb blast and the heat it created burned the faces of those not yet evacuated. The violent wind thrust hair from side to side. And like falling boxes, buildings exploded into mountains of smoldering wreckage. Clouds of choking dust consumed every unit of available air space. Spokane falls was irretrievable in the fiend's mouth.

Chapter Twenty

By the next morning, my knee was an eggplant. I had to see a doctor. Benny offered to take me into town, but I insisted on going alone. I wasn't in my right mind. He saddled up Cyrus and brought him around to the front door. Sadie helped me out. My leg was wrapped in splints and bandages. She was not happy with my decision to go it alone.

"Let Benny take you," said Sadie.

"I'll be all right," I said through my teeth.

Sadie looked annoyed. "What's gotten into you?" she said, placing a hand on her hip, "You'd never allow me to do such a thing."

I flinched, too proud to admit I didn't want to appear helpless. "I'll be fine. Stop worrying."

Benny fidgeted nervously. "Mr. Jones, let me take you."

Cyrus sensed there was a problem and raised his head in protest.

Just then, a man on a black horse galloped up the driveway, spun around, pulled out an envelope, and handed it to me. "You, Jones?"

I reached for the envelope. "Yeah."

"This is for you," he said, then took off down the driveway without waiting for a response.

I handed it to Sadie. "Could you read it?"

Sadie tore open the envelope and read the note. "It's a summons from the mayor. There's a town hall meeting in the big tent." Sadie scratched her head. "What tent?" She looked at Benny, who shrugged a shoulder.

"Must be a tent," said Benny.

"It's scheduled for three p.m.," said Sadie, folding up the letter. "You're expected to attend."

I drew a big breath and bit my lip. "Benny, give me a leg up."

"Sure, Mr. Jones, but I think she's right. You're in no shape to go it alone."

I shouted, "I can do this!"

Grasping the letter to her chest, Sadie stepped back. "Stubborn fool."

"Benny, please." I didn't want anyone telling me what I couldn't do. I was determined not to be in this diminished state.

Benny shook his head and made a sling with his hands. I stepped in and tried to swing my bad leg over Cyrus. A sudden scream burst from me as pain shot through my leg. I fell back against Benny.

Sadie took over. "Get him on the porch, and get Cyrus hooked up to the wagon."

"We've got to elevate the leg," said Benny as he set me in a rocker on the porch.

Sadie rushed into the house. "I'll get blankets and pillows."

Daniel came to stand beside me and took my hand. "Are you going to die Dada?" His eyes were worried and glossy.

I squeezed his hand. "Oh, no, I am not going to die. I just need to see a doctor for my leg." I pulled him to me and held him tight. "Dada will be back before the end of the day. I love you."

"Are you sure, Dada?" whispered Daniel.

I held him tighter, kissed his head, and nodded.

Benny brought Cyrus and the wagon forward. Sadie set up the bedding. Benny lifted me over his shoulder, set me on the edge of the cart, and dragged me in.

Sadie propped pillows under my knee and another behind my back then covered me with several blankets. "Better, you stubborn mule?"

Sheepishly I nodded. "I'm sorry." I waved goodbye to Daniel and Sadie as we headed for the hospital.

We took the Maple Street Bridge on the far west end of town because the Howard had burned and fallen into the river. As we reached the city, smoke stood motionless over the city like a derelict unwilling to vacate. A powerful enemy had marched in and demolished everything. Spokane Falls had suffered hard and died a horrible death. Everything in me wanted to flee. A gut-pull so hard it left me nauseous. No man wants to admit when they're afraid, but I was. My heart revved at each terrifying memory skating before my eyes. My breathing became short and shallow. A grabbing sensation clutched my chest. I tried to calm myself, but panic kept rising. I wished Benny would turn the wagon around or just keep going out of town, anything but deliver me to my fate.

Monday, August 5,1889

The Spokesman-Review

VOL. XI No. 1026 © 1889 The Spokesman-Review

MILLIONS LOST

An Appalling Calamity Visits the Proud City of Spokane Falls

Thirty Blocks of Its Most Magnificent Buildings Devoured by Flames

---

The Entire Business Portion of the City Wiped Out of Existence

---

A Night of Terror Devastation, Suffering and Awful Woe

Hundreds of Dwellers Downtown Turned into the Streets Destitute

---

One Man Killed and Many Others

Severely and Painfully Injured

An Official to Be Investigated for an
Apparently Inexcusable Blunder

The People Not Discouraged and the
City Will Be Rebuilt Better Than Ever

Notes and Incidences of the Disaster and a
History of Many Heroic Deeds

A List of the Sufferers, with Amounts of
Losses So Far Received

We entered a section of town where a crew of men was hard at work patching wires to the damaged telegraph system. Another team loaded burned debris into a caravan of wagons. I read a sign that ordered a state of martial law, a sensible way to keep an appearance of law and order. Meanwhile, tents were coming in by train and by wagon. It wouldn't be long until Spokane Falls would be a city of tents. I later found out a dozen National Guardsmen from Fort Wright, an all-negro company of soldiers, were on their way to supervise the removal of the debris and prevent looting.

When we arrived at the hospital, Benny went to find a wheelchair. He came back empty-handed. "They're all being used." I scooted to the end of the wagon, and he lifted me over his shoulder and carried me in like a sack of potatoes.

Gurneys and wheelchairs were filled with people who had made makeshift bandages to cover their burns and lacerations. Others wandered about coughing and hacking. I didn't see any sheeted bodies. Nurses with clipboards and pencils walked around, taking down names and triaging the injured.

A boy of about fourteen entered the hallway and called, "Mrs. Hutchinson, Mrs. Adelaide Hutchinson?" A shaky woman rose with the aid of her husband and followed the boy into an examination room. Another volunteer with long hair tied at the back stopped and asked for my name.

"Your name, please?"

"Rolla Jones." I winced as a crack of pain skittered through me.

"Rolla Jones, you say?"

"Yes, why?"

"Oh, nothing, I heard your name mentioned a few times, is all. You look in a bad way. I'll get you a room as soon as I can." He stepped away, looking back over his shoulder with an indignant expression. Dread rolled over me like the spread of measles. The gossip had begun. No one ever fared well under the eye of that tornado.

Teams of priests, nuns, and Red Cross workers, a little way down the hallway, searched for places to shelter the homeless. One more table down, a group of volunteers was busy reuniting lost family members. Between the two tables, a wall phone sat. One of only six phones in Spokane fewer now was in near-constant use by the Red Cross workers. “Call the folks in Coeur d’Alene. See if they can take thirty more people," said a nun with a superior voice. Families asleep in the corridor were ten deep. Mothers quieted their wearied and hungry children. Others shared stories of heroism with whoever would listen.

"I was on my way out of town when I saw two children screaming in frozen terror. I had to help," said the cowboy. The young couple listening was wide-eyed and transfixed.

I tried to take my mind off the gossip mill, but it kept reeling it in. My leg pain was still so intense I could barely think in a straight line. I wanted to pace the floor or punch walls, something to distract the pain. I settled on reviewing the protocols the city council had approved for the system I had designed and built. That process provided no relief whatsoever.

Sometime later, I got a wheelchair and was wheeled into a room split by a curtain and helped onto a gurney. I was desperate for sleep. On the other side of the curtain, a sheet lay over a body. I saw the doctor standing over it saying to a man with a notebook.

"George S. Davis, our only fatality, died from jumping through fire out a window, like some kind of circus animal."

I covered my arm over my face and squeezed my eyes closed. My dream had foretold the event. Tears began rolling. I could have warned people, but instead, I had skated on my merry way, ignoring the omen.

"Well, it's early still," said the doctor. "There's likely to be more."

"Hear tell the man with the only key to the pump station was out of town fishing," said the reporter. "Astonishing that more deaths haven't been reported."

"Was that why no water came through the fire hose?" said the doctor.

The reporter tapped on his writing pad. "That's what I hear. I'd like to string that bastard up by his gonads."

"You and many others, I suspect," said the doctor. "Now, if you've no more questions, I've got others to treat."

"Thanks for your time, doc," said the reporter. "Say, when's the last time you had a break?"

"Don't worry about me. I'm fine," said the doctor.

Overwhelmed by the poor man's death, I started sobbing. The curtain slid back along the ceiling track. My face was wet by the torrent of tears.

"Mr. Jones, I'm Dr. Van der Flies. I understand you've sustained a leg injury." The doctor saw my tears and handed over a tissue. "There, there," he said. "You must be in a great deal of pain. I'll get you some pain relief but first, let's have a look." He grabbed a pair of scissors and cut away the bandages Sadie had wrapped around my knee. The doctor appeared about ten years older than me and had a swipe of white in his dark hair.

"Oh, my, that is substantial," said the doctor as he touched my knee with two fingers. I swallowed hard and tried to let the pain wash over me. "Try and relax. Everything is going to be fine."

I soldiered up. "Okay, doc."

He poked on either side of my knee then on top. "You're lucky the bones are still under the skin. You'll need thorough cleansing, sutures, and a cast to stabilize the leg. You broke the knee cap right in half."

I turned to him. "I heard it snap."

He raised his eyebrows. "I'll bet you did," he said, patting my arm. "I'm going to give you a laudanum tincture for the pain. I'll send you home with two weeks' supply. In the meantime, complete bed rest. If the infection gets worse, come back and see me. Do you have bromine at home to wash the wound daily?"

"Mm-hmm," I said, biting my lip.

The doctor turned to leave. "I'll send some with you just in case."

When he returned with the syringe and sewing kit, he asked, "Are you Rolla Jones, the water superintendent?"

I peeked at him from the corner of an eye. "Yes, but you have your story wrong."

"Oh, so you weren't fishing?" said the doctor as he pulled the syringe full of liquid.

"My assistant was on duty as scheduled."

He inserted the needle. "What happened to the water?" he asked.

I blubbered for a minute as droplets rolled down the sides of my face and into my ears. "I don't know, but I'm going to find out."

"One more poke," said the doctor injecting the needle into the leg where the flesh and muscle had torn.

That's the last thing I remember until waking up as the doctor finished wrapping my leg from thigh to foot with plaster of Paris. The cast was massive and needed to dry for a long while. Once released from the hospital, my loyal friend Benny was waiting. "Hey, Ben," I said through a drug-induced grin, "I don't think I can maneuver this cast on my own."

Benny knocked on the cast with his knuckles. "Probably not a good time to go swimming either."

I laughed and put my arm around his neck. "Sure, am glad you're here." Benny rolled me back to the wagon. The pain was gone, but so was my mind. I had never had a drug like that before. This was a moonshine like no other. Keeping my wits about me during the meeting would be difficult.

Benny and I rolled down the street slowly. I struggled to stay coherent. People stumbled around, dazed and listless. Bloody bandages were wrapped around hands, legs, and heads. Every manner of clothing wore sections of burned marks.

Benny pulled up alongside the only tent amongst the many burned-out buildings and helped me into the oatmeal-colored canvas tent. There must have been fifty people inside standing around, their arms crossed, demanding answers. I struggled to keep my head up and eyes open. A hazy covering distorted everything I saw. A warped racket of voices bellowed and bulged and squawked and whinged.

A man huddled beside his young family cried, "How will I recover from this disaster?"

An older man with a white beard talked in slow motion. His voice was deep and dark, and bits of spittle foamed at his mouth corners. "You…gotta…fix…this."

Then a screeching voice pierced the wigwam. "I've got no home to go to."

I went to hold my ears but couldn't quite reach them.

Mayor Nicholls whacked a stick on a box until it broke in half. "Order! Come to order!"

Rossiter, who was his usual tactless self blurted. "Bellyachers, shut your traps."

Captain Everett pulled out his whistle and blew it hard and long. Eventually, the crowd quieted. Nicholls stared down a few of the relentless loudmouths. I knew that look of irritation all too well. "We're here to form committees to deal with the many questions before us and,"

Rossiter interrupted and pointed at me. "I dare say the first matter is to determine who's to blame for this catastrophe as if we don't already know."

The crowd roared and brandished their tattered hats in the air.

Through the haze of opioids, I stiffened my back and lifted my head. I flashed back to the opossum I had found in the corner of my fruit stand one evening: frightened, ferocious, undeniably trapped. I, too, felt trapped by what seemed a schoolyard of bullies.

Nicholls looked furious and yelled over the crowd. "We are going to follow the law. That's what civilized people do."

But his assertions were useless. The crowd was beyond reason.

Everett blew his whistle again, and again the people quieted.

"What we're going to do is conduct an investigation," said Nicholls holding his fists tight, "a full investigation. We will get to the truth. You have my word."

Rossiter raised his hand. "I volunteer to lead the investigation."

Though I was blurry-eyed and dizzy from the drug, I wasn't going to let that go uncontested. "No way! You are incapable of being fair-minded." By the looks on their faces, I must have slurred my words.

Nicholls paused and took stock of Rossiter's demeanor. "He's right. It must be a completely unbiased examination."

Rossiter spluttered in astonishment. "I will be objective. You have my word."

"How will we know you'll employ scrupulous fact-finding methodology?" said Thomas looking toward Rossiter. "No, I think it's better I lead the study."

The crowd grumbled.

Rossiter puffed up like a cornered snake. "I'll do my due diligence, as I always have. Furthermore, I resent the implication that I've ever done otherwise."

Florence Rossiter, who had been standing slightly behind her husband, stepped forward. Her face twisted, and her eyes jeered at me. "Everyone knows Mr. Jones is more concerned about his many businesses than paying attention to his city duties."

Her words set off a litany of accusations followed by a volley of shouts from the townspeople. I wasn't surprised considering who she was married to, but the ache of betrayal was bruising. All the times she'd flirted with me, in front of her friends and her husband. All the times I had to politely deflect her advances. And that night at the party when she tried to seduce me into going upstairs, saying, "I wanted you from the first time we met."

There is never a way to say no to an aristocrat who is used to getting her way. This was her way of getting back at me. The rumor mill surely would feast on her assertions for weeks to come. Her accusations didn't hurt as much as they humiliated me. She was the last woman I would have ever considered straying with. If Sadie had been here, she would have been crazed out of her mind. It would have hurt her, our marriage, her trust in me. Such an ungodly and unfounded hurt for her to endure.

Thomas punched the air with his right hand. "That indictment is unfounded. And you can be sure I will be checking your every fact, every conclusion."

The mayor turned to Thomas. "Why do you say such a thing?"

Thomas crossed his arms and paused. "I believe her motives to be disingenuous. I have witnessed advances by this lady on Mr.

Jones. Dare I say she may be a scorned woman seeking revenge. Let us not assert a fall guy for the convenience of petty motives."

That was a bold and possibly reckless statement for Thomas to make. He had the integrity of ten men. I hoped his integrity would not be to his detriment. Nevertheless, I couldn't help but be profoundly grateful.

"Fine, you do that," said Rossiter glaring at his wife. "And as for my wife's unbefitting conduct, you can be sure there will be repercussions."

By this time, Florence Rossiter, whose jaw was agape, had scurried indignantly out of the tent with two of her cohorts in tow.

Rossiter faced the crowd. "Now, who will join me?"

A slew of hands went up. Rossiter pointed at three of his regular cronies and three or four other townsmen. "You, you, you two, and the rest of you with your hands up, meet me after the meeting."

Thomas's promise of oversight lessened my anxieties but did not alleviate them.

Nicholls turned to me, his eyes cast low. "In light of the impending investigation, I believe it is fitting to ask you for your resignation."

The crowd roared.

My heart sank as I erupted inside: my hands shook, sweat leaked from every pore, every muscle was tense as iron. I had to hold it together. Otherwise, my defense would be futile. An overreaction would be seen as a sign of guilt.

This was the last thing I expected from Nicholls. I kept a stiff upper lip, turning my hat in my hand, trying to find the right words.

"Do you have anything to say?" said Nicholls, a bit strangled himself.

My mind raced back and forth, trying to put something together that made sense. My head was fuzzy. A drilling sound bore into my left ear. I looked at the many people I had come to know and care about. Francis from the livery stable, Jeremy from the land office, both of whom were at my wedding, were now unwilling to look at my beseeching stare. Stuart from the general store and Stan from the bakery also seemed to be in agreement with the others. Then as if outside my body, I heard myself say, "I followed all the protocols."

The crowd clamored.

Nicholls spun around and yelled, "Let him speak."

Most quieted except for a few final insults: "Liar." "Lazy, good for nothing."

"My assistant was on duty. It was my rightful day off," I said emphatically.

"You had the only key to the pump house, and your assistant was nowhere to be found," said Rossiter.

I jerked and screamed, "Not true."

The crowd roared.

Nicholls stepped forward, his arms spreading out. "We sent Thomas there. He found no one, and the door was locked. How do you explain that?"

Thomas tried to speak but was motioned by the mayor to keep quiet. Thomas seemed flummoxed. My trusted confidant was now forbidden to stand up for me. I thought Nicholls would be fair with me, but I guess I was wrong.

The sense of betrayal was murderous, like the day Renaldo died the day my father implied that the fire that killed my brother may have been my fault. I was five years old. We had been playing with wood matches in the barn loft when one fell between the floorboards. I left to go to the W.C. When I got back, the barn was on fire. Recollections of that horrible day took all the fight from me. Drained of hope, depleted of strength, I couldn't go on. "I guess I have no other choice but to hope that the truth will come out."

Applause broke out.

A woman with a crooked cane stood up. "That's right, you have no other choice, just as we had no choice when our businesses and homes burned."

I starred at the ground and choked out. "I hereby resign my position."

Rossiter snickered through his teeth. "Well, at least he's handling it like a man."

Both Thomas and Nicholls avoided my gaze as I turned to leave. I'd never felt more alone in my life. Everything I had worked for had just disintegrated. I deflected Benny's help at first, trying to get myself out of the tent, but every muscle in me trembled. Spots twinkled before my eyes.

Nicholls followed me out. When Benny and I reached the wagon, Nicholls reached out his hand and touched my shoulder in a fatherly manner. "Listen, Jones, resigning was the right thing to do."

His hand on my shoulder disgusted me. I moved from it.

"Rebuilding this town is going to take an enormous effort," said Nicholls. "We need everyone working together. Can't you see that?"

I looked him dead in the eye, forcing myself to focus. "Any perversion of the truth, I'll be hiring an attorney. Do you get that?"

Nicholls stepped back, astonished.

I'd worked with Nicholls for five years. This was out of character for him. I knew him to be an honorable man. Then it came to me. "Rossiter, put you up to this?"

Nicholls waffled. "No, he hasn't."

I grabbed onto the wagon and spat back at him. "Only a coward blames an innocent man."

Nicholls puffed up his chest and wagged a finger. "Someone has to take responsibility for this calamity."

I stared at his finger and the black dirt under his nail. "You're pointing in the wrong direction."

I had nothing left in me. My head pounded, my bowels a twisted towel. "Damn you to hell. You know I'm telling the truth."

On the ride back, I slipped in and out of drug-induced euphoria and a macabre string of nightmarish thoughts. One question haunted me to the core. Would I ever be forgiven?

Chapter Twenty-One

When I woke, I was rested and stronger, and the pain was minimal. I rubbed my eyes and stretched my leg and arms a while before noticing I wasn't in my bedroom. I was in the front parlor on a cot. A washbasin and a neatly folded towel sat on the table beside me. The air smelled light and clean of smoke. The house was quiet except for the sound of dishes clanking in the kitchen. A moment later, Daniel wandered in and found me leaning on my elbows. He rushed and hugged me.

"What did I do to deserve such a hug?"

Daniel leaned away from me. "Yucky, Daddy, you smell." He took off squealing as little children do when excited. "Daddy's awake," I heard him say.

Sadie's footsteps clicked across the floor. As she entered the parlor, her face was rife with concern. With teary eyes and a big smile, she kneeled beside me. "Oh, Rolla, you're finally awake."

"Yes, darling," I said, kissing her hand and wondering what the big deal was. "How long have I been sleeping?"

"Eight long days," said Sadie.

"Eight days…how is that possible?" I said, moving back onto my elbows again.

Sadie folded back my covers. "The daily dose of the tincture sent home with you got you to sleep through a lot of the healing pain."

I took Sadie's hand." I'm sorry. It must have given you a horrible fright."

She lowered her head and nodded, "Horrible."

I pulled her to me and held her tight with one arm.

Daniel came back with his favorite toy horse and snuggled up to me, laying his head on my chest. "You've been asleep too long."

I hugged them both and touched her tummy. "I had no idea. Is everything else all right?"

"I am fine," she said.

"And the baby?"

She smiled. "Fine."

"The harvest?"

"Benny and a part-timer have been a big help," said Sadie. "Listen, why don't I heat some water for a bath, and we can talk over dinner?"

Behind the glee in her eyes, I could see I had genuinely worried her. Everything was on her shoulders:—me, Daniel, the store, the harvest, the house. I don't know how she did it. I would have never asked so much of her, particularly since she was in her first three months of our third child.

I soaked in the hot soothing water. The soap cast-off days of dead skin and leftover soot. I needed a shave and a haircut, but the hair would have to wait another day. Being at home felt right. Good to have some time to sort things out. Jeb Thomas had been right that day on the street after the fire: "Be thankful you still have a home to go to." I was thankful. Only now, I was also riddled with humiliation and fear—humiliation to have the entire town against me and fear I'd be blamed for the fire forever. I practiced pushing that thought from my mind. It worked some of the time.

Sadie bathed and shaved me. Afterward, we sat down for a hot meal, my leg propped up on a pillow. Benny joined us for dinner.

"Sure glad you're up and around, Mr. Jones. The harvest is right on schedule. Mrs. Jones made sure of that. She's more bullheaded than you are." He lowered his eyes. "I hope you don't mind me saying, Mrs. Jones?"

She smiled wide. "Not in the least, Benjamin."

Daniel looked relieved and just happy to have us all together at one table again.

Famished and forgetting my manners, I grabbed a slice of bread and tore it in half. I looked around and noticed they hadn't begun eating. I stopped chewing and wiped the corners of my mouth. "It was a good thing you were here. You were the help Sadie needed while I was out of it. I owe you."

Benny shook his head. "Glad I was here to help."

How did such a loyal and modest man come from the likes of Rossiter? Whatever their disagreement, I was sure to be on Benny's side. "Shall we eat?" I said, eager to continue.

Daniel picked up his fork and looked at his mother. "Can we?"

"If you don't, I'll have to eat it all myself," said Sadie, "but first grab hands."

We took each other's hands and squeezed. She said, "Thank you, God, for this meal. Thank you for our friend Benny who watches after us so well, for the health of my son Daniel and for healing my love!"

Everyone at the table smiled broadly.

Daniel threw his head back and giggled.

The food tasted like Christmas. Rump roast, juicy, and fork-tender. Gravy, perfectly salted, and creamy. Boiled potatoes with freshly churned butter, tangy tomatoes from the garden, and a pie from Mrs. Clifton next door. Even the water was beyond compare, like ice cream in the summer —soft, cold, sweet. I cleaned my plate but couldn't eat a second helping. My stomach had shrunk.

When Daniel had gone to bed, and Benny had left, Sadie came back to the table with a wet cloth and began wiping it clean.

"Tell me, how are store sales?" I said.

She leaned over, holding her skirt back from touching the table, and took several long swipes across it. I watched as she dropped her skirt and swept the crumbs into her hand as if they were precious morsels worth saving. She then folded the damp towel onto itself, rested it on the table carefully, and rubbed her hands together. "We haven't had a customer since the fire. The people whom I thought were our friends have vanished. Only Benny, Sam, Mary, and their boys talk to us." She picked the rag back up and wiped the edges of the oak tabletop where Daniel had sat. "I guess we're no longer welcome here." She stopped cleaning. "What are we to do?"

I looked out the window at the diminishing light and searched my mind for an answer. Sadly, I turned to her. "I don't know. I'll figure something out. Try not to worry too much." Blamed for a fire. I didn't start, asked to resign, store sales gone, my knee was broken, and Sadie needed more of me than at any time since we had married. Yet at that moment, all I wanted was to sleep, my body too weary to continue sitting. "I have to go back to bed. I'm sorry." I put down my half-empty coffee cup. "What about the city council? Heard from them?"

"Not a peep," said Sadie helping me to the cot.

I patted her hand. "The whole matter will be settled in a few days. Don't worry." My head fell heavy on the pillow. I had no real confidence in my words and fell asleep mid-sentence with a lingering sense of guilt.

Days later, we still hadn't heard about the findings of the fire investigation. It was all I could think about, dream about. It's all Sadie, and I talked about; we were consumed with it. It was the tick we couldn't extract. It had hooked its teeth deep. The harder we tried to remove it, the more it screwed in. I needed a way to get it off my mind. Benny pushed me in a wheelbarrow to my workshop in the back corner of the barn. It felt good to get out of the house. Many a night after work and weekends, I'd steal away to repair tools or modify broken ones. When I could, I'd work on a few of my inventions. One, in particular, had promise. It was an invention that would solve a big problem for me—well, every farmer—an irrigation sprayer.

I'd been in the barn for an hour when Benny wandered back as he often did to watch me work, chat or go to his quarters in the upper barn. We had built him a nice room in the loft and installed a wood stove to keep him and the horses warm in the winter.

Benny knocked on a post. "The Mrs. asked me to check on you."

"You can tell her I'm fine." My cast was deteriorating into crumbly bits. I was regaining my strength little by little, and as long as I kept my leg in a specific position, it didn't hurt.

"What are you working on?" Benny said.

"I call it a garden sprayer. It will water gardens and crops when I get it figured out. Here, hold this for me."

Benny stepped over and took hold of the channel-lock pliers I held out for him. "Down a little. Hold it there."

"Like that?" Benny said.

"That's it. Now a ninety-degree bend to the left." We applied equal pressure and bent the copper band into what I hoped would be the correct circumference. "The idea is to slip this device over it so it'll slide the length of the hose and return, all the while spraying water."

Benny leaned in. "What propels it?"

"Water pressure," I said.

"How are you going to pressurize the water?" said Benny.

I looked at him, surprised by the question, "With a small pump."

"That's clever as all get-out, Mr. Jones."

I paused and looked at Benny. "When are you going to start calling me Rolla? You've been around long enough. I think of you more like a brother than a farmhand."

"Hard to break a habit," he said with a smile.

I hadn't put much thought into those words, but he was like a brother. Only in this case, instead of me being the younger brother, I was the elder. It never occurred to me I could feel this way after losing Renaldo. It was renewing, and yet a sense of disloyalty flickered in me.

I reached for a can of oil. "Have you talked with your family lately?" I wanted to appear mildly curious but not nosey. Benny had revealed who his father was a while back. I told him I already knew and was not concerned as long as it didn't cause problems. So far, Rossiter had kept his distance from his son. He avoided mention of Benny when I was around except for an occasional off-color remark.

Benny leaned in closer to see what I was greasing up. "I saw my stepmother, Florence, from across the road a few days back when I was in town for supplies."

I was incensed by the mere mention of her name. I muttered under my breath but kept working. After a few minutes, I got up the gumption to ask, "Did you talk to her?"

Benny lifted his chin and stared into space blankly. "I don't talk to her."

Still trying to keep the conversation casual, I put down the oil can and wiped the excess oil onto a rag. "Can I ask why?"

Benny exhaled the way Cyrus does when he's impatient to move on. "She doesn't want me around. Says I make her tense."

"Hmm. What about your father?" I said.

"He's too busy running the town, or so he thinks, to be bothered with me. I figure he thinks I'm old enough to make it on my own. He told me he moved away from his parents when he was around my age and never went back."

This time I made eye contact. "Maybe he needs a reason to talk again."

He dropped his hands at his sides. "No, he's happy to be rid of me."

I turned the device upside down. "Here, you clamp that end down while I hold this part. You see, this sleeve has to be free to move—nothing can restrict it, or it will stop and soak one area only."

Benny shook his head in agreement. "When it reaches the end, how will it retract?"

"Ha, I'm still working that out." I was slightly embarrassed at my lack of progress. "Do you like numbers?"

"Oh yeah, numbers have always made sense to me," Benny said.

I snapped my fingers and pointed at him. "Maybe there's an engineer in you."

"Thanks, Mr. Jones —Rolla. Nobody ever thought of me as having potential." He slid his hands in his pant pockets. "Except maybe my mom. She died when I was twelve."

I could see by his sullen eyes he missed the one person in the world who had loved him no matter what.

"I can teach you some engineering concepts?"

His eyes brightened. We shook hands.

"Let's start with velocity," I said.

****

When I got back to the house, I went to lie down. Sadie's face peered over me just as I began to drop off.

"Rolla, before you sleep, I have a proposal I want you to think on."

I stirred awake and stretched out my hand to touch her. "What?"

Sadie twisted a hand towel in her hands and sat in the chair. Pausing, she smiled. "Let's sell this place and move to Walla Walla, where my parents are now. It'll be a new beginning, a new start. It's easy when we're young, not as easy when we're older."

I jerked up.

She continued. "Daniel will be in school soon. Our baby would be in a calmer environment. Mom can help me."

"For criminy sakes Sadie, do you understand what you're asking? We can't just sell the homestead, our home, our children's birthright, and go off with our tail between our legs."

Sadie leaned back. "Why not? Spokane isn't the only place to live a good life."

I felt my muscles pull taut and a deep hole open in my chest. "You think I'm at fault?"

Sadie slapped her hands on her knees. "No, of course not. But you know how people are when they make up their minds."

"It would be an admission of guilt," I heard my voice get louder. "I will never admit to something I haven't done."

"If you didn't always think about yourself," said Sadie with a pursed mouth and outrage in her eyes, "you might be able to see this as a good idea."

I yelled. "That's how you see it, do you?" A storm of anger rose in me. "Everything I do is for you and Daniel, everything." I stopped to catch my breath, my heart beating in my throat.

Sadie's erect posture and glare told me she was searching for a comeback. Then her countenance changed, and she slumped low in the chair like a disgruntled teenager. I pulled her to me. "Come here. I'm sorry. This must be awful for you." I squeezed her. "It's going to be all right. We should hear from the committee soon, and it'll be over with. Try not to worry so much, please."

She searched my eyes and patted my hand with trepidation the way her mother did her father's, a placating subservient touch of resignation mastered over the years. She propped her chin onto one hand and stared at the floor. "Stop worrying? That's an impossible request."

Chapter Twenty-Two

By the time we did hear from the committee, it was day sixteen post-fire, August 20. Fortunately, much of the heatwave had diminished. Mornings were cooler. A man on horseback delivered a note saying I was to attend the reading of the committee's findings. I asked Sadie not to come. I didn't want her to see me exposed, but she insisted. Benny drove us in. Daniel stayed with the Clifton's.

As we came across the bridge, I could see that the town was clear of its burned debris. Only a few chimneys and brick walls were left standing. More than fifty canvas tents were erected and lined up one after another where Mill and Howards Streets once were. Insurance companies, bankers, cigar shops, the railroad ticket office, clothing stores, and food tents were open for business. In the middle of the makeshift town, a large tent with a crowd of people packed the temporary city hall. Rossiter was out in front when we arrived. Neither Benny nor Rossiter acknowledged the other.

Still unable to straighten my knee, Benny and Sadie helped me down from the wagon. I crutched into the crowded tent. Astir of voices rose as I entered. We made our way down the center aisle. As if disturbing a hornet's nest, another rumble of voices bristled as Benny asked someone to give up their seat for me. The priest who had married Sadie and me offered his.

Scanning the crowd, it seemed a wake of buzzards with macabre eyes were glaring at me. Their harsh stares stung as they looked down their noses at my leg. Did they think I was pretending?

God, I wished I wasn't there. We found a corner near where the tent flap was open. Always good to have an escape route. Sadie stood on one side of me, Benny on the other.

People stood shoulder to shoulder on both sides of the enclosure. Many had gathered outside at either side of the tent where the flaps were cinched up. The city council, positioned at the front, had brought their own chairs to sit on.

The accusation of guilt rattled in me. Nothing in my experience felt as horrific as being blamed for such a calamity. I wondered what could have surpassed it. Then it came to me: being called a baby killer would top it. I hung my head in the horror of that thought and felt my chest convulse. It was all I could do just to sit there. Feelings and emotions tumbled in me like marbles in a jar. Part of me wanted to cuss everyone out. To take them by the shirt collar and shake them. The next minute I wanted to beg forgiveness. I started to hyperventilate. What was taking so damn long? I stopped looking into the many faces that avoided my pleading glance. It was plain what they had concluded. Why did I have to endure more public humiliation? Send me a letter. You know where I live. Maybe Sadie was right. We should leave this place.

Then I recalled the pep talk Sadie had delivered before we left, her nose touching mine, her eyes looking deep inside: "Be strong. I believe in you. We know the truth. I am right by your side. Remember, we are free to go anywhere in the world."

A little whimper slipped out. I didn't deserve her.

Fred Nicholls, Jeb Thomas, Frank Rossiter, and the other councilmen stood shoulder to shoulder. Everett and four of his officers, two firemen, a handful of journalists from the Spokane Review and the Gazette were stationed toward the back. On one side of the aisle, a crowd of prominent citizens—William Blythe for one and Abigail Cowley, president of the WCTU and suffrage advocate for another—were there. Francis from the livery stable and Jeremy from the land office were off in a corner, two friends I had most assuredly lost. Lady Colleen and Big Wilbur Johnson and his wife Matilda stood beside each other in solidarity. Lady Colleen waved her handkerchief at me. I couldn't remember a time when she was anything but amicable. God bless her.

Mayor Nicholls tipped his hat to me. If he knew the findings, his face wasn't letting on. He took a wide stance and cleared his throat while shuffling through several documents in hand. "Today, the results from the Fire and Water Committee endowed with investigating the cause and culpability of the fire will be read."

The energy in the tent rose like a hot air balloon. Sadie squeezed my arm. Benny smirked irreverently and stuck his hands in his pockets.

"After the findings are read, we will be discussing another critical issue, the Northwestern Industrial Expo contract the city signed shortly before the fire occurred." Nicholls stopped and peered as sternly as a schoolmaster at several whispering residents. He was always intensely annoyed when people talked while he had the floor. "All present are asked to conduct themselves appropriately. There will be no fights and no profanity, understood?"

Many shook their heads in agreement. Nearby a woman shushed the whisperers.

A man in the back called out, "Get on with it."

Nicholls folded the documents in his hand. "Sir, if you cannot restrain yourself, the police will remove you."

I tried to see who spoke out, but several others blocked him.

"All right," conceded the faceless man.

Nicholls turned to Rossiter. "Chairman Rossiter, you ready?"

Rossiter scratched his groin and postured from side to side. He removed his spectacles from his coat pocket and wrapped both wire temple pieces around his ears. The nose pad rested low against his bulbous nose.

"On Sunday, August 4, a fire began at 6:15 p.m. and in four short hours burned the entire city down, thirty-two square blocks."

Mayor Nicholls threw out a hand in frustration. "Everyone knows that. Move on to the report."

A little red-faced, Rossiter started again. "Right. After a rigorous investigation of all contributing factors: weather and wind conditions, obligations of the superintendent," Rossiter pivoted in my direction, "the functionality of the water system, and the fire department's handling of the incident, we submit the following findings." Rossiter raised one finger. "Number one, the dry, hot summer contributed to an abundant source of dry tinder that any random spark could have ignited. Many cities in the region have burned down under similar conditions."

With crossed arms and contrary expressions, those in attendance listened intensely— women in black bonnets with scornful faces and men with dubious grins.

Rossiter bent the papers out and back. "The wind, which initially came from the southwest, blew across the city toward the river. Its trajectory created ideal conditions for the spread of fire. Around nine o'clock in the evening, the wind changed directions and headed back on itself in a serpentine pattern. Whatever hadn't caught fire did so then. The number of flammables stored in the alleyways from the many shanties built next to mills and hotels made for excellent fire kindling, a practice that will be outlawed when we rebuild."

Rossiter raised a second finger. "Number two, the volunteer fire department's response time was sadly lacking. Twenty-two minutes to get on site." The firefighters stood stone-faced like granite statues. No admissions came forth. "An unacceptable response time for a town of our size. Mind you, part of the delay was due to residents stacking furniture and personal belongings in the middle of the streets." Rossiter slapped the papers with one hand and looked disgusted. "An insane attempt to salvage dining room tables and hutches. Those obstructions stole precious minutes from firefighters trying to get on site. However, there can be no denying; that the firefighters were a disorganized and rudderless group. Additionally, the equipment was poorly maintained, as evidenced by the number of holes later found in the hoses. Any fool knows if there's a hole, the pressure will be flaccid at best."

One firefighter who appeared particularly miffed spoke out. "I hope we'll have a chance to defend ourselves."

Rossiter turned toward the firefighter and laughed. "Your opportunity passed days ago. Number three, many had thought the water pump system had been left unattended. That turns out to be false. The assistant to the superintendent, Andrew Akin, was left in charge of the station during the absence of Superintendent Jones, who was on a weekend jaunt to Lake Coeur d'Alene. Furthermore, Akin has been deemed competent and reliable with twenty-years of practical experience in machinery and pumps."

A murmur of voices stirred.

"Who led us to believe otherwise?" asked an old-timer sitting on one of the few benches brought in, his white beard stained dark with tobacco juice.

To my surprise, Sadie blurted, "I heard the rumor came from the council itself." I turned to her, amazed and thrown off by her boldness. This was not the time to poke the bear.

"Dear lady, it's quite impossible to determine who started the rumor," said Rossiter.

"Maybe you're just covering for one of your own," said Zhang Wei, the Chinese launderer pushing through the crowd.

Rossiter walked a few steps up the aisle and turned back. "Although I may not personally agree with all of these conclusions, I present them as facts."

Sadie spoke out again. "Could you clarify that last statement?" Her eyes mocking him.

I was glad she spoke up then. I didn't care for the inference either.

Rossiter lifted his upper lip to reveal a glimpse of teeth and cleared his throat.

Nicholls crossed his arms and lowered his chin. "Do you not have faith in the findings that you have collected? The findings you claimed were gathered through rigorous methods?"

Rossiter stammered. "Of course, but there may be other facts we were unable to discover given the amount of time we were allotted for the exploration."

Nicholls' face deepened in color. "If there were more facts to be found, you would have found them."

A rugged man with a corncob pipe between his teeth stepped forward. "If there had been sufficient water, we could have put out the fire. I know, I was there. That's why my mustache and sideburns got singed to the skin."

"That's not what the findings reveal," said Rossiter backing down from his attempt to cast doubt on the conclusions.

"Let's move on," said Nicholls.

"Number four, the fires which originated in Wilbur Johnson's kitchen and Lady Colleen's room, can only be viewed as unintentional. We can find no malice aforethought in either case."

Rossiter bowed slightly and looked for concurrence.

Nicholls interjected again. "Go on."

Rossiter spread his entire right hand out. "Number five, it should be noted that city policy is to keep the water pump system at half capacity. Therefore, there may have been some delay in getting the water pressure up to its maximum potential."

Dismay fanned out through the crowd.

One woman's voice could be heard above them all. "Half capacity?"

Rossiter turned her way. "Its standard procedure to maintain a pressure of sixty-five pounds per square inch across all municipalities."

The woman shrieked. "Why in tarnation?"

Rossiter pointed at me. "Mr. Jones, do you want to explain the reasoning?"

I moved forward in my seat. The humidity was starting to pull on me. "The pressure is maintained at sixty-five psi because more would put too much stress on the system, therefore dramatically shortening its useful life."

The crowd grumbled. A few men barked at each other, and a pushing fight erupted. Two police officers hurried over and tossed the rousers onto the street.

"Does everyone understand?" said Rossiter. He waited for other questions about the water pressure, but none came forward. "Number six, if there had been adequate water pressure, could the fire have been extinguished? That, I am sorry to say, we'll never know. If we look at the Ellensburg and Seattle fires as evidence, both cities suffered major in-town fires that became unstoppable. Nothing impeded their system. It seems that once a fire gets hot enough to blow windows out, there's no stopping it."

Sadie slipped her hand into mine and squeezed. I was relieved and glad she had come after all.

I heard Benny let out a sigh of relief.

"Number seven, to stop the fire from advancing beyond the downtown area, buildings were dynamited to create fire breaks."

Jeremy shouted, "Whose idea was that?"

"Well," said Rossiter, somewhat apologetically. A rarity if there ever was one. "We did what we thought was right at the time."

A few sniggers rolled over the crowd.

"It is, therefore, the judgment of the Fire and Water Committee and the city council that no one person is to blame for this horrific event."

The crowd whispered and grumbled.

I rubbed the heels of my hands together. My rib cage expanded and locked as I waited to hear the rest of my fate.

Rossiter and the mayor turned and faced me while motioning for the crowd to quiet. "Rolla Alan Jones, you are exonerated of all charges. You followed the protocols. You are not to blame."

My breath let out as Sadie embraced me. Benny shook my hand and slapped me on the back. I wanted to cheer, but that would have been immodest. Many had suffered significant losses, but oh, to be cleared of all wrongdoing was magnificent. Now our lives could return to normal, hallelujah!

A townsman lunged forward, waving his hat wildly. "This is a farce if I've ever heard one. You're just protecting your own."

Some in the crowd roared, fists high in the air.

I was dumbfounded; all I could do was stand with my mouth agape.

The mayor moved in. "You've heard the findings. The committee found the truth and did a damn fine job. Now let it go."

Rossiter gave the mayor an "I told you so look." A few men walked out of the tent, shaking their heads.

A woman fanning herself vigorously stood up. "All right then, what are we to do now? We've lost everything. Should we pack up and leave it all behind?"

Mayor Nicholls looked relieved. "Thank you, madame, for asking that question. What we are going to do, my fellow citizens is what any civilized community should do: work together and rebuild a better town. The insurance companies are hard at work, as are the bankers. We will reconstruct this town to become the touchstone for which it was poised. This time, however, we advocate all buildings be constructed of stone and brick—no more wood structures. It's what Chicago did thirty years ago. I know that may not sit well with the sawmills in the area, but it's prudent. Our streets and alleys will be clear of flammables and widened for easier passage. Any man not interested in working to rebuild the town will be escorted out. The mayor paused. "No wolf will ever blow this town down again."

Hoping the matter was settled, I nodded in relief. But the crowd continued to shout its disapproval. What more did they want? Why wasn't the truth good enough? Did they want me to bleed more to satisfy the injustice of a calamity?

A tiny smirk on Rossiter's face telegraphed his true colors as he retreated into his group of cronies and committee members. What did he know I didn't? Did he understand human nature better? Did he see that a tangle of findings and facts would never satisfy their need for blood? If they accepted the truth, they'd have to admit they were wrong and had jumped to conclusions. As if their gut instinct was flawless in every circumstance. They'd have to retract their stories and appear foolish. Or is it that once a person accepts a version of the truth, the brain won't release it. Isn't that why the law exists innocent until proven guilty? Obviously, people don't change their minds quickly. Keeping an open mind requires effort. I hoped I was wrong. Intuitively, I knew I was not.

William Blythe stepped forward and pulled a cigar from his mouth. Out of respect, the crowd quieted. "Let's move the discussion to our future, the Expo."

Nicholls stepped up, eager to leave the fire discussion behind. "Thank you, Founder Blythe. As many are aware, an industrial revolution has swept across America across the world, a revolution that has already improved our lives and will continue to do so for decades to come. Days before the fire, the city signed a contract to host the Northwestern Industrial Expo on October 1, 1890. We must decide to honor the commitment or shut it down."

Nicholls held his head high. "I say, let's show the country that the people of Spokane Falls are no quitters. Show them we are leaders in commerce, industrialization, and expansion." Nicholls paused as a handful of townspeople departed. "In light of our circumstances, we need a majority to pass the agreement. Hosting the expo requires building a grand structure. An impressive building, one that will take many working hours and many dollars to build. We have the money set aside for it. So I put it to you now: Should Spokane Falls move ahead or relinquish its contract?"

Nicholls pivoted back toward the council members. Councilman Bender stood up.

"The council will now hear arguments, answer questions, and vote. Those who have something to say may form a line."

Nicholls interjected, "But let it be known: I believe we must honor the contract. Let's show the world what tough and honorable people we are. Are you with me?" His face was turning red as his neck veins bulged.

William Blythe grabbed Nicholl's hand and raised it like a prizefighter. "I agree. Honor the contract. Seize this opportunity. Come on, join us?"

A barrage of yips and hollers tolled.

Nicholls chimed in, "If we pull together, nothing can stop us —not even, dare I say, a great fire." He spread his arms out wide and looked to the many faces. "We can be greater than before. Those who stand with me shout out now!"

Shouts of agreement echoed from inside and outside the tent. Handshakes, back-slaps, and nodding heads confirmed the deal. Spokane would rebuild itself. The city would honor its contract and reclaim its position as the financial hub of the Northwest and unofficial capital of the Inland Empire.

When Sadie, Benny, and I left the tent, eyes darted off, smiles shut down, faces turned away as we passed. I had hoped the accusations of wrongdoing would be gone. The next day the newspaper headline read, "Exonerated Yes, Blameless No." When I read it, I knew I wasn't free, and our lives would not be as before.

Chapter Twenty-Three

When summer ebbed and fall crawled nearer, an Indian summer entered for a brief yet beautiful stretch — a time to reflect with gratitude for the long summer days of light. For the bounty, the land had graciously given forth. We welcomed the cooler nights and crisp mornings of autumn. Clear skies and warm afternoons would soon submit to the chilly fingers of October. Meanwhile, my soul was content to forget the devastation summer had shepherded in for me and so many others. These were the moments when time moved forward, not mired in the past.

Apple Varieties

Duchess Oldenburg—Large, striped red, very hardy, an excellent bearer. Season: late summer.

Red Astrachan—Large, crimson striped, good cooker, very robust. Season: early summer.

Gravensteins—the best apple of the season and cannot be surpassed. Beautiful yellow and red.

Season: September and October.

Maiden's Blush—Good size, yellow with red cheeks, excellent. Season: September.

Transcendent Crab—Best crabapple ever introduced. Season: August to September.

That's how I described some of the apples in my catalog. I stacked the fruit on a U-shaped table in the store, each in its own pyramid. Above, a raceway of fruit flies flew. The floor below was cluttered with shriveled maple leaves. The color of summer was gone, but the smell of green was held faintly within their membranes. Drifts of road dust the consistency of ground coriander and allspice, and spring grass splintered into whiskers of pale straw crowded into every corner. The store needed sweeping. I couldn't care less. The spider season had arrived, a sure sign of autumn's arrival. Their nests were strung meticulously in every nook of the rafters above me.

I leafed through the ledger on my lap —no sales or deliveries recorded for seven weeks. The plums, cherries, and pears had all rotted. Cuthbert raspberries went early in the summer, before the fire. Sadie canned as much as she could every chance she got, given her regular duties and the growing life inside her. I had packed most of the apples into cold storage. Walnuts and hazelnuts were in the dryer on the top tier of the barn. I gleaned the apples ready for animal feed into a basket covered and pulled the door shut. Looking through the narrow space between door and frame, a part of me wanted to stay holed up inside the rickety stand, to hunker down the way an injured animal would. Sadness and loss required solitude.

I headed toward the house. Up ahead, just beyond the porch, Sadie pulled wind-dried linens off the line. Daniel played cowboy in his toy outfit: a pretend Stetson, flimsy chaps held together with elastic and a gun. As I reached the door, she and I fixed on each other for a time but did not speak. I set down the basket on the porch and pointed with my cane that I was going inside.

When dinner came that night, we ate in silence. More and more of our meals went that way. I'd start to speak—but a shelling of thoughts and arguments and memories gagged me. The fight in my head, the constant chatter that stormed over everything I wanted to say, never let up. Daniel ate with his elbows on the table, his fork, and mouth close to the plate as a dog does until Sadie corrected him.

The silence followed us into the bedroom like skunk fumes. In bed, I'd turn one way. She'd turn the other. I'd stare out the window at the moon and bruised clouds above. I was heart sluggish. My breath diminished until an inward draw of air, coupled with the outward release of a moan, came from my dearest. Being shunned by the townspeople pained her deeply. I turned back and fit my body alongside hers. I fought my heart to let go of the lingering loss that threatened to kill us—our lives were broken, our future walked toward an unavoidable ravine.

Overnight the air cooled. A steady rain came in and washed the Indian summer away. I got up, put on my poncho, and left the house for my weekly check of the property's perimeter. Cyrus and I scrutinized it together. The jarring motion of trotting was still off-limits for my leg. I had missed spending time with Cyrus. A good horse is a great friend. We sensed each other's moods and agreed on most of our interactions. God knows he was patient and gentle with me, avoiding trees and bushes that could bump my leg. I guess we just liked being together.

When I got back, Sadie set down a plate of food and walked back to the kitchen without saying anything. A proper country breakfast: three strips of bacon, a mound of beef slices from last night's roast, two eggs over easy, cornbread, butter, and raw honey. I was hungry in the morning. The ride with Cyrus and a plate of hot food was an excellent way to start every day. That is until Daniel began to cry and wouldn't let up.

"Daniel, what's the problem?" I said as he hid in his mother's skirt, continuing to whimper. "Is he sick?"

She stroked his head softly. "No," she said, giving me the eye. "The problem is you."

My tongue pushed hard against my front teeth. I set my fork down on the folded napkin and moved it to the center of the cloth. This compulsive positioning gave me time to think and calm myself before reacting. "Tell me."

She expelled her held breath. "Daniel thinks you don't like him because you've stopped saying good morning or howdy, partner, or reading to him at night." With one hand she scrunched her collar tight around her neck as if to choke herself. "You haven't played with him in days."

I sighed and reached out to him. "Come here, son."

Daniel inched over. I swept him up and set him on my lap. "Daddy's been grumpy, hasn't he?"

He nodded.

"I am sorry. It's not your fault. I love you as big as ever. Big, big!"

"Big?" parroted Daniel through glassy eyes and a tiny voice.

Covering his face with kisses until he squealed, I said, "Big as a barn." I knew that would satisfy him, but it wouldn't appease his mother. A fight was brewing, and time was running short. "Want to play cowboys and Indians after breakfast?" Daniel smiled and snatched a piece of cornbread dripping in honey, stuffed it in his mouth, then rocked his little body in agreement.

I poked his belly with a finger. "Good. Let's eat so we can play."

For a time, I worried about the impending fight. How would I defend myself? Could I persuade her to give things more time? Thankfully she let the rest of the day go without revisiting the issue.

That night, a family of five rapped on our front door. They huddled on the porch, rain-soaked and shivering.

I grabbed my cane and opened the door.

"Howdy. You looking for produce?"

"No, sir, we're on our way to our in-laws in Idaho. We'd be much obliged if you could put us up for a night?" said the man in his late thirties, and a scar clear across his forehead. His wife, stood back a few feet held her jaw tight beneath her faded bonnet.

The two girls were between eight and ten, the boy about four lined up next to their mother. Their little hands looked chapped and bony. Their ghoulish expressions over pallid skin and tired eyes looked like so many of the orphans in Spokane that walked the streets for handouts.

"You can stay in the barn," I said. "Give me a second."

I went back inside and grabbed my coat. "A family of travelers needs shelter. Can you put some food together?"

Sadie bit her lip. "Are you sure?"

"Of course," I said as I grabbed an oil lamp and departed.

I stepped off the porch heedfully. "Follow me," I said, as the mother tossed a quizzical look. Sixty feet from the house was the barn. Benny and I had proudly built it to last. I shoved one side of the nine-foot sliding door over. Once inside, I pointed to a hay-filled corner. "You're welcome to bed down on the hay. My wife is preparing some food. I'll build a fire in the stove. We'll pull together what blankets we have. A few may have to use some horse blankets."

The father rubbed his hands together to warm them. "We've been living in a tent ever since the fire. The mud and the cold have become too much for my wife. Lucky you live way out here. A terrible thing that fire."

I nodded politely, noticing another strange look on the woman's face. The children had clustered together and were trembling. "We can talk after I get the fire started." I returned with an arm full of firewood just as Benny scaled down the steps from his loft.

"I'll get the blankets," he said, darting off into the darkness.

The oldest girl came nearer with desperation in her eyes. "Do you have any milk?"

The mother barked, "Leave him be. Can't you see he's busy?"

I whispered. "Let me see what I can do."

Not long after, Sadie and Daniel came in with a food basket. Benny followed with a pile of blankets and pillows in his arms and set them on the hay.

"Grab the table outside and bring it here. Would you please Benny," I said.

He stepped out and soon returned, brushing it off with his coat sleeve. Next, Sadie set out the food. A pan of fried chicken, a loaf of sliced bread, a bag of apples, a pot of baked beans, and a large jar of milk. When she brought out the milk, I saw the children's eyes come to life. Sadie stepped aside and said, "Help yourself."

The homeless family closed in on the food just as shivering kittens do when desperate to lap up a bit of warm cow's milk. The four of us stood and watched the travelers gorge on the food.

"Okay, we'll leave you to your supper," I said. The family's plight was awful. I was glad my family didn't have to endure that hardship. The homeless father bit into a chicken breast and waved. Then, with frequent backward glances, Benny crawled back up to his room in the barn. Daniel followed Sadie back to the house. As I pulled the barn door closed until the homeless mother approached, clutching a drumstick and wiping her mouth with her skirt hem.

"I know who you are." Her teeth were brown from years of tobacco use and black coffee. "We're homeless because of you."

I lowered the brim of my hat and raised the collar of my jacket against my neck. "Madame, I was exonerated."

She spit between my boots. "We know better, and dare I say, so do you." She swallowed the food in her mouth. "We're grateful for your hospitality, but we'll be gone before the sun is up."

I backed up and pulled the door shut. Standing there in the black night, I stared at the tiny points of light that peeked through the barn door. My fogged breath jutted puffs of steam. A knot burned hard in my throat. Why do they insist on blaming me? Everyone now knows the truth. It was in both newspapers, plain as anything. How the hell can I fix something I didn't break? Will this ever end?

If screaming could have helped, I would have until my lungs bled. Until the rage in me was expelled and lay on the ground like some foul mucous. But I stuffed the need to scream down as I would castor oil. I turned and stomped down the driveway, trying to cool off. After six trips down and back, I entered the house stone-faced. Thankfully, Sadie was upstairs with Daniel. I headed to the fireplace and let the heat warm my shaking fists.

When I got into bed that night after pacing for an hour and drinking too much whiskey, I continued to wrestle with the woman's words. I tried every argument to invalidate her. And I probably could have if the images of her children's faces had left me alone. Instead, I stared at the ceiling, unable to sleep for what seemed like forever.

Sadie rolled toward me and slipped her hand into mine. "Don't shut me out. Let's talk. We'll both feel better."

"Nothing to tell," I said as flatly as I could.

Sadie squeezed me. "The nothing you speak of required whiskey to ease through it?"

I wanted to scream out something fierce. To tell Sadie what had happened would have created an uproar. Let her see the blackness of our situation would be terrorizing for her. I couldn't do that. I had to spare her at least this anguish. I patted her hand, deciding that it was better she thought I was a cold prick for now. "I need to sleep, dear."

Cyrus, Benny, and I wagoned into town the next day hoping to find the supplies Sadie wanted—flour, oats, molasses, string, paraffin, soap, and antiseptic. Since the pardon, I hadn't been in town and was curious to see its progress. As I got closer, the sound of hammers striking wood, logs being sawed, and the slop of mortar on bricks filled my ears. The air contained a pleasing scent of progress. Wagon after wagon loaded with building goods trudged through the muddy streets. The hustle and bustle about town were impressive. Spokane was on a mission to reinvent itself. I ached to be a part of it but knew I wasn't welcome.

Benny pulled in front of the general store tent and pushed his hat back. "I have a few things of my own to do. I'll meet you at Jake's in an hour."

I scanned the street before climbing carefully down from the wagon. "Sounds good."

Stuart had a tent selling just about everything he had before. I was nervous to see him, stressed about coming face to face with him and his feelings about the fire, about me. I ducked under the tent flap and paid careful attention to my boots, given there was no boot brush. He noticed me and approached with a pensive expression on his face.

"What do you need?"

I felt myself stuttering and wished we could talk man to man. He didn't seem open to it. "Sadie needs these things," I said, handing him the list she made.

"I don't accept credit any longer," said Stuart abruptly, keeping his gaze on the list to avoid looking at me.

Lowering my eyes, I said, "I have cash."

Stuart turned away and went to work pulling the items in stock. I got what I needed except the paraffin, which he'd run out of three days prior. The discomfort of talking to Stuart made me thankful, I still had Sadie and Daniel and Benny and Cyrus, my parents, the Cliftons, and hopefully the Withers in my corner. This small tribe of people gave me the will to carry on. I didn't know how long I could sustain this brave act; I only knew I must. Undoubtedly every soul in pain seeks to be free of its anguish.

Much to Sadie's dismay, I'd gotten into the habit of drinking whiskey. If the ladies of the temperance movement knew, it would constitute a double shunning. But I needed it—first to soften the leg pain, then to numb my unhappiness. Jake's Saloon was open after being closed by the mayor for weeks. He had decided the town's need for drinking would only heighten despair and provoke unnecessary violence in the streets. He was probably right.

I pulled back the tent flap of the makeshift Saloon and scanned the many patrons sitting on barrels and wood boxes. Benny was at the bar waiting. Lady Colleen standing nearby saw us and sauntered over.

"You two are a welcome sight." She passed a knowing wink to Benny. "How's 'bout a drink?"

"I'll buy," said Benny eagerly.

"Naw, it's my shout," I said, thankful for the friendly greeting. I held up three fingers and mouthed the word "whiskey" to Harry, the half-owner.

Lady Colleen moved in closer and swirled her finger around the top of Benny's shoulder. "You know, Benny here's my little fire starter."

I stopped and gaped at him, uncertain as to what she was implying. "What do you mean?"

Benny grinned and covered his face with his hand.

"Oh, he didn't tell you? He's the one who barged into my room that fateful night and knocked the lamp over," said Lady Colleen with a teasing tone in her voice.

Her words took time to register. Fitting that bit of information into the vast puzzle I had been constructing and deconstructing every day was as complicated as inventing a machine to make men fly.

My jaw clenched. My heart sickened. "You? You never told me that."

Benny touched my shoulder and stammered. "I...tried to, but...."

I stared at him. The hurt of being shunned, the indignation of blame, and the immense sense of failure I felt were meager compared to Benny's betrayal. He'd probably had a good laugh over it.

Harry, a muscular man with a beer gut, grabbed two glasses and a bottle of whiskey. "I got no liquor for you," Harry said with an icy stare at me as he poured. "That'll be two bits, now."

My gut clenched and my back stiffened as I repaid Harry's frosty stare. I reached into my pocket, pulled out a fifty-cent piece, and slapped it on the bar.

"I'll take the change, now."

Lady Colleen rested an elbow on the bar. "Ah now Harry, what's wrong with you?"

Harry crossed his arms over his gut. "This is the carpetbagger who let the town burn."

Benny piped up. "You know, he was exonerated. Everyone was exonerated."

Harry shook his head. "Not in my book, he ain't."

I motioned to Lady Colleen. "It's all right. I'm no longer thirsty."

"Well, good, then you can leave," said Harry

Lady Colleen leaned in. "Sorry, darling, guess we oughta be treated the same as you, huh, Benny?"

Right then I wanted to smash something to destroy. That's when I knew I had to get away before I did something appalling. Yet, it was at that moment that Renaldo's lifeless body flashed before me, an image that always shattered me. I guess I thought Benny was some kind of clemency from God that I wasn't doomed to a life of guilt over the fire that Renaldo died in.

I spun around and shoved Benny. "I was wrong about you. You are your father."

Benny fell against the bar, eked out a whine, and pinched his eyes shut. His failure to disclose his part in the fire was unforgivable, an omission only a coward would have done. With a broken heart, I drove out of town that afternoon alone. The diminishing number of people I counted as friends opened an even broader hole in my heart.

Chapter-Twenty-Four

The following morning the rain came sideways and tore leaves from branches. The beautiful yellows, reds, and oranges of autumn swam away in the mud, never to be noble again. With a book of Keats, a blazing fire, and a shot of whiskey, I was almost numb to the wretchedness the last few months had brought. A fortnight of nightmares, trying to fix everything frantically, but too out-of-sorts to accomplish any of it. Of the dead man under the sheet lifting it to say, "You did this." Of flames crawling over everything in their path. I hoped for an uneventful day. Forget about Benny, no longer a trusted and loyal friend; now, he was just a dirty, low-down betrayer, as many others had become. I needed my solitude to recover from yesterday, the day before, the weeks back, and the month before that.

The pinewood fire heated the house to a balmy summer's glow — a paradise of warmth, particularly to my leg, which now reacted adversely to the cold. I got up from my chair to feed the greedy blaze and feel its biting heat up close. I turned my face from side to side and felt the heat melt my dark thoughts into something lighter. Not long after setting the last damp log on top of the others, smalls puffs of smoke and geysers of steam set from it. I watched with fascination each gush of steam. It started small, just a bubble or two, then faint bursts, until a surge blew tall like a whale's blowhole. I could watch it all day. Sit, listen, watch —just wander through the misty air before my eyes. I didn't want to talk to anyone. But, when

Sadie came into the room and put her hands on the back of my chair. Somehow I knew serenity was over.

"How long will this silence continue?"

I looked through the fireplace flames and said nothing.

I heard her dig her fingernails into the chair's upholstery. "How long will laughter and joy be absent from our home?"

I dropped my head and muttered. "I don't know." A sudden pressure drew up between my eyes. I tried to rub it out.

Sadie threw up her hands. Her energy was fierce. "This is intolerable."

I could feel her angst spin around the room like some kind of trapped hornet. Her desperate glare, her pinched mouth, unnerved me. She was committed to battle.

"And poor Daniel is beside himself," said Sadie raking her fingernails down her arms from her elbows.

This fight had been festering below the surface for weeks. There was no stopping it now. I forced myself into a standing position and made one last attempt to retrench it, "Could we not do this today?"

She came around the chair toward me. "No, the time has come. I have something to say, and I will have my say." Her hair wrapped on top of her head was oily and unclean, so out of character for her.

I took a wider stance and continued rubbing my eyes. "Woman, I don't know what you want me to say."

Her shoulders pulled back broad as if she was ready to throw a punch. "You could start by not shutting me out. You could start by considering my proposal to leave this place. Start new, start again. We're still young."

Regrettably I swung around. "Jesus, do you understand? I've lost everything."

Sadie rushed forward, raised her fists, and pounded on my chest. "This didn't just happen to you. We're suffering too." Her eyes were fierce on me. "Daniel can't verbalize what he's feeling, but he's feeling as exposed as I am."

I looked away for a moment then clutched her fists. "What do you expect me to do, laugh it off? Pretend as if nothing happened."

Sadie teared up. "I don't know."

"I don't know who I am anymore." I let go of her slender fists and yelled. "Tell me what to do, and I'll do it."

She spoke with a horrified expression, her lower lip trembling. "I don't believe I know you anymore." She stepped back as if afraid of me. "Daniel and I are going to my parents."

"Oh no, you're not," I said, balling my fists. "You're going to stay here and endure this with me as you promised in our vows."

She covered her pronounced womb as if to shield the baby from what was about to come. Then came a wail so pitiful it buckled my knees. "I'm not going to deliver another dead baby," said Sadie, "not even for you."

Sadie had spoken the truth, and her words stung. I was buried in failure. "I suppose… that's my fault too?"

She whimpered and wiped her eyes with her apron. "We'll be back after the baby is born. Let's hope you've come to your senses."

Her mournful eyes, the saddest I'd ever seen, ruined me. But how could she leave me when I needed her so much? I had disappointed her, failed every test. Now my all vision for the future, even for the next step, was gone. I was in the middle of the ocean. No land visible from any direction, every orientation leading nowhere.

All the words I could have used to explain myself up and vanished as if they had fallen off the back end of a wagon, like one of Daniel's socks. Sadie would leave me.

I grabbed my coat and headed for the workshop. "Do what you think is right."

On November 12, 1889, I hitched Cyrus and loaded in the luggage. It was cold and threatening rain. I made sure Daniel's hat was tied snug, kissed his icy cheek, and lifted him into the wagon. Then, turning back, I took Sadie's hand and pleaded once more, "Sadie, please reconsider. Things won't get better without you. I need you."

But she held her eyes on the horizon, unwilling to meet my gaze. "Help me up," she said in a deflated voice.

On our way through town, though we marveled at the many structures in progress, we did so in silence. The newspapers had reported five hundred buildings were under construction, and I believed it.

A light dusting of snow covered the platform, benches, and awnings at the station. The wind blew in from the north and turned the snow into tiny prisms of ice. The real cold was en route and would arrive soon. The Farmer's Almanac had predicted a bitterly cold winter as evidenced by the early departure of ducks and geese, the heavy steam in the valley floor, and the larger than usual spiderwebs. I told myself that Sadie and Daniel would be warmer down south in Walla Walla. Their departure would give me time to sort through things and see what I couldn't see now. I could construct a new life plan in their absence, but I was too heartsick to do much of anything. I couldn't muster even a smile for Daniel.

The train pulled in, and soon it was time for them to board. I tried to make light of it. "Have a good time with grandpa and grandma. Don't eat too many cookies."

Daniel didn't understand what was happening, but I could tell he knew things weren't right.

In a quiet voice, Sadie asked. "Will you come for Christmas?"

"I'll see how things go," I said.

"No Christmas?" said, Daniel tearing up.

I kissed his cheek. "Daddy has much to do. I'll see you before you know it."

I stood up, still holding his hand. Sadie looked at me with ambivalence. Then, finally, I cast my eyes to the ground and expelled my breath, which turned to steam and hovered between us. "You better board."

Once boarded, they found a seat by the window and moved close to the glass. We kept our eyes on each other, never once looking elsewhere. Sadie's tortured face told me this was as difficult for her as it was for me. As the train moved, I walked beside it. Daniel planted his palms on the window as tears ran down his face. A icy wind blew through as the train pulled away. I tugged down my hat and hiked up my collar in defense of it. The train shrank further along the tree-lined track, and the wind moaned a hollow voice. At the end of a ragged breath, I uttered, “Forgive me."

Steam

The period of transition between two states of being

Chapter Twenty-Five

At home all alone, I wandered about like an abandoned fawn, my boot heels thumping the floorboards. I rambled from room to room and back again, feeling Sadie and Daniel's presence, smelling their essence—hearing their voices. Sometimes whispers. Other times it was as if they were calling from upstairs.

"Dinner," I heard Sadie say.

In the hallway, a haunting air turbulence moved past me. I shuddered and tried to shrug it off until Daniel ran across the floor like a panel of cartoon sketches illustrating each movement. Sadie nudged her hip against my shoulder and poured coffee into my favorite cup, a veil of steam faintly rose. They're not there. It's my heart's invention. I want what I can't have because they're not coming back, and it's my fault.

If it was my fault that Renaldo died in the barn fire and my fault the town burned down, how does an honorable man atone for such transgressions? Is there even a way to make up for it? Would his own death be sufficient?

I had no idea nor the strength to put my broken life back together. It all seemed too impossible. As unfeasible as breathing life into a taxidermied fox. The mere thought of reconstructing my life depleted me. All I wanted to do was drink and cry and drink some more. A bottle of whiskey hidden in the barn was my answer.

Whiskey—my new friend—would numb the pain, blur reality, erase confusion, and help me forget for a time.

The first shot of whiskey went down hard. Soon enough, the toffee liquid slid down like warm milk. The initial inebriation snuck up on me with a tickle. Light as a gossamer of steam, I floated about the room, hearing music from every direction. Giddiness suddenly pounced in like a puppy at play. The world was right once more—everything headed in a dandy direction. Laughter bubbled up in me as I moved around the house. Shrieks, whoops, howls, hisses—hysterical laughter flooded in from voices outside my head. They laughed at me. I cackled back. They laughed more. I tee-heed. Everything was funny. Until the whisper of Sadie's ghostly voice fell over me.

"Why won't you talk to me?" shouted Sadie.

I heard the roar of Satan's laugh and shivered. His bellow seemed to come from the bottom of the water well, wickedly low and perversely mean.

I began bawling like a motherless calf. I cried in silent screams. The pain, a bullet in my stomach gushing out —no way to stop it. A moaning boomed from my gut. Cries of regret. Cries of humiliation. I had let everyone down. My father and mother, and Alice for dishonoring our family name. I had let down my brother, Renaldo, and my sisters, Clara and Cora, for not living a life worthy of their young deaths. I had wasted time and money on a high-priced education. I let the entire city of Spokane Falls down, and they hated me for it. Once, I could do no wrong, now I was dammed. Most of all, I failed Sadie, Daniel, and our unborn baby. For that, there was no forgiveness. My miscalculations would curse them the rest of their days.

The euphoria of whiskey soon became snarls and hisses. More drink seemed the best remedy until a bonfire appeared even better. I threw open the front door and went searching for things to burn: a mound of dried leaves, logs from the front porch, a handful of boards propped against the barn. Good wood, but too short to do much with. Broken chairs. Bales of hay. Dead tree branches. I kept adding to the pile until it towered above me. I stuffed crumpled newspaper into open spots and splashed on lamp oil. Before I struck the wood match, my mind raced back to that evening at Delmonico's when I explained how matches work. I was young and thought I knew it all. I guess Sadie thought so too. James Withers knew better, son of a bitch. When I threw it on the pile flames rose up.

Soon the fire cracked and swelled. I threw on one of the porch rocking chairs I had built—chairs Sadie and I sat on most evenings after Daniel was in bed. Then I threw on the other one. We loved those chairs. They fed the fire well.

As the fire grew taller, heaps of light rippled upon the house and barn. I downed a few more swigs, looked around for more to burn. Leftover newspapers yellowed the flames. Pieces of it as thin as skin floated into the treetops. I found the volley of cracks, pops and sizzling squeals strangely comforting.

But barbarian faces in flames brought me back to misery, a far easier foe than being made the scapegoat of Spokane Falls. Hell, anything was easier than that reality. I reached for my new friend and sucked more of it down. Blurry-eyed and wobbly, I went looking for more to burn. I threw on loose straw; it was a pathetic show. I needed something longer-burning to kill this inner demon. A wagon wheel Benny had tried to fix. I stumbled, lifting the heavy wood wheel onto the pile, and watched it become enveloped in flames. I saw in triples and fumbled about. Delight came to me when I found three wooden fruit crates. The boxes pushed the blaze above the tops of the trees. Then it became a game—how high could I get the flames? I started seeing movement in the shadows and worried it could be wolves or cougars drawn to the light. I got out my gun, set it close by, piled on more fire nourishment, and downed more whiskey.

It wasn't long before I went through the house for more things to burn: wood logs kept in the kitchen next to the stove. An old shawl left behind was used only for runs to the barn. A photo of James Withers on the sideboard was something I'd always wanted to burn. Daniel's pushbike was too small for him now. Then I came upon it, hanging on the wall —my diploma from Cornell. If I hadn't studied engineering, I wouldn't be in this situation. My father was a successful merchant. I could have been a merchant, stayed in New York, and not come out to the fucking Wild West. I took another gulp. What good did this degree do for me now? My reputation was disgraced. No one will ever give me a second chance. I tore it off the wall, walked it out like an unruly customer, and tossed it onto the burning mass. The flames swallowed it in one bite. I was stinking drunk.

The flames got bigger. The smoke billowed higher. My eyes watered and stung. I remembered the night of the great fire and how my eyes wept incessantly. I remembered the burning in my throat, the violent hacking to expel the black smoke from my lungs. I recalled the night my world collided with Lachesis, the Greek determiner of fate, who, without consultation, changed the life plans I had so meticulously made. A life once filled with love and family and prosperity and community prominence. I took another swig, collapsed to the ground, and screamed. I screamed south toward the city where

Rossiter sat unfazed by my destruction. I yelled to the north where most of my property lay—just another underachiever I spit. I screamed at hell. I yelled at the heavens. "Fuck you." I had no plan, no idea where to go from here, and I didn't care.

That was the last thing I remembered until I woke the next day in my bed still in my smoky clothes. My boots were thrown against the wall, a chair on its side. Sick as a dog, I wished I was dead and out of misery.

Chapter Twenty-Six

I woke in an attack of nausea, pulled the washbasin over, and ralphed every ounce of me out. But that wasn't enough for Lachesis, daughter of Zeus. She was responsible for deciding how much life thread each living being on earth was granted. Oh no, the misery was not over yet. I braced my way on chair tops, door frames, walls and, banisters to the outhouse, where I continued to heave—erupting from both ends. I had never spent that much time in the shed; who would? An oblong box, three feet square with a hole in the ground, a wretched fly-swarming shack. I should do something about the dam thing.

My mouth was so dry I couldn't use my tongue to speak. I needed water. I stood up, fastened my pants and, took one wonky step at a time toward the well. The ground was bumpy and tilted like a carousel. Eventually, I got to the well, lowered the bucket, and drew it up. The bucket seemed heavier than I remembered. I dipped the metal cup we kept nearby into the water and drank cup after cup then poured it over my head. It was cold and sent a low and irksome vibration through my body. Cup after cup ran down my twitching body until I was soaked to my socks. Finally, I rested to let the water run its diminishing course.

My head had started to clear up when a pair of worn boots appeared on the ground before me. I looked up to find Sam Clifton holding his hat in one hand and scratching his head with the other.

"You feeling human yet?" His coveralls were hooked on one side, a shirttail was out.

"Not yet," I said, wiping my face with my shirt collar.

Clifton collected his hanging hair and stuffed it back under his hat. "My boys and I found you passed out. We got you to bed and put the fire out. You can thank me later."

I looked back at the burn pile, still smoldering like the remnant of a tiny fiend. "Doesn't look completely out."

With an annoyed smirk, Clifton walked over to the well and dropped the bucket. He drew it up, walked over to the burn pile, and poured the contents onto the fuming mound of ashes. Steam rose quickly and floated off in a huff. A cauldron of repressed anger had been fizzing right below the surface in me. I probably should have been embarrassed that they saw me in such a state, but I didn't care anymore. I should have been thankful for their help. Instead, I wished he'd go away.

Clifton picked up a basket he'd set on the ground with a gingham towel covering the contents and motioned to the house. "Come on, let's get some food in you."

I got up gingerly and stumbled toward the house. "I don't think I can eat."

He watched my pitiful zigzagging before grabbing my arm and guiding me into the house.

"You'se walking a Virginia fence boy," he said.

"Yep," I said, not knowing what he meant.

Clifton snorted. "Serves you right."

I sat hard on a chair at the dining table. Sam put down the basket and pulled out the contents. He dished up a plate of cornbread, beans, and pork back still warm and slid it over.

"Eat," he said.

I looked up in defiance, grabbed a fork, and took a bite. I closed my eyes and savored the buttery corn and salty bacon. It was good. I hoped my stomach agreed.

Clifton, chewing on a homemade toothpick, leaned against the door frame. “Why the bonfire?”

I grunted.

“Sheer stupidity, if you don’t mind me saying. You could have burned down your house and mine,” said Clifton with irritation in his voice.

I started to feel better with every bite. “It won’t happen again.” After all, it was me I wanted to destroy. Not that I would tell him that.

He walked to the door and looked back at me. “If you need someone to talk to, my Mrs. is a good listener. She listens to the boys all the time.”

I motioned goodbye, not appreciating the child reference. I continued eating until all the food was gone. I was licking my fingers when Cyrus began neighing and snorting in the barn. It was past his feeding time and high time to be let out of his stall. When I opened the stall door, he head bumped me and let out a big fluttering breath.

“Sorry, Cy, let’s get you out of here.” I led him out into the sunlight. He instinctively seemed to pick up on my mood and settled. “You’re a damn good horse. I don’t deserve you.”

After feeding Cyrus and the cows, I threw some feed out for the chickens. No reason they had to suffer too. At the edge of the porch, I sat and watched the day pass into darkness. I watched my thoughts — a gristly thread tromping past like criminals scouting for nefarious opportunities. An audible moan slipped out now and again whenever I heard Sadie’s voice or Daniel’s laughter. It was useless trying to contain myself. I teared up and sobbed frequently. When the cold moved in, I went inside, grabbed my coat, sawed off a hunk of bread, cut a chunk of cheese, and wrapped the two together for dinner. Silence echoed in my ears. Not an ocean, just cavities of silence, a deafening clamor of nothing.

I fell asleep on the porch with my wool jacket tight around me as the night turned into morning. When dawn's light surged over the land, the sun crept around the house and poked me in the eye. Roosters crowed; chickens cackled their customary morning zing for the eastern sun. Their optimism pissed me off. I wanted to get up, but my eyeballs felt as if they were in a frying skillet.

Cyrus and I moped around the property for the better part of the day leaving the daily chores undone. The silence in my head became shouting voices. Sadie's persistent voice kept banging around like a rock in an empty can.

"Don't shut me out," I heard her say repeatedly.

I heard my father's voice too. "What have you done, boy?"

The whiskey was gone, and reality was more than I could stand. I needed more, more whiskey oblivion. I donned a disguise and snuck into town with my mare. She was slow and uncooperative. It was an arduous ride. The costume wasn't good—a scruffy beard, a cowboy hat, and a scarf high on my neck. Nevertheless, it was sufficient enough to get the grog. When I got back, I plunged into one of the two jugs as if I was dying of thirst.

From there, one day blurred into another until finally, the whiskey no longer masked my grief. I was miserable drunk and miserable sober. There was no fork in the road. No resolution within sight. No defense, I hadn't argued. What could I do? I could change nothing. My life had been blown to smithereens. "What's the use?"

was all I could come up with, "It doesn't matter —nothing matters. You don't matter."

So I got out my shotgun. Loaded it and began pacing the floor. I was ready to end this shit existence. One-shot would end it— the humiliation, the pain. The easy solution —one shot to stop the frustration. One chance to finish my utter disillusionment. One hole in my head, and bam. It would be over.

I sat down on my dining room chair, the chair I had sat at for meals, planning sessions, talks with Sadie, coloring with Daniel, the afternoon long ago when Sadie and I made crazy love on it. I positioned the stock on the ground, braced the barrel between my knees, and propped the end of it under my jaw. I took hold of the trigger. It was cold and foreign in that position. Daniel spoke to me in his hardened cowboy voice. "Want to rustle up the grub, partner?" Then I saw beautiful Sadie resting under the moonlight. Renaldo running to catch a ball. When I imagined the blood on the floor, on the walls behind me, I hung my head in defeat. I couldn't do it this way. I had a large hunting knife that could end my life. But I was pretty sure I couldn't get it far enough inside to pierce my heart before passing out.

Instead, I went to the barn, threw a rope over a rafter, and tied a hangman's knot. Stepped onto one of the few remaining boxes I hadn't burned in the bonfire. I placed the rope around my neck. Its woody odor drifted by my nose. The last time I had used the cord was when Benny and I pulled a tree stump from the ground. It was a good strong rope. It saddened me to use it this way. Teetering on the crate not built to hold my weight, I began to sweat, then hyperventilate. But, the nerve to step off the box came and went. I needed punishment. I needed it bad. But, suicide would hurt my family for the rest of their days. I had already done too much of that.

Across the barn in the workroom, I spotted a bridle hanging from a hook. Quickly I loosened the rope and got down from the box. Pulling the leather straps from its perch. I knew the metal buckles would inflict real pain. I held it to my chest, shaking. Never could I have imagined I would do such a thing when I was a boy, or when I accepted my degree, or when Daniel was born. But here I was contemplating whipping myself like a mad dog.

I stripped off my jacket, then my shirt. Agony had overtaken every breath, every thought. I had no choice. I had to stop it. The unfixable disaster that was now my life could not continue. I threw the bridle in front of me then back against my skin. It slapped hard leaving a numbness, and seconds later, a tingling sensation but not in a good way. Then an intolerable itch crawled up as horrible as any poison ivy. Stinging rushed in like alcohol in an open wound. I panted then drooled, but I continued lashing. Sometimes the bridle would flip back and strike my face. Other times it struck either side of my neck. Drops of blood ran down warm. A scream tore out from me when my skin split open under the lash. I hit harder.

I had to get the physical pain to surpass the inner pain. Only then could I put things right. Only then could I defeat it. Only feeling free when the inner and outer pain became equal. Both worlds colliding together would cancel each other out. Over and over and over, I swung the straps over my shoulders until I couldn't anymore.

A grinding hum enveloped my skull as I dropped to the dirt floor. A blanket of frigid air rolled over me as I slipped into an indigo abyss, sinking deep into a vastness, a vastness of no return. A flash of Sadie's doleful eyes; Benny's face the night Lady Colleen told him he was her fire starter; the sweet innocence of Daniel dressed as a cowboy; and the lifeless body of Renaldo smoking on the ground perforated my brain. Then, around and around, I spun, cascading into damnation.

Chapter Twenty-Seven

The following morning, I peeled my eyes open a little at a time as the sun poked through the half-opened barn door. Three light shafts filled with floating particulates caught my attention. Suddenly a cold cloth stabbed at the skin. I twitched up to see Mary on the other end of that cloth, tending my lacerations. Benny was there, too, coaxing me to wake.

"Mr. Jones, wake up."

I cringed. Why can't they leave me alone? "I want to be alone." I didn't want anyone to see me at my most depraved. I tried to summon my muscles to roll up to a sitting position, but Benny pushed me back down.

"Stop saving me." I pleaded.

Mary gasped.

"He's delirious. Don't listen to him," said Benny.

"Poor man," she whispered, stroking my head. "He'll scar if he doesn't get stitches."

I grunted. "I'm fine."

Mary continued to clean the wounds by drenching my back in whiskey. Searing pain bubbled over my skin the way boiling water steams on a hot grill, another penance I deserved. It seemed a waste of good alcohol.

"He's gonna regret not gettin' stitched," she said. "I've done worse than you, Mr. Jones."

"Do it. I'll hold him down," said Benny.

Mary hesitated for a moment. "Let's get him in the house before we start."

Opposing was useless, but complaining helped. "I didn't ask for your help, you damn liar."

Benny ignored me.

"What's he talking about?" asked Mary.

Benny said nothing.

"Poor man is out of his mind," murmured Mary.

"Am not," I blurted as they took me into the house, my arms lifeless, my legs too weak to lift.

Benny stuffed a scrap of leather in my mouth as Mary poked through my skin with what felt like a fish hook. Rockets of pain fired off across my back at each new piercing. In defense, every muscle raised as the needle entered then released once it was through. When she pulled the thread, the nails of that young mother who scratched me on the street returned. My stomach knotted. Saliva oozed into my mouth and drooled out at the edges. When she finished stitching, she applied honey to each suture. A pleasant sensation began to spread over the wounds.

Benny helped me sit up on the cot while she wrapped my torso in long strips of torn linens. "I'll be back tomorrow to change the dressing."

I lifted my index finger. "Thank you." What I wanted to say was. Don't bother. You've done enough.

She returned every day for two weeks to change my bandages, often bringing fried chicken, pie, and milk. Although I assumed she'd try, she never attempted to get me to talk.

The smell of hot coffee stirred me awake.

"Want some coffee?" said Benny.

The worst of the pain had subsided, and numbness had set in. I inched into a semi-sitting position and winced as I attempted to get into a sitting position. Then, I slurped the coffee with closed eyes, not knowing what to say to Benny.

Benny spoke in a low voice. "How's the coffee?"

I nodded with my eyes closed. "Not bad."

We sat in silence until his chair creaked. "I saw the fire from across the river."

I peeked out with a sideways glance. "Just burning brush."

Benny nodded nervously.

"I got to go to the crapper," I said, carefully standing. I deflected his helping hand and made my way outside one shaky step at a time. It was raining, and several drops penetrated through the dressing. The drips were icy and bone-chilling.

When I returned, I stopped at the table and finished the last few swallows of coffee. My jaw was locked so hard it was a struggle to speak. "Come to get your things?"

Benny rubbed his palms together. "I came to apologize."

"Hmm," I said. I sat back down and tried to summon the gumption to care.

He chattered on as I stared out the front window. Color had vacated every leaf, every blade of grass. Everything wood —the trees, fences, and house siding—seemed to have sucked its luster back into itself to hide from the cold.

Benny cleared his throat. "Since I was unnamed in the newspaper and at the exoneration, I figured I could just let it go."

I pulled the scratchy wool blanket Mary had fetched from upstairs closer, "Easy for you."

With sincere eyes, Benny continued, "I know, and I'm ashamed. I took the coward's way. I didn't think about anybody but myself."

I stewed for a time before pushing my foot against the leg of his chair. "Can you even imagine what I've been through? Do you have any idea?" I held back, then blurted, "Sadie and Daniel are gone." Tears filled my eyes and rolled down my shaggy face.

Benny sniffled and wiped his eyes. "Not for good?"

I slumped down in the chair. "I don't know. There was a time I knew stuff. I don't know a damn thing."

"It's not just that I'm sorry." Benny rested a hand on the table. "You've been there when no one else was. I owe you. Can you see to forgive me?"

Once more, I looked out on the listless landscape. "I can't work out why you didn't tell me in the first place."

He ran his hand through his hair. "When we talked in the barn that day about your invention, I wanted to, but I chickened out. I don't have your courage."

"Ha, what's that supposed to mean?" I said. "Have you been laughing at me behind my back?"

He sat up indignantly. "No, never, I wrote you letters, then tore them up." He cast his gaze back to the floor. "Look, you and I aren't the same."

"No fooling," I said, shaking my head, still not wanting to forgive him.

"I run from my responsibilities, hide from what I know I should do. That's what I've done all my life. My father will confirm it." Benny tucked his feet under the chair he sat on. "You're strong and face problems head-on. I can't do that."

I snorted. "You wouldn't say that if you had been around the past few weeks."

"I'm nothing without you and this place," said Benny. "When you said I was like a brother, I felt right in my skin for the first time."

I turned away, half hoping he'd leave. If I can't trust him, then I'm done. Leaning back, I said. "I can't help you. Everything I've planned, everything I've worked for is lost. I have nothing to give you."

Benny paused pulled off his hat. "Maybe it's my turn to give."

We looked at each other for a long moment. I wondered how Benny could help me do anything. On the other hand, it was lonely here. His words sounded earnest and remorseful.

"I don't want to fight with you," I said. "I don't know what to do."

Benny dropped his gaze and stared at the ground. "Eyes see only that which they seek. If you're on the hunt for one thing, you don't see what else is before you."

His words surprised me. He sounded as though he was reading a passage from a book. "Who told you that?"

His chin puckered. "My mom did, but I never understood it until just now." He interlaced his fingers. "Seeking means having a destination. But finding means: being free, being open to possibilities."

"Your mom was pretty smart," I said.

He looked at me squarely. "You told me that."

"Huh."

"I believed in your words," he said. "Maybe if you reclaim your beliefs, you'll find your way home."

We fell silent. I tested Benny's words every which way, trying to unearth the hole, the rock, the defect. In the end, I knew he was right. The truth had rung its bell. Now, it was he who provided a firm hand. I shrugged my shoulders until a snap of pain ran across my back. "I'm not sure how to get beyond this."

"Your answers are within you," said Benny.

I leaned back gingerly against the chair and closed my eyes. "I want them back. I want Sadie and Daniel back. They're all that matters."

"That's the first step," said Benny with wisdom in his voice. I had never heard from him before. "Let's make it happen."

I bent down to pull up a sock. "I wish I could put things," another blast of pain shuddered up my spine, and I stiffened, "back the way they were?"

He cocked his head. "Is that possible?"

I took a deep breath and shook my head.

"Maybe there's another way, a different way," Benny said, "I'll help you find it if you let me."

The hopefulness in his voice comforted me. I looked out the front window once more. A muted mosaic of winter grays interlaced, and touches of sunlight danced on bare limbs. “Got some more coffee?"

Chapter Twenty-Eight

Winter was on the prowl. Benny and I worked hard to harvest before frost covered the fruit. If fruit freezes on the tree before being picked, it may not be a total loss, but the damage will be significant. What's more, temperatures in the twenties leave apples edible after they thaw, but their storage life is drastically shortened. At this point, I no longer had an income from the city, so long storage life was critical for my survival.

The wounds on my back and the bone in my leg were healing. Strength returned to me in shovelfuls. No longer did I feel old and worn. I was strong again, as a man of thirty-four would naturally feel. I still used a cane and thought it might be a permanent appendage. I got up every day, put on my boots, and went to work. I kept a close eye on the town's rebuilding progress through the Spokesman-Review and the Gazette newspapers. Spokane was making headway, and morale was reportedly high. Sadie and Daniel remained in Walla Walla. I wrote regularly.

Dearest one, How are you? Is the baby keeping you up at night? How is Daniel fairing? I miss you both more than I can say. You were right to leave. I am glad you're safe and being looked after.

The rebirth of Spokane Falls continues at a galloping pace. I clipped several recent photographs from the Spokesmen Review for you. Spokanites are a hardy bunch. There seems to be no slowing them down. Unfortunately, the tents are ordered removed by the end of the year due to widespread sanitation problems.

Cyrus has grown a healthy coat in preparation for this year's winter. I had to repair the kitchen stove again. It doesn't want to work for me. Most of the apples have been picked, but we'll lose some to frost. Tree pruning is going slow. Not to worry, we'll get it done before January arrives.

I'll write again soon. Please know, I love you and Daniel with all my heart.

Better times are ahead of us. Shall I come for Christmas?

Your ever-loving Rolla

Meanwhile, every minute of the day, every dream I dreamed, I sorted. Sorted through the fire events, sorted through my regretful resignation, the contentious exoneration, and Sadie's departure. It was a drawerful of events where the outcomes had no favorable assemblage. I didn't know if I could even sequence the pieces together. Could I stitch these torn segments back into place? Did I have the tenacity to clear the roadblocks in my way? To say I had doubts would be to trivialize the hole I stood in; the top of the pit was far out of reach, the walls graded too sharp to climb. But, either way, doubts and unsavory resolutions remained a constant swarm in my mind. All I knew for sure, I had to get myself right, and I had to try to get my family back.

Benny and I worked well together. His friendship and his professed loyalty saved me from many negative beliefs. Beliefs that I now see have imprisoned me most of my life. One day he said to me, "Blaming one person makes life easier for others. Don't take it personally."

A heaviness began lifting when I considered that new yet somewhat convoluted idea. Still, I yearned not to wear this stain of wrong-doing. One day while we were laying down apples in cold storage, Benny blew on his fingertips to warm them. "Why do you accept the guilt of others?" I stopped working. Benny's impertinence irked me. Who do you think you are, I almost said. But, on the other hand, he had a point. I pondered his question for a while. When did I start accepting others' guilt? A person keeps breathing not because it feels good but because it's an unavoidable response. What false beliefs did I accept without question as my duty?

"That's a good question," I said. "I'm not sure the answer to that question. I have come to understand that it doesn't need to be your fault to break you. There needs only to be an accusation."

A foggy landscape obscured my knowing. I wanted answers. Was there a place in Spokane for me to repair the damaged water system, to be part of the city again? Was my underutilized nursery and orchard the best direction to head? Should we leave Spokane and put roots down elsewhere? Would the people of Spokane ever stop blaming me, or would I forever be their scapegoat? The continual sorting and questioning for answers exhausted me.

Sleep was fitful. I'd pull the covers over my weary body, ready for a solid night's sleep. Soon I was running through flames, jumping off trains, hanging from bridges, and strung up by a mob. I saw my life flashing before me over and over again. I dreamed of being back in the tent on the day of my exoneration—people with clenched teeth, jeering eyes, and fists shaking in my face. Other nights I'd dreamed of saying goodbye to Sadie and Daniel at the station, his wee face scrunched up and his hand clawing the window; Sadie's angry eyes; and the shrinking train moving quickly out of sight. When I did sleep, I woke in sweat and tears.

When all the apples were picked and stored, it was three days before Christmas Eve. I hadn't heard back from Sadie. Did she not get my last letter? Had it been purposely hidden from her? Would her father do such a thing? I paced the floor, deliberating all the possibilities, a compulsive habit I had taken on and needed to stop once Sadie was home.

The next morning, I couldn't wait any longer. I rode into town to send Sadie a telegraph. I waited outside the office for two hours, hoping for a quick response. Rain mixed with snow came down in waves. I huddled inside my coat and tucked myself as far as I could under the awning. I would have gone for a cup of coffee, but I didn't think I'd be welcome anywhere. Finally, when no telegraph had come in, Cy and I slumped home in the miserable weather. I ate three cold pork chops and drank whiskey for dinner while standing in front of the fireplace, trying to control my obsessive thinking. It was of little use.

My demeanor and outlook on life were better since Benny returned. And I was certain Sadie would see the improvement if she came back. Maybe there were other problems I hadn't realized—problems Sadie kept to herself. I wanted her back in my life more than anything, and I didn't want to spend Christmas alone.

I woke the following day feeling I had gotten all of fifteen minutes of sleep when I heard a knock at the door. I hopped downstairs and swung open the door to find a telegraph clerk. I snatched the envelope out of his hand and tore it open. It read:

Expecting you for Christmas Eve

Confirm arrival time

Sadie

Though her brevity left me cold, but I went ahead and made preparations to leave anyway. I struggled in earnest to hold down the nagging sense that things weren't right. Over coffee, I made a list of unfinished tasks for Benny to complete. I pulled down a suitcase from the downstairs closet and opened it on the bed. The mighty maple stood in hibernation outside the bedroom window, its arms wrapped around itself to keep warm and fully rooted. Was a bomb set to go off in my lap when I arrived in Walla Walla? Had Sadie decided to end our marriage? James Withers could be pretty persuasive. I'd read the most effective brainwashing was done with subtlety, but James Withers was rarely that. Nonetheless, letting her go down there alone was like sending her to enemy lines without a gun. Lord, if she had any idea how I felt about her father, she'd be unnerved.

The day before I was to take the train to Walla Walla, I went to town to search for gifts. I didn't bother to shave off my beard. I hoped it would be enough of a disguise to avoid altercations with townspeople. Viola-flowered stationery and a white cashmere scarf with a lace border seemed right for Sadie at John Graham's store. He had opened for business in a ten-by-twelve-foot tent two days after the fire. Its motto: "If it's made of paper, we have it." In addition to paper products, they sold everything from art supplies to cameras, sporting goods, to furniture.

Hearing the old stories of young drummer boys leading troops into a battle between the North and South had every boy clamoring for a toy drum or bugle. I would get a drum for Daniel. The drum John Graham was selling had a metal shell painted in red and blue with brass fittings. It was heavy but small enough to pack. But when I saw the zoetrope reel and the viviscope, I had to have it. The machine created the illusion of movement by spinning still drawings inside a drum, an invention I wished I had imagined. A bottle of Jack Daniel's for James Withers and a fashionable woman's hat for Mrs. Harriet were sure bets. The cap had a band of gray satin and a smartly tied bow at the front. On one side, a rose was hand-stitched. The clerk packed it in a sturdy hat box with a handle.

The very next day, Benny drove me to the train station. I was as nervous as a jackrabbit and found it nearly impossible to sit still. I adjusted my hat and pulled out my collar for more breathing room. I rested my cane on one side of me then the other. I couldn't leave things alone.

Benny was his usual quiet self, piping up once in a while. "I got a good feeling about this." His beaver-skin hat was tightened securely to his head. His beard was scruffy, but at the right angle, his baby face still showed through. "You seem nervous."

"Nervous and excited," I said, fidgeting with my gloves where the holes let in the frigid air.

"She's going to stay until after the baby is born," said Benny.

"Well, that's her plan," I said. A plan I was not too fond of at all.

"Maybe she'll change her mind?"

"That would make it the best Christmas of my life," I said with a smile. "Say, what are you doing for Christmas?"

Benny touched Cyrus on the back with the quirt as the horse slowed to eat some of the last remaining green grass. "Don't worry about me. The Cliftons invited me to dinner. I'll be well-fed, and between the boys and Mary, I'll be talked out before the night is through."

I rapped my cane on the wagon floor. "Darn good of them."

"Yep, them's good people," said Benny.

At the train, I shook Benny's hand and thanked him. I would see Sadie and Daniel in about three hours. Trust in the love you share, I repeated to myself. Although outwardly I grinned from ear to ear, waves of doubt came and went. It was like the night of our wedding when I was excited and nervous about our impending consummation. Would it be blissful, awkward, clumsy? Would I fail to perform? Would I falter at expressing how deeply I loved her, particularly if the animal in me became unleashed? I didn't know any more then than I knew now. God, how I detest blindspots.

The train ride took forever. But, I kept telling myself, it's just around this corner, then that corner. The compartment rattled and shook its way down the track. I wished it was warmer inside the cabin. I supposed the few others on the train felt the same. A handful of men coming home from the mines or logging camps was all there were besides me. I tried to occupy myself by looking out the window at the scenery and reading from Keats. There was some relief just getting out of Spokane. The idea of walking around a town where no one knew my face was freeing.

As we pulled into the modest Walla Walla train station, I searched for Sadie or Daniel but did not see them. I interlaced my fingers and wrung my hands. Would I have to find my way to the house alone? A pang of hurt rushed through me like an all-too-familiar gloom. Life continually tested my will—to what end, I didn't know. I'm sure there were lessons from which to glean. I hoped I was learning some of them. On the other hand, I had grown strong as a great oak. On the other, I was as weak as a seedling. I had to trust in the love we shared, that our desire was as strong in her as it was in me. I visualized exercising patience like a tulip bulb does under the earth holding its fervor until the soil of spring warms up.

When I stepped down from the cab, a curtain of steam parted. Sadie and Daniel stood hand in hand before me quiet as falling snow. I swallowed hard. My heart grew big and bountiful. Daniel ran to me, his little feet pounding the boards like a toy hammer. He wrapped his arms around my legs and cried out.

"Daddy, Daddy, you're here."

His grip was better than I remembered. I swept him up and kissed him. Gathered a breath of him big enough for all the days we'd been apart. His little boy's smell of cotton and cookies was like nothing else. Hugging my son put the whole world right. All the pain of the past four months evaporated like mist.

Sadie moved in closer with a radiant smile. Her eyes set with a dreamy look. "Is it you, my darling?"

I put my arm around her and pulled her close. My heart just about exploded. Trembling, we fell into each other's caress. Whatever she wanted me to do, I was going to do. I wanted my family back more than a job, more than a homestead, more than anything. And it was at that precise moment when the fog I had been caught in cleared off. I could see again.

Chapter Twenty-Nine

We kissed, drawing oxygen from each other. I wanted to consume Sadie, to pull her into my body, into my bones. I needed her as I've never needed anyone in my life. I required her muscles; mine were disabled. I wanted her eyes; mine had fogged. I yearned for her loving touch to heal the wretched scars on my body and my broken heart. But when Daniel squealed, a pitch so high it hurt my ears, we came back from our retreat. He pushed our faces apart. We covered his face in kisses, which brought forth a ticklish giggle. Sadie lowered her gaze and placed her hands on akimbo.

"How do I look?" said Sadie.

The baby had grown significantly. Sadie's face was fuller, and her complexion pinker than before. "You look rested and well fed," I said, taking her hands.

"Do you mean fat?" she said, pushing away playfully.

Embarrassed, I said, "No, no, you look beautiful. As beautiful as I've ever seen you."

Sadie laughed. "You should see the expression on your face, priceless."

I broke into a smile.

"Mother has a new young cook who makes the best crumpets." She pulled out my vest. "You've lost weight. Are you all right?"

I placed my hands akimbo, as she had. My hip bones were noticeable through my clothes. "I've surely missed your cooking." Tonight when we got undressed for bed, she'd see how scraggy I'd become. And when she ran her hands over my scars, she'd cry. Then she'd yell with alarm.

She stepped back and gave me an appraising look. "Well, fortunately, all we're going to be doing for the next two days is eat."

I brightened. "Well, let's get to it." We laughed and started on our way with buoyancy.

Daniel ran ahead. "Come this way, Daddy. I'll show you the way."

"It's true. Daniel knows the way," said Sadie proudly.

I squeezed her hand. "He's grown." Eight weeks of Daniel's life were forever lost. I'd never get that time back. Never know what made him laugh, what made him cry or what questions he had that I should have been there to answer.

She nodded. "Yes, soon enough, he'll be a big boy."

We strolled toward her parents' home. Christmas decorations adorned every shop window. Passersby greeted us with friendly nods. The candlelit decorations through polished glass gave us a chance to catch each other's gaze. There was a shy glance here, a peek there, a smile, a wink — desire surged. She loved me. I could see it. I stopped and kissed her gloved hands and recited our favorite sonnet, by John Keats:

I am certain of nothing but the
holiness of the heart's affections,
and the truth of imagination

When we arrived at her parents' gate, I held back. "Do we have to go in so soon?"

"Come on, Daddy," said Daniel, halfway to the door.

I stretched my hand out for him to return. "Wait a minute."

Sadie patted my arm. "Father's promised to be on his best behavior. So it'll be all right."

"It's not that," I said. But of course, it was. "Having the three of us together, alone, is glorious. I don't want it to end."

"Don't worry." Sadie tugged on my hand to follow her. "There'll be time for us."

I pointed. "Can we stroll the grounds a bit?"

She stopped pulling. "Of course. Daniel, we're going for a walk around the yard."

The Witherses' had purchased a somewhat inferior home compared to their New York estate. Nonetheless, it was the best Victorian on the block: Two stories painted custard yellow with white trim and black details. Boxwood bushes lined the walkway, the sides, and tops cut with precision. Rhododendrons, unruly in these parts, had been adequately neatened. An expansive porch spanned both sides of the front door with rattan furniture on display. It appeared as if they had lived there for years rather than a year since relocating from the East. The back and side yard were meticulously groomed. An expanse of green lawn and patches of snow covered the ground. A few giant conifers and a row of weeping birch trees populated the south side. Within view of the kitchen, under a sycamore tree, hung a swing at the perfect height for a small boy. A nearby sandpit sat undisturbed.

"Daniel, you have such a big yard to play in," I said.

Daniel's shoulders slumped. "But no one to play with," he said with a frown.

"Well, I'd like to do some playing, partner," I said, taking a cowboy's stance and pretending to spit.

Daniel laughed with his mouth wide open and he hugged my legs again. Sadie and I smiled at each other, giving each other a quick peck.

When we made it back to the front steps, my knee started to ache. I squeezed Sadie's hand on the approach of the front door when somehow it opened on its own volition. On the other side, James Withers and Mrs. Harriet stood. Her hands were clasped neatly in front: His feet were set in a wide stance and his hands in his pant pockets.

"Come in, dear, come in," said Mrs. Harriet. Her arms stretched out wide.

I stepped in and air-kissed her like the media crowd of New York who lunches and gossip with each other.

"You're using a cane," said James Withers, taking the bag of gifts from my hand.

"I'll be rid of it soon," I said, jostling. I extended my hand. "How are you, Father?"

"Couldn't be better," said James Withers. "Shall I put these under the tree, Mother?

"Thank you, dear," said Mrs. Harriet taking hold of Daniel's hand. "Daniel, do you want to show your daddy his room?"

Daniel, who had his eye on the bag of gifts, broke his gaze. "Daddy, come on. Come on, Dad, come on."

"I'm coming," I said, hoping they didn't expect me to sleep any-place other than with my wife.

Sadie stepped in. ”I'll show him our room. Daniel, you can play with some of your toys for a short while."

"But I want to go with Daddy."

"I know, but for now, let me show Daddy the room."

"Okay," said Daniel, with his lower lip protruding.

Taking Daniel's hand, Mrs. Harriet said. "Come on, let's find one of your toys."

I followed Sadie upstairs to the second-floor landing, around the banister, and down the hallway to our room. She moved with grace. Her floral scent aroused me. To hold her again would be to quell the angst and uncertainty I had lugged around these past months.

I followed her into the room. She closed and locked the door behind her. My heart leaped. All the months I worried seemed to be for naught. She was her old self. Could it be true? Was our love as reliable as before, no worse for the wear? I sat down on the bed and dropped my shoulders in total surrender. Her eyes dazzled me with intent. She pushed me back onto the bed and stuck a finger in my mouth, drawing out my lower lip. A hunger rose. The heat of her hand against my face flooded me with zeal. I wanted to caress every bit of her, kiss every plain, every valley, glide my hands down every slope of her silken skin. She knew what she was doing to me. She knew well.

Sadie moved in closer and looked deep into my eyes. "You know we can't do this right now?"

I burrowed my head back into the pillow. "I know." Unbuttoning the top button of her shirtwaist and kissing the tops of her breasts. "I find you irresistible, Mrs. Jones." Being here with her, in that way, told me life would someday be as it was—a life filled with laughter and harmony. "Can you tell I'm making every effort to control myself?"

She arched her back and moved against me. "I can tell." Then in the sweetest yet cruelest voice ever: "But we should probably go down."

I closed my eyes and bit my lip. "I think I'll need a few minutes before I am presentable again," I said with a strained smile.

A roar of laughter bubbled between us.

Giggling, she ran her hand down and squeezed me tight for a moment. "Oh, my, you are happy to see me."

A gush of air came forward. "Before you go downstairs, my love, your telegraph was rather terse and now this."

She kissed my mouth, her lips wet and warm. "Mother sent it."

I sighed. "That explains it." My worries about divorce disappeared. I was so relieved and pushed away my doubts.

She got up from the bed, fanned herself briefly, and smoothed down her dress. "Let me put your things away for you."

"Don't trouble yourself. I can do it." I said, sitting on the edge of the bed. "I'll meet you downstairs in a few minutes."

Sadie tilted her head with a coy smile. "As you wish."

When she reached for the door, she turned back and fluttered her fingers seductively. That's the playfulness I have missed so much. "You better go before we can't stop ourselves," I said.

She scooted out the door with a moan.

I sat there in joyous amazement. If we were together again, we could manage anything no matter what came our way. I flopped back on the bed and chuckled. I hadn't felt this good in months. Relief settled in, and soon I drifted off. Then, in what seemed like no time at all, I awoke to a poke in my arm.

"Daddy, I've come to collect you for dinner."

With my eyes not yet open, I pulled him onto the bed. "Oh, you have, have you?" I said, tickling him under his chin, behind his neck, under his arm and finally his knee. He laughed loudly with shrieks of glee. His blond hair was turning darker. His knees had grown more significant than his leg bones.

"Do it again, Daddy. Tickle me again."

When Sadie entered the room, I had him laughing so hard; he hadn't taken a breath for at least five-seconds. We looked up, knowing we were in trouble and trying to bottle our giddiness into some semblance of restraint.

"Come quick. It's time for dinner," said Sadie, her hand outstretched and a happy grin on her face.

"My sweet boy, we must now do as we are told," I said to Daniel.

He rubbed his nose. "Oh, mom," he said and slid off the bed.

Quickly, I combed my hair and Daniel's and followed Sadie downstairs, still straightening my crumpled suit. Before we reached the foyer, I noticed his pants were twisted to one side. "Wait a minute. Let's get your knickers straight." I straightened him without a second thought, as I had done so many times before. "Now we're ready for dinner." It's funny how that little action made me feel in tune. The three of us smiled at one another and walked into the dining room, holding hands. I felt whole—not shattered by the fire and the events of the last few months. I was not tormented with worry that everything was gone for good. Not blind to the next step. Things were going well. I was happy to be there.

Mrs. Harriet was busy adjusting the cutlery to her precise specifications on the table. At the same time, Mr. Withers sat waiting to be served.

"There they are," Mrs. Harriet said. "Rolla, please sit on this side, the second chair down. Sadie, you will sit across from him, and Daniel, please, take a seat next to your father."

"I much prefer to sit next to my husband," said Sadie.

Her mother fondled her elbow nervously. "All right, have it your way."

"Thank you, Mother."

I said nothing and did what they agreed I should do.

A center cloth of embroidered linen lay on the highly polished oak table, which sat eight. A shallow dish of ferns mingled with white carnations sat in the center on a round mirror base. A few stray leaves were set around it as if placed there by Mother Nature herself.

A young Indian woman of about sixteen with a white apron and a thick braid of hair at the back stepped through the swinging door holding the first course, raw oysters. There were six shells to a plate with two or three slices of lemon and a ramekin of hot sauce on each.

Daniel looked to his mother and made a face. "Do I have to eat those?"

"No, darling," said Sadie.

Daniel wriggled his legs back and forth in relief.

James went straight for the oysters and slurped down two before either Sadie or I had a chance to prepare one.

The Indian girl stood unblinking, her chin low, her eyes staring into blankness. She soon disappeared into the kitchen, the door swinging behind her with a whack. Minutes later, she carried out a goose on a platter and placed it on the sideboard. James Withers stuffed his napkin behind his Farnsworth necktie and readied himself to eat more. "Looks delicious Abey."

Abey appeared pleased. "Thank you, Mr. Withers. It's best to give it time to rest before serving."

James Withers thumped his round belly. "Of course, no reason to rush. Although I must admit, I have worked up a mighty fine appetite," said Mr. Withers, "Rolla, do you fancy goose?"

I chuckled at what I knew must be a rhetorical question. "It is beyond splendid."

Mrs. Harriet smiled widely and asked, "Rolla, would you like to say grace?"

"I'd be delighted." I was getting the royal treatment.

James Withers cleared his throat. "I'll say grace. This is my home."

That's the James Withers I knew.

"Yes, Father," said Mrs. Harriet lowering her linen napkin.

Sadie bowed her head and threw a sideways glance at me.

I winked with understanding.

"Dear Lord," Father began, "we are gathered here on the eve of your birthday to celebrate family, new beginnings, and big decisions. Thank you for your bounty and your wisdom. In Christ, our savior, we give thee thanks, amen."

"Amen," we responded together. I wondered what he meant by new beginnings and big decisions. Was I being forewarned? Was he up to something? That thought opened a door into old suspicions and fears. I became on edge. Was I about to be ambushed? Drawn into his web, forced to do things his way again? That night at Delmonico's five years prior came rushing back. He had taken control and told us how we were to proceed. I quickly slurped down my first oyster to divert my thoughts. Its smooth texture and lemon wash, beautifully spiced with a dash of Tabasco, were exquisite. Still, James Withers's prayer made me sure something distasteful was headed my way.

With a nearly inaudible slurp, Sadie imbibed her oyster. "Oh, Mother, the oysters are just divine."

"Simply wonderful," said James Withers.

"Absolutely," I said.

"A toast to oysters," said Mrs. Harriet raising her champagne glass high and releasing a gale of honking laughter. We couldn't help but join in with her.

Sometime later Abey brought out dishes of steaming food and set them on the table. She started to carve the goose. Each slice oozed with seasoned juices. The scented steam of rosemary, garlic, and sage circled the room. French peas and boiled cauliflower with drawn butter sent out a rich, savory aroma. The cranberry sauce was spiked with orange slices and cinnamon sticks. There was also a haunch of venison wrapped in pastry dough, pickled beetroot, mashed turnips, and sweet potatoes. So much food for four people. On the buffet sat an array of mince pies, plates of fresh oranges, grapes, nuts, raisins, and cheese.

By the end of the eight-course meal, I was heartily satiated. I had enough food in me to last until dinner the next day. We finished up with cups of strong black coffee and snifters of brandy. I remembered what my mother said at the end of every grand dinner: Sensible people do not affect pale and watery liquor after a hearty dinner.

I was thankful to be dining in this elegant house with Sadie, Daniel, and her parents. Still, I couldn't help but wonder what James Withers meant by new beginnings and big decisions. Sadie and Daniel were relaxed and happy. Mrs. Harriet was chatty and repeatedly expressed sympathy for my injuries. Father ate a second helping of the frosted spice cake. Even so, my gut told me something was on the prowl.

Chapter Thirty

I grappled with James Withers's words, "new beginnings, and big decisions," for the remainder of the evening. I knew him well enough to know that it wouldn't be trivial if he brought it up on Christmas Eve.

I was glad the undisclosed subject was put off. Daniel deserved to have a magical Christmas, unspoiled by family differences. It was fitting for him to experience the fascination of an ancient myth so lovingly carried down through the ages. It had been my own first introduction, as I am sure it was for so many children, to the world of enchantment. That sense of wonder for me developed into engineering and the invention of ideas. When I could work out a mathematical problem, finish construction on an intricate design, or invent a new time-saving device, a fizz of magic would burst into the air. It was as if Santa had just come down the chimney in one fell swoop and covered me in sparkling dust.

James Withers warranted respect for his role as the grandfather of the family. He'd done well financially and supported a wife and three daughters. However, over the past five years, I had been unable to garner the kind of affection I would have preferred to have for him. With my own father, although gruff at times, I knew he had my best interest at heart. Like the time I was short on spring tuition. He told me, "Get out and find some work. It'll be good for you." I was angry at first with exams being around the corner. Fortunately, the school agreed to give me an extra thirty days to raise the money. For four weeks, I worked every job I could find. I washed dishes at a nearby pub. I ran errands for shop owners. I drew blueprints for a woman who wanted to remodel her kitchen. I chopped wood for hours. Every night I studied into the wee hours of the morning. Eventually, I got the money and passed the exams. My marks could have been better but, I learned there are always trade offs with every decision. You don't give up; you find another way. It certainly did me no harm. I felt proud of myself afterward and respected my father even more.

It's not that James Withers's opinions didn't hold value. It was his autocratic manner that chafed my nerves. My father expected me to make my own decisions and suffer the consequences. James Withers assumed he knew a better way and would vehemently force his will upon us. It was a constant battle, deflecting demands disguised as advice. If he had a new plan for our lives, a fight was inevitable.

After dinner, the ceremonial opening of one gift commenced. Daniel loved the drum I bought for him and banged on it until bedtime. Sadie and I put him to bed as we had many times before by reading him one of his favorite bedtime stories. That night it was the famous Goldilocks and the Three Bears.

When we finished, he pulled the cover under his chin and asked, "Are you sure Santa knows I'm at Papa's and Grammy's?"

I furrowed my brow humorously. "Santa knows where you are and will not forget you."

Daniel smiled with renewed excitement. His unfiltered innocence made my throat tighten, my heart warm. He soon drifted off to sleep, a sailboat nudged by a tailwind. Sadie and I sauntered back to our room, arm over arm, and retired for the evening.

In our room alone, a wondrous push of sensations rushed in. Outside, snow fell quietly, padding every surface in a pristine blanket. We stood in our nightclothes, Sadie's back against me. I listened as she inhaled gentle sweeps of air. With my arms around her, my hands rested on her bulging abdomen. The baby moved.

She cupped her hands over mine. "You know, we must get up in a few hours to set out the gifts for Daniel."

"I know," I said, kissing her temple. The heavenly smell of her hair, clean and perfumed, filled my senses. "Say, have you come up with any names for the baby?"

Sadie squeezed my hand and turned to face me. "If it's a girl, I was thinking Hazel Blue."

"Like the color of your eyes?" I said.

She meowed, "Maybe."

"I don't care what others think," I said. We falsely chuckled at that untruth. Of course I cared, but I wanted to care less. "It's a perfect name. You might get some resistance on Blue, but so what. It's our baby."

"Precisely," she murmured.

I moved my mouth to the curve of her neck. "And if it's a boy?"

She snuggled in closer. "What do you think of John, after my granddad, or Joseph after yours?"

I nodded to her sensibility. "Good choices, but maybe we should wait until we meet the baby to make a final decision."

"Probably a good idea," she said.

The moonlight from the window illuminated one side of her face as I caressed her slender shoulders. It was sublime to be close to her again. "During grace, your father referred to new beginnings and big decisions. Do you know what he meant?"

She shook her head. "I hardly listened. Most of what he says I ignore. You should too."

She pulled my arms tighter around her. Her attitude about her father had changed and gave me some relief.

She turned and stared up at me with dreamy eyes. "Should we talk about us?"

I leaned down and kissed her mouth. Then circled my tongue around her shoulder, over her swollen breasts, and around her tender nipples. "Let's talk tomorrow." She moaned. We kissed until a craving for connection swelled in us. We clawed at each other. Her scent filled my mind with a bouquet of eroticism. At that moment, with her so close, I knew we would survive. I was not going to rot in the West alone. I felt as happy as I ever had in my life. We made love discreetly, afraid someone might hear. We made love gently, although the desire was to do the opposite. Our intertwined bodies were taut. It was our destiny to be together, to be one. My heart sang out in elation like sun coming over the horizon. The parts of me I'd lost came back. I felt whole again. I was a man, strong and in control.

Not but a few minutes later, a soft purr escaped from her mouth as she floated off to sleep. The warmth of her body, the luxury of the bedding was a blissful cocoon. Through the bedroom window, way up yonder, a moon glowed brightly. It was plain to see. She and Daniel had it good here. The house was better than our rustic homestead—everything polished, everything clean and crisp. Everything she needed was here just for the asking. Rather than worry, I decided to be grateful. I shut my eyes and peacefully drifted off.

Chapter Thirty-One

Sadie and I had slept soundly, waking only minutes before we were to rise in a panic, afraid we were too late to set the Christmas scene. We snuck downstairs and back again without hardly making a sound. We woke the second time with Daniel running downstairs to see that Santa had left hoards of gifts. He was so excited that he ran up and down the hallway, banging on doors and begging us to get up.

He barged into our room. "Come on, he's come and gone."

"Give us a few minutes," I said. "Go ahead and wait for us downstairs. Don't touch anything."

Daniel jumped, turned, and ran down the stairs.

Sadie scooted to the bathroom. I put on a clean shirt, clean undershorts, and clean socks with the only suit I brought with me. We crowded down the staircase. James and Mrs. Harriet strolled just ahead of us in satin robes and smooth leather slippers. I held us back for a moment to straighten our hair and clothes. When we were presentable, we giggled and quickly kissed.

James Withers had already settled on his settee as we entered the room. "Mr. Jones, you're looking chipper this morning. You must have slept well."

I knew he was hinting at coitus, and I chose to ignore his impertinence. "Yes, we both did, didn't we, darling?"

Sadie nodded in agreement and threw me a sideways glance.

Abey was back on the job and quickly served James Withers his coffee.

"Rolla, would you do the honors of handing out gifts?" said Father.

I cocked my head. "Are you sure?" I hoped he'd decline my offer.

James Withers paused a moment.

I wished I hadn't said anything except yes.

"You go ahead, he said. "It'll serve as a good memory for Daniel."

Another obtuse remark that left me questioning. Oh, how I detested her father's games.

Daniel was down on all fours, eyeing each gift, a little poke, a little shake. "I wonder what this is?" He lifted one corner of a package with a bow. "Who's this for?"

Mrs. Harriet bent down. "Who do you think?" she said, her eyes smiling.

Daniel took a big breath, eyes the size of moons. "For me? Can I open it?"

She wagged her finger. "Not yet, we have to wait for your mother."

Beside the eight-foot tree dressed in baubles and lit candles, a carafe of coffee and cups had been set out. The smell filled the house with a robust aroma. Abey handed Mrs. Harriet a steamy cup of coffee and cream.

"I know how everybody prefers their coffee except you, Mr. Jones," Abey said.

"Straight black," I said.

She poured a cup and brought it over. "You don't want some of this cream to lighten it?" said Abey. "Makes it nice."

I shook my head. "No, thank you," and took a quick sip. "Abey, will you be celebrating Christmas today?"

Abey raised her head. "Yes, sir, my parents will come to collect me this evening . I'll go home for a few days."

"When was the last time you were home?" I asked.

Abey dropped her eyes and looked as though she was holding back tears. "It's been months. I came here right after school let out."

After the Civil War, Indian children were sent to boarding schools away from their families. Americans who once regarded native people with fear or loathing transformed their feelings to reformation. Reformers felt that with the proper education and treatment, Indians could become regular citizens. They convinced the leaders of Congress that education could change at least some of the Indian population into patriotic and productive members of society. Most of the girls were required to cook traditional American cuisine and clean everything from linens to China.

Mrs. Harriet eyed Abey then jiggled her cup for more coffee. "How will I do without her? I don't know," she said, rolling her eyes.

Abey quickly filled her cup and poured more cream.

"That will be enough. You are excused," said Mrs. Harriet.

Abey curtsied. "Yes, ma'am," she said and returned to the kitchen.

I watched her leave, her tiny body shuffling solemnly out of the room.

I finished my first cup of coffee and went for another. A few more savory sips and I was ready for Santa duty. But Sadie was back in the bathroom. The wait nearly drove Daniel wild. He couldn't stop repeating, "Mommy, present time."

She was ten weeks to term. The best part of the pregnancy was over. Sadie had once told me, "The last three months make you so miserable you're willing to go through the pain of labor."

I believed her.

Sadie was finally ready to open gifts. Sitting beside me, she whispered, "Give Daniel that one." She pointed to an oblong box wrapped in red tissue paper with a green silk bow. I reached under the tree. "This gift is for...Daniel, from...Santa," I said, handing it over to Daniel, who was standing erect. He rushed over, grabbed it, and sat with a thud.

"Don't tear the box. You may want it when you're not playing with it," said Mrs. Harriet.

Daniel pulled off the ribbon and let it fall. "I won't." When he got most of the paper off, his eyes lit up. A replica train was printed on the box. "Look, Dada, a train just like what we have at home."

Father smiled. "This one has four axles and a large fanned grate at its front."

I examined the box. "And it's a 2-8-0 model, impressive," I said, looking to the Witherses. "Well done."

Mrs. Harriet and Father beamed.

To maintain Father's positive demeanor, I passed my gift to him.

He peeled the tape from the heavy brown wrapping paper to reveal a decent bottle of whiskey. He screwed off the top and poured a slug in his coffee cup, then mine. I didn't care for whiskey and coffee, but I wasn't about to disclose my feelings. Father lifted his cup and leaned over to clink cups with me. "Cheers," he said with a wry smile.

Next, I handed Mrs. Harriet the hatbox I had brought for her. She opened it parsimoniously with wide eyes. "Oh my," she said, removing the lid, "what a splendid color, Rolla, thank you."

Sadie fetched a hand mirror, and the two spent a good long time fitting the hat to its perfect angle.

Her acceptance gave me relief.

I presented Sadie with her gift wrapped in thick brown paper but with a red and green plaid bow. Sadie gasped when she saw the soft white down of cashmere and the lace trim. She pulled it out and immediately cloaked it around her neck.

"Oh, I love this. Isn't beautiful, Mother?"

"Just lovely," chimed Mrs. Harriet. "You have good taste, Mr. Jones."

I bowed modestly.

"I think Daniel needs another gift," I said.

"But, darling, there's a gift or two for you under the tree," exclaimed Sadie.

"For me? Really?"

"Well, of course," chimed Mrs. Harriet.

James Withers poured more whiskey into his coffee cup, raised the bottle, and waved his cup loosely.

I searched and found a gift the size of a tie box. "This one?" I asked, holding it up as I sat back on the floor. Sadie and her parent's eyes twinkled. Daniel crawled onto my lap as I opened the box covered in white tissue paper with a linen bow. Inside, a charcoal-gray wool neck scarf with threads of lighter gray running through it rested between folded parchment. "Why, thank you, I've been wanting one and almost bought myself one before coming here."

Daniel loved the viviscope and watched in fascination as a cowboy rode past the screen on horseback. Sadie presented me with a set of monogrammed handkerchiefs every gentleman was expected to carry, as well as a book of poems by William Wadsworth, which I had long desired. I gave her the stationery with the idea she could write to her mother from home.

When we were finished opening gifts, Abey neatly folded up the discarded wrapping paper and ribbons. She set the bows to one side but burned the gift wrap in the fireplace.

James Withers bobbed his head from side to side. "Abey, please take Daniel upstairs. We have a family matter to discuss."

The hair at the back of my neck stood up. The mystery behind the remarks would soon be unveiled.

Daniel's lower lip poked out. "Why do I have to leave? I want to stay with Mommy and Dada."

"What's this about?" said Sadie, straightening the viviscope.

"Do as you're told," said James Withers.

She looked at her father suspiciously and muttered, "Mmm."

Abey took Daniel's hand. "We won't be long, honey," said Sadie.

"I'll come and get you as soon as we're finished," I said. I patted the back of his head as he passed. "Everything's all right, son." My stomach knotted.

Daniel grabbed the new toy train his grandparents had given him in a huff and climbed the garland-wrapped staircase with Abey.

I looked at Sadie and mouthed the words, "What now?" She looked cross-eyed at me, a sure sign that she thought this would be one of those talks he bestowed upon us from time to time. Positioning myself behind her chair, I could feel the doom descending just as sure as when Rossiter tapped his pipe in his hand, threw the contents on the floor, stuck the mouthpiece between his teeth, and unloaded a barrage of criticisms on me or some other poor sap.

James Withers's preamble was far less evident. He blew his nose, wiped it with his cotton handkerchief, folded it neatly, and slid it back into his robe pocket. "Harriet and I have decided the logical next step as it pertains to our daughter and our grandson."

Mrs. Harriet spat a short honk of laughter. "You mean, you've decided. I'm not at all sure about it."

Appearing irritated, James Withers whispered, "You are my wife, and I am head of the house."

She sighed. "Yes, dear," folded her hands in her lap with a miffed expression.

Looking sternly down his nose, Mr. Withers said, "Mr. Jones, since you have seen fit to destroy your reputation by way of a terrible fire—which I grant you was not entirely your fault—I have decided the best thing for my daughter and my grandson is for them to live here with us. You can remain in Spokane or where ever, but not with them. You may come and visit Daniel from time to time until Sadie has found a serious suitor."

In that instant, the kid gloves came off. My mind raced about frantically trying to get a grip on the insanity of what I had just heard. I looked at Sadie, her eyes bulging, her cheeks flushed.

I moved from behind the chair. "Who do you think you are?"

Sadie put out her hand. I pushed it aside.

James Withers withdrew a cigar from a wood box beside him and searched for a match. "In destroying your reputation, you have also destroyed my daughter's. That shame is too much to ask of her. For her to recover from this, she has but one choice: divorce you so that she can find a more suitable husband. A husband who offers a clean dossier." He stood halfway up, searching for a match on the side table. "It's too bad. I rather liked you."

"Father, you're quite hostile," said Mrs. Harriet.

James Withers flashed an angry eye. "I am merely presenting the reality of their lives."

Rage flew as high as a winged bird of prey. I bolted forward. Every fiber in my body was on fire. "You're out of your cotton-picking mind."

James Withers crossed his ankles as if my reaction did not affect him. "Quite the contrary, Mr. Jones, I believe you are the one who is out of your mind, as evidenced by what my sources have told me."

"Your sources?" I howled.

Sadie grabbed my hand. That old archenemy betrayal marched through me. At that moment, the recovery I made evaporated like steam. The pain of being blamed yet exonerated was again sharp.

"Have you been spying on me?" I said, bracing myself on the chair's back. I searched for words to shut him down. I had to defend myself. Yet defeatism lurked in every corner. I was completely thrown off, just as I had been the day I was blamed and nearly strung up to die. I couldn't find a vantage point from which to quash his accusation. "Sadie, did you know about this?" I spat.

Sadie looked wild-eyed. "I did not."

"Your binge drinking and nearly setting the house on fire are unacceptable responses to a tragedy. My God, you're supposed to be the man of the house, not an adolescent in rebellion," said James Withers.

"Rolla, is this true?" said Sadie.

I bit my tongue and squeezed the chair back. "It was a difficult time. It's behind me now."

"Oh, sweetheart," said Sadie with a look of deep compassion.

James Withers leaned in. "He's weak. Can't you see? He has destroyed your future. I won't stand for it."

I took a step toward him. James Withers sat with his legs spread wide, the outline of his gonads for all to see. "You have no right to say such things to me. I don't take orders from you. We make our own decisions. Just as we did when we decided to marry."

"You asked for my permission," said James Withers.

I planted my fists on my hips. "A mere formality, I assure you."

James Withers pointed at me. "Look at his hands. He wants to fight me. How very mature of you, Mr. Jones."

I was now a few feet from him. "I get it. The great James Withers is above all feelings. Everything is rooted in logic. No one could accuse you of following your heart, oh, no sir, not you. I'll say one thing for you, you've got bigger balls than most—or is it presumption?"

Sadie and her mother gasped.

James Withers looked down at his open legs and covered himself up.

Sadie got to her feet, grabbed my shoulder, and held it back. "Enough, I have had enough."

"Watch it," said James Withers pointing a shaky finger.

I reached for her hand. "I'll handle this."

Sadie swept my hand aside and pointed to herself. "No, this is not your fight alone."

I stared at her, baffled, not knowing what she meant. "Sadie, let me handle this."

Mrs. Harriet moved forward on the settee. "Now, don't get too excited. It's not good for the baby."

Sadie spun around. She glared at her father, then her mother. "This fight isn't only my husband's. This is not about what happened in Spokane. This here's an assault because my father believes I am a child unable to care for myself. Unable to make proper decisions. Why? Because I am a woman and inferior to his great intellect and power. He believes I am weak and lack the proper temperament as all women do. Right, Father?"

James Withers feigned. "Don't be ridiculous."

I had seen this kind of scrap in her before. But she didn't have to fight for me. I could defend myself. To be honest, she made me nervous. Never would I have asked my wife to do such a thing. Why that would have been disgraceful. I stood over James Withers, every muscle taut.

Mr. Withers folded his arms over his chest, sneered at Sadie, and blurted, "you're getting mighty close to making a mistake."

Sadie moved beside me again. "I am going to tell you how things are, Father. I am a grown woman, owned by no man, not him, not you." She pointed to me, then to him. "I will have the legal right to vote. I will have the right, like every American, to live life my way." Her hands grabbed her dress cloth. "No one tells me what to do.

Furthermore, I have had enough of your old-fashioned thinking. Rolla and I are the new generation. Your insistent need to coerce, as well-intentioned as it may be, has got to stop. I made a commitment when I married Rolla to honor him until death. To share our lives in good and bad times. I am not quitting this marriage. What we are going to do is leave Spokane as soon as we figure out where."

My jaw dropped. "We what?"

Sadie continued. "Maybe we'll go back to New York. Either way, we'll find our way, with or without your help."

I crossed my arms over my chest. Sadie and her father had usurped my right to decide, and I wasn't happy. "I have agreed to no such thing."

"There, you see what I mean?" said James Withers looking for acknowledgment from his wife.

Sadie turned sharply. "Rolla, we talked it over, remember?"

"It was mentioned," I said, "but we have much more to discuss before such a decision can be made." She may have been the thread that stitched our hearts, convictions, and beliefs together, but some things still required both parties to agree. In an attempt to calm her down, I said, "When we get home, we'll have a proper discussion."

Mrs. Harriet dabbed her weepy eyes. "But, she could lose the baby."

Sadie paused, appearing to have lost her momentum. She dropped her arms to her sides and swayed back. "The baby is strong. And I thank you for the time to collect my wits and recover from the fire. But I am going home with Rolla, my husband, on the very next train."

"Daniel stays here," yelled James Withers, his fingers perched high on his knees. "I can do it. You know I can."

Simultaneously Sadie and I rebuked his threat. "Not on your life."

James Withers bared his teeth. "If you don't do as I say, I will cut you out of the will."

With a bizarre honk, Mrs. Harriet scoffed. "Like hell, you will."

James and Mrs. Harriet looked at each other liked two wolves ready for battle.

Sadie threw up her hands. "Do what you have to do, Father. I'm not your possession. Rolla is not an indentured servant. We are free. We are as emancipated as anyone in America."

Sadie took my sleeve and pulled me into the middle of the room before I turned back for one final word. "Try having a little faith, a little trust, in your daughter and her husband."

James Withers got up and stormed out the front door into the snow without a coat or a match for his cigar. He went out into the bitter cold, where he stomped around like a spoiled child steaming over the derailment of his scheme. Would he threaten us further through legal methods, or would he back off?

Chapter Thirty-Two

I can't wait to get home and sleep in my bed," said Sadie, gazing at the snow-covered landscape out the dining car window.

"I've had more sleepless nights than I care to admit," I said. "With you home, those are behind me."

Sadie smiled over at Daniel, lying on the opposing seat, his feet up reading picture books. "A good night's sleep is such a blessing, isn't it, darling?"

I drew in closer and whispered, "We're going to be fine, don't worry."

She nodded her head and took on a prideful glare. "We're strong and independent."

"Strong," I confirmed.

But when she said, "My father will come around," her eyes filled with misgivings.

A moment later, she stiffened, her eyes cast in frustration. "I don't know about the people of Spokane."

I patted her hand. "I pray they will come around too," I said. "We must give them more time."

"I will, but remember, we have options."

"I know, I know."

****

Sadie and I were cautiously happy on the train ride home. We had closed down James Withers unequivocally. My family was reunited. Harmony was ours again. The struggle to regain them had been punishing. Between the fire, Sadie leaving me, and her father deciding we must divorce—I felt as if I had been to hell and back. Now, on the other side of despair, a renewed inspiration seized me. I had a second chance, and new ideas popped up like grasshoppers.

Thoughts about a timber dam kept circling my mind. Was it a vision or a fantasy? I'd give it some time before letting my imagination play with it on the drawing board. For now, just being with my wife and son was all I required.

Sadie's argument for moving away from Spokane sat with me as a skin rash might. She felt betrayed by the people of Spokane Falls. One minute we were the rising dynamic couple hobnobbing with high society; smiles and handshakes came from everyone. The next minute we were in the dirt without so much as a howdy-do. She was hurt and angry, as was I, but pulling up our ties, leaving the homestead, and moving away was a gigantic step.

How much of her father's disapproval motivated her desire to leave? All the years we'd been together, she had couched her true feelings about his controlling ways. She was too much a lady to speak ill of him. She was a modern woman and believed in it proudly. Her father's chauvinism was the standard. For Sadie, being under any man's thumb was intolerable. I did my best to be the kind of husband and friend she expected. But, I also had a lot to learn.

Honestly, the idea of another life-changing event scared the hell out of me. It could very well be a decision we'd come to regret. I had relied on her judgment during those days after the fire. I was sure her ability to see through the steamy vista was better than mine. Her happiness was all-important to me. I would do whatever was necessary to protect it, but leaving the homestead did not sit right with me. I hoped for a better way.

When we pulled into Spokane Falls depot, Benny greeted us with the biggest smile ever. "Welcome home, Jones's family," he said with a big grin, the kind you might see on a smiling dog.

Daniel reached up and shook Benny's hand like a little man.

"Howdy partner, you look as good as blueberry pie," said Benny.

Daniel laughed at the idea. "That's silly."

Sadie rested her hand on his shoulder and gazed at him fondly, "Dear Benny."

When we gripped hands, he smiled like an old comrade. We shook earnestly and embraced briefly. Our friendship was sturdy. Looking back on that first day when I found him squatting on the property turned out to be a blessing for us all. He had become a brother.

We loaded our luggage into the wagon, including the viviscope and the toy train set. On our way through town, Sadie was astonished at the town's progress.

"It looks more like New York every time I see it," she said. "So many skyscrapers going up. Look, there's a five-story building. Let's drive around a little."

Benny winced. "We'll get stuck in the mud."

I surveyed the streets. "Ah, come on, take us for a jaunt."

"Yes, please," said Daniel, wiggling between us.

We were stuck in the mud ten minutes later in front of the Northwestern Industrial Expo building site. The expo will open on the first day of October. It was a big deal for Spokane to prove we were still on the map.

"Our civic leaders decided to put on this exposition—to awaken the nation to the matchless advantages of this resurrected city," I said, "in the brand-new state of Washington."

Benny pulled back on the brake. “A bit too ambitious if you ask me."

I jumped down from the wagon. "Hard to argue with you on that." With only the foundation framed and nine months to go before opening day, Spokane's vision for the future was shaky at best. The building's design would favor a state building, flags on every corner of a multilayered roof, and a turret big enough to hold a dozen or more.

Benny followed me to the back of the wagon and pulled out shovels and boards, tools everyone kept in their carts to navigate the interminable muddy roads. He shoveled mud while I wedged the board under the wheel. My boots sunk into the muck just like that first day when I arrived in town—trying so hard to look good in my best suit and polished Wellingtons. Now, I know how ridiculous that was.

"Go ahead, Ben, give it a try."

He jumped in and quickly rolled onto a dry patch.

As soon as I put the tools in the back, Sadie perked up. "So many banks. Is Spokane trying to be the Wall Street of the West?"

I scanned the many construction sites within view. "It is curious."

"Too extravagant, if you ask me," said Benny. "They must be expecting a whole lot of outsiders."

"You know the Dutch and European financiers are leading the charge on the rebuild," I said. "Maybe they know something we don't."

Benny shrugged. "Yeah."

I lifted Daniel onto my lap. "Many new people will settle here."

"No matter, it's of little concern to us," said Sadie in an uncompromising tone.

Her presumption that we would leave Spokane made me heartsick as did her insensitivity to Benny, who cocked his head and stared at me for an answer. I kept quiet and shrugged it off as a passing comment. The last thing I wanted to do was divulge our discussions about moving elsewhere to him today. He wouldn't take it lightly, not after all he had invested in the property and our friendship.

Ever since the fire, life seemed to throw one scorching fireball after another. Each day was an exhausting battle to keep upright. A reprieve had arrived. Once I got my family back under one roof, then everything would be right. But there was always some unforeseen twist. I guess life is that way for everyone.

Chapter Thirty-Three

A few weeks later, unable to get the dam project out of my mind, I started to sketch it out. Secretly I had been disappointed in the inconsistency of the water pressure of the system I had built. I believed a dam would resolve the issue. It would also curb the unwieldy torrent of water coming through town, creating a more serviceable river for all. I kept the project to myself for fear Sadie would feel I had been disingenuous about the decision to relocate. I didn't want to do anything that would drive another wedge between us. At the end of each day, after dinner and before bed, I worked on the design. I plowed through the books I had on the subject. When done, I'd roll the blueprints up and tuck them out of sight.

During the day, I sent telegraphs to my professors at Cornell and scouted possible locations on the river. I made hundreds of calculations of volume versus pressure. I determined the size of the induction pipes and the pump capacity needed to deliver the desired pressure. I was on to something. I was sure of it. I wanted to share my drawings with Sadie, but this close to her due date, it would likely upset her.

Meanwhile, Ben and I talked at length about expanding the nursery and orchard in the workshop. He took it upon himself to map out the best sections for roses and marigolds, meticulously figuring the optimum climate and irrigation requirements for each perennial and annual.

He sat on the workbench, reading the Farmer's Almanac, while I wrapped a split hammer handle. "Farmer's Almanac says burying seedling trees under stress in the wet ground for two weeks saves them."

I continued wrapping the handle. "Read on."

"Berries need lots of sunshine and their feet to be wet, but not soaked," said Benny, "Apple trees and stone fruit need to be planted in sections where they can cross-pollinate. And if I read this right, we're going to need more beehives."

We made every consideration in planting for maximum output. Meanwhile the expansion of the railroad coming in and going out of Spokane provided the perfect vehicle to transport the products regionally, maybe even nationally. I read up on the science of pruning and grafting for hardier varieties. I studied which apples flourished in these parts and which did not. I was fascinated by life again. An obsessiveness ran through me as good stories do, unable to put it down until the wee hours of the morning.

With more than a foot of snow on the ground, I'd walk sections of the property and listen for its wisdom. It was beautiful even then. Its stillness, its simplicity, its white bleakness—spoke to me. I heard its promise for next season. It vowed to be better than the year before. It had stored up its potential in seeds. I listened to its invitation to stay, to devote myself to it. Without consulting Sadie, I accepted. The American Indians did not believe the land belonged to them but belonged to the earth. This property had a commanding presence, a forever knowing of where I belonged in this world. My soul, my heart, and all that I was had become imbued to this western patch of soil. Leaving this land was utterly criminal to me.

It became impossible to shut my brain off at night—so many inspiring ideas, inventions, and tasks that needed doing. Every five or six days, I'd sleep long to catch up like a bear hibernating in winter. Sadie would wake me with fear that I was coming down with influenza.

Once a week or so, Sadie would bring out the map of the United States to discuss places to which we could relocate. The city of Walla Walla was not an option for Sadie or me. Neither of us wanted to be that close to her father. New York was not a choice for me. Going back home was out of the question. I couldn't face my father and mother as a failure. What gave me the most significant pain? I had not lived up to my mandate of living well for my siblings. Leaving the land and admitting defeat would cause them to anguish in their graves, an unforgivable legacy that haunted me daily. I knew it was unreasonable to think in such a way, yet it was the truth in my heart. How could I get Sadie to see it if she didn't share the devotion to the land?

Anyplace north was not an option for either of us. We had all the winter we could stand in Spokane. Portland or one of its outlying areas had potential. Hood River, Oregon, celebrated for its fruit fertility, had possibilities. We thought about northern California, but the gold rush mob was known for lawlessness. I had committed to move. I hid my discord as well as I could. Emotionally Sadie was vulnerable, and I didn't want to make matters worse. But, each time we discussed it, we ended up at odds with each other. It had become an obstacle of impossible proportions.

On Valentine's Day, an idea came to me, and I proposed it to her. "What if we found a place in Coeur d' Alene? It's only a thirty-mile train ride from here, but it's far enough not to be recognized by townspeople."

Poking the logs in the fireplace, she stopped. "Why Coeur d' Alene?"

I shifted my chair toward her. "It would get us out of Spokane. I could commute to work the property."

She walked to the dining room table where I sat. "How often would you commute?"

Our eyes locked. For the first time in a long time, I saw hope there. "Three days a week should do it."

She squeezed my shoulder. "The rest of the time, we'd be in Coeur d' Alene?

"You could run the steamboat," I said. "I mean, manage the captain and the tour schedule."

She gazed out the ice-etched windows in silence and picked at her fingernails. "Let me think on it."

I was excited. A compromise was possible. It wasn't but a few hours later when Sadie came back. "I like your idea about Coeur d'Alene."

We embraced. "Good," I said. Finally, we had an agreement—an agreement where I could remain devoted to the land and honor my siblings' lost lives. Sadie would get her fresh start unencumbered by the past.

"We should look around to see what's for rent in Coeur d' Alene," said Sadie.

"Do you want to wait until after the baby is born?" I said.

Sadie nodded. "That's probably wise."

We smiled in relief and kissed with rediscovered passion. I could see Sadie was happy, and so was I.

The next day, I received a letter from Mayor Nicholls asking if I was interested in a small job to extend the four-inch water main on Elm Street. He was throwing me a scrap. And I said yes, for the money. Although I didn't see much change in attitudes, especially with Rossiter, Benny thought it was a sign that tides were changing. Sadie was reluctant to see it as progress. I swore off all expectations. I did my job to the best of my ability, as my father had taught me, and left the rest alone.

Selling fruit out of wagons on the streets in Spokane had recently been prohibited. Consequently, customers started showing up at our door, desperate for apple pie, apple sauce, and canned peaches. Sadie usually took care of the rambling stream of returning customers. Today, so close to delivering, she had lain down for a nap. Three women from different families stopped by.

"We're wondering if you have any apples," said a blond woman with dark eyes and a pink bonnet.

I hurried from the barn, eager to sell all I could. "Yes, which varieties were you interested in?"

A stout woman wearing a swarthy dress spoke. "Need some good eatin' apples for my kids."

The blond woman nodded enthusiastically. "And do you have Pink Lady's? They're my husband's favorite."

The other woman, tall —thin with dark brown hair parted in the middle, waited in silence, her hands clasped around a small coin purse. Her shifty eyes made me uncomfortable.

"Give us a few minutes. We'll bring down an assortment."

I called up to Benny, who was in his loft quarters. "You hear that, Ben?"

"I'm already on it."

I scaled the ladder, my knee still wonky from the injury. "Bring down one tray, and I'll bring down another," I said as I reached the platform.

We both grabbed a tray and filled them with an assortment of apples, mostly Gala's, because they were of the greatest value and brought the highest price. "Be sure to throw in hand full of Gravensteins, Duchess, and Jonathan's, oh, and a few Baldwins." Ben and I held back our delight. Life was returning to normal; we knew it.

We got down from the ladder and laid out the trays of apples. "We've brought down an array of apples perfect for eating, baking pies and apple sauce," I said. "There's more if you don't see what you like." I removed my cap and scratched my head while they looked the apples over.

The women picked through the assortment and put the ones they wanted in their baskets.

"Are these pink lady's?" asked the woman with the bonnet.

"Yes, ma'am, those are the ones," said Benny with his toothy smile.

"He'll be so pleased I found them," said the blond woman.

The tall shifty woman approached and inspected the apples. "I prefer red apples."

With my hands in my pockets, I said, "If these aren't the ones you want, I have others."

"Do you have Red Junes?" she asked.

“I don’t grow them," I said. "How about Empires? They're perfect!”

"All right, I'll give them a try," she said, reaching into her coin purse. "How many can I get for twenty-seven cents?"

"Twenty-seven cents will get you seven apples, but I'll throw in an eighth for good measure," I said. "How's that?"

"Fine," said the woman, now staring at me.

I hoped she wasn't going to say something about the fire. I remembered the other woman traveling through with her family months before. She made me nervous. I was glad to see her go, even if she did wave goodbye on her way out.

When they left, we had made a total of $2.05. Not bad for a few minutes work.

Sadie could see that customers were slowly returning. She said it was a sign that some had accepted the pardon. Still, she felt uncomfortable around them and thought their attitude was off-putting. Her stubbornness made me cross. A trait inherited from her father. What more could I do to convince her? I didn't know. The not knowing resided in a dark and lonely place in me.

One windy February morning, the house filled with hot, fragrant bread just out of the oven, my impatience gnawed for a piece. I scanned through a pile of old Spokane *Review* newspapers I had neglected for weeks. Road regrading was underway from First to Riverside —a hard, tedious job. New concrete sidewalks, curbs, and gutters were going in. Approved for installation, one hundred electric light posts from the Edison Light Company.

A new steam fire engine would cost the city a whopping $4,395.00, but it offered the kind of speed no horse-drawn wagon could ever provide. Three new firehouses had approval. Firefighters now had to be elected by the townspeople.

T. J. Pedicord and G. Gardiner received saloon licenses. After the incident at Jake's in September when he refused to serve me, I wasn't at all unhappy when someone challenged his domain. The city issued another pawnbroker's license. I guess people still had to sell off their possessions to survive. At the foot of Center Street, a new bridge would go in. This new bridge would replace the Howard Street Bridge. I'd never forgotten watching in horror as it fell into the river.

The police force got twenty-four new officers. An outbreak of typhoid swept the city, the source of the disease discovered to be a cesspool near the hospital. Immediately, a new cesspool built of concrete and brick was in the works. Double trolley tracks for the Spokane Street Railway Company were approved. A two-foot plank beside the routes for pedestrians entering and exiting the cars got approved. F. P. Weymouth became the new city water superintendent. I wished him well.

Interestingly, an ordinance initiated to create and regulate the fire department with new officers and employees defining its powers and duties was in place. Before the fire, I had told them the department was inadequate. They wouldn't listen. Now the new chief engineer of the city was ordered to be the executive officer of the fire department. A district overseer would bring necessary change.

I was nearly half-finished with the dam's design, except for a few critical unanswered questions: the makeup and quantity of the bedrock and backfill necessary to build an impenetrable barrier. I mailed my soils professor with my calculations to double-check the numbers. By my computations, I would need two-hundred mature logs to build a dam strong enough to withstand the constant water pressure of this forceful river. I would also need three hundred tons of river rock to backfill the dam. There could be no margin for error in my design. It had to be perfect. Taking risks was not an option. Then again, the smartest thing to do with so many variables would probably be to walk away from it entirely.

Chapter Thirty-Four

Sadie sat up in bed, pressed her hand against her belly, and groaned. It was five in the morning on March 25, 1890. I watched her slide out of bed and grab the bedpost.

"Rolla!"

"Is it the baby?" I asked, stretching out my legs.

Bent over and panting, she eked out, "Yep," then moaned through a rush of pain.

I got up and scooted from the bed. "I'll hook up on the wagon and fetch the midwife."

A shaky hand caught my nightshirt. With eyes doleful and a pinched brow, she drew in a deep breath and started to weep. "I'm scared."

I pulled her to me. "I know, honey, so am I," and with fervency, I kissed her hand. "This is completely different from last time. The baby is well. Everything is going to be fine."

Sadie kissed my cheek. "You're right, you're right." She pulled herself up to a standing position. "I've got to go to the bathroom."

"Let me help you," I said.

"I think I can do this by myself."

"Probably, but I'm coming with you anyway," I chirped.

We proceeded slowly out of the room. Halfway down the stairs, Sadie stopped. Water trickled down the step. "My water just broke."

"Don't worry about it. I'll clean it up."

Sadie touched my shoulder." Have Benny collect Mary. I don't think we have time for the midwife."

"Yes, ma'am."

She let go a tiny smile.

While Sadie was using the bathroom, I raced to the barn still in my nightshirt.

Drawing open one barn door, I stopped and cupped my hands around my mouth.

"Benny, you awake?"

"Yeah, what's up?"

"Baby's coming. Can you get Mary? There's no time for a midwife."

I heard Benny rustling around. "Give me a second," said Benny.

I helped Sadie back upstairs, rested her on the bedroom chair, grabbed all the clean sheets and towels I could find, and set them on the bed. Daniel came out of his bedroom with his thumb in his mouth. I swept him up in my arms and twirled. "Today, you're going to get a new baby sister or brother."

"Mmm?" said Daniel pulling out his thumb, his eyes startled.

I kissed his cheek. "Yep, today."

Daniel wriggled down and approached his mother. "The baby's ready to come out?"

Just then a contraction stopped Sadie from answering. Daniel looked worried. When it subsided, she pulled Daniel over. "Mommy is fine. Don't worry."

In less than ten minutes, our Mary was there to help. She walked to the bedroom door and held it open. "You two can wait outside."

Daniel and I sat on the hallway bench. Daniel swung his legs back and forth in anticipation. The murmur of their voices was all we heard for what seemed an eternity. I ran down to the kitchen to grab some cheese and bread. I started a fire in the stove, set the coffee pot on it, and ran back upstairs.

With my ear to the door, I heard Mary say, "You're doing fine."

Sadie moaned. I sat down beside Daniel.

"Is mommy going to die?"

I took his chin in my hand. "No, she's having a baby, the most natural thing in the world."

His chin wobbled. "Does it hurt?"

"Yes, but she's strong," I said with a smile.

Then things got quiet again for a long time. I bolted downstairs for coffee and walked back two steps at a time. Daniel and I ate our cheese and bread, tearing a piece of each off and putting them together. I listened to every sound. I didn't want to interrupt with questions, but I was desperate to know something. The baby had been active all through the pregnancy. We'd lost a son last year. It wasn't uncommon to lose a baby—or the mother, for that matter. The thought of losing another baby, or worse, losing Sadie, made my head hurt. I prayed for their safety. Given everything that had happened, I couldn't fathom the idea of another tragedy.

I tried to stay seated but couldn't. I put my ear to the door again and heard Mary say, "On the next contraction, give me a good push."

I heard Sadie bear down.

"The baby is moving," said Mary.

Sadie stayed quiet during the delivery except for some hard panting and a whimper or two. She had such strength.

"You're a soldier," said Mary. "This baby will be out in a few more pushes. Now rest a bit. Next time push harder."

A deep moan rose from Sadie.

"Ok, here we go, pull your knees up. There's the head. Now rest a minute more until the next contraction, then give it all you've got."

Minutes later, Sadie grunted as if she was pulling a heavy weight.

"One, two, three, four—there we go," said Mary. "Baby's out."

Sadie tee-heed.

I knocked on the door, eager to see my baby and wife. "Can we come in yet?"

Mary cracked open the door and stuck her nose out, her hair a muss. I quickly picked up Daniel, ready to go in.

"Give us a few more minutes. You have a daughter, and you," she pointed to Daniel, "have a baby sister." She closed the door.

I spun around in excitement. "A girl! I've always wanted a daughter."

"Yay," said Daniel.

We twirled around and danced until Mary poked her head out the door.

"Quiet down you two."

Daniel and I covered our mouths and stared at each other, then broke into giggles.

Finally, the door opened, and we were let in. We tiptoed so as not to startle the baby. A glow befell Sadie as she gazed upon the baby's face, so small, so delicate. I remember that glow when Daniel was born. We rested on the bed. Sadie looked pale and yellow. Even so, bliss was in her eyes, a gaze that took my breath away. I ran the back of my finger on the baby's cheek. "You've done well, Mrs. Jones." We touched noses and kissed.

When the baby wrapped her tiny hand around my finger, tears welled up. "Well, hello, Hazel Blue," I said.

Daniel took a serious pose. "Mom, did she come from your tummy?"

"Yes, she did," said Sadie.

"Your tummy's still big. Is there another baby?" said Daniel, lifting a corner of the bedsheet.

"Just one baby. My tummy will get smaller," she said. "Do you want to give her a hello kiss?"

Daniel leaned over and kissed her ear. "When can she play?"

We chuckled, "Not for a long while," we said together.

Daniel whined, then touched her forehead with one fingertip. "Soft."

"And beautiful," I said, kissing the baby's hand. "Welcome to the family Hazel Blue."

Chapter Thirty-Five

The months flew by as we got to know our baby girl. Hazel was a peaceful baby, smiling at everyone, most especially Daniel. He entertained her with his toys and bouncing on the rocking horse beside her bassinet. The two would get laughing, making it impossible for Sadie and me not to join in. Benny whittled a little doll out of wood. Hazel put it straight in her mouth and used it for teething. Sadie's figure had returned, and spirits were high. The trees had leafed out. Buds were bursting. Bees worked in earnest. What I had lost didn't pain me as it once had. I was resigned to moving to Coeur d' Alene. We were building a new life. My heart was almost content.

Every week we'd scan the newspaper for rentals. We planned to go to Coeur d'Alene in early July when Hazel was four months old, locate an acceptable rental, and put down a deposit for a September move-in.

I avoided telling Sadie about the dam proposal or appointment with the city council in two weeks. I was searching for the right time to bring it up. I planned to slip it into a conversation when we were talking about apples or mending fences. Anyway, I looked at it, telling her about a project I'd been working on in secret was dicey. I knew no matter how I told her, it would be cause for a wrangle. Maybe, I'd tell her while Hazel was napping. Or after dinner, when the children were both in bed. I settled on a family picnic beside the river where the dam could be constructed. I knew she'd be angry, cross that I was putting myself in a position to have my head lopped off. Of course, I didn't believe that would happen. I thought the past was behind us; everyone had moved on. So much had changed for the better. Spokane Falls had transformed itself from a muddy, stick-built town with shanties, lean-tos, and clogged streets to a financially vibrant village with wide paved streets, concrete sidewalks, and stone skyscrapers. The Spokane Review reported:

Citizens soon realized that those fiery red clouds indeed had a silver lining.

The great fire never leaped outside the business district, which spared all of the city's

schools and churches and most of the city's homes.

Spokane Falls is coming of age.

To support its continued growth and its exceptional resources, I believed that Spokane River needed taming. Electricity was in significant demand. The industrial revolution was booming. The many mills, farms, ranches, businesses, and townspeople needed a river that could provide electricity and constant water pressure. I hoped Sadie would see it my way. I dreaded the thought of her not being in favor of the project. I didn't want any more upheaval in our marriage.

A week later, on a Saturday, I loaded up the wagon with a picnic basket and blanket. Once everyone was on board, we took off as the sun shined bright across the big blue sky.

"How do you know about this spot?" said Sadie, looking down the road while holding onto her bonnet as we bumped along the road. "How far is it?"

I avoided her first question. "Not far, maybe two miles."

Cyrus, who had become notorious for randomly stopping to eat choice grass, had to be urged repeatedly to move along. Sadie shifted Hazel in the child seat I had made for her to a more secure position on the floor between us.

"I hope the roads aren't too rough," said Sadie.

Baby Hazel looked up at me just as one wheel dipped into a pothole, and she squealed. I giggled back at her.

We followed Crescent Drive until it turned into Upriver Road and then a few hundred feet beyond that point. When we pulled off the road, Sadie scanned the area. The river was full of equal spans of marshland on both sides.

Sadie shook her head. "We can't swim here."

"I told you, not a swimming hole—too swift, too deep," I said. "Just a nice place to relax and get some sun."

"Look, a big bird," said Daniel. "Can I get down?"

I pulled back on the brake and locked it down. "Hold on."

Daniel crawled down from the wagon. Sadie took off her bonnet and pushed her face into the sunlight. I grabbed the blanket and picnic basket from the back, helped Sadie down, and lifted Hazel out. Sadie opened the blanket with a few shakes and set it on the grassy ground. Daniel wore his cowboy outfit and stomped around as someone fierce. I set Hazel down in her baby seat on the blanket. A minute later, she began sucking her hand. Sadie sat beside her, lifted her out of the child seat, unbuttoned a few hooks, and started nursing.

My nerves got shaky.

Daniel stomped over and removed his gun from his holster. "Howdy partner might be Indians in these parts."

"I reckon you'se right. Let's have us a look around," I said, and off we went to play. I was glad for the diversion but wary of prolonging the agony.

During lunch, consisting of butter and jelly sandwiches and apple-walnut salad, I had started to tell her about the dam when she interrupted me.

"I remember the last picnic we had, do you?" she said with a coy expression.

I searched my memory: making love behind a tree at Lake Coeur d'Alene came to mind. I murmured something unintelligible. Sadie snickered under her breath, and Daniel appeared puzzled. But, unfortunately, I had also remembered it was the last day before our lives were changed forever, and fire destroyed everything. The day before, I was blamed for the great fire of 1889. Yet here I remain in need of redeeming myself in the eyes of those who accused me.

Maybe the dam was a stupid idea. Would I come to regret ever thinking of it? I was either courageous, a gambler, or a fool.

Sadie burped Hazel and set her back in the seat. "Something on your mind?"

I took a deep breath and surveyed the landscape. Bald eagles, red-tailed hawks, egrets, and robins were busy scavenging for food. Cattails and blue swamp grass sprouted along the river's edge. I moved close to her." Why do you say that?"

Sadie swept a clump of hair from my forehead. "You're preoccupied."

I should have known she'd see through me. I took her hand and set my misgivings aside. "A dam could be built here. A dam that Spokane would garner its electricity from and provide constant water pressure."

"Speak English," said Sadie.

I shut my eyes and blurted. "Spokane needs a dam, and I've designed one. I have an appointment with the mayor and the city council."

As soon as I opened my eyes, she snatched her hand back. "What? Rolla! No!"

Jerking away from me, she said, "How long have you been working on this?"

Here it comes, the moment I've dreaded. The moment she throws the towel in on me. "Since we got back from Walla Walla," I said. "I'm sorry I didn't tell you. I didn't want to upset you any more than I already had. I just couldn't help myself. It was a project that wouldn't let go of me."

"You're unbelievable, you know," said Sadie. "You're obsessed. Do you hear me?"

I slumped down and nodded.

"We agreed. We're moving to Coeur d'Alene. We're getting out of here. We're done with this place, remember?"

"And we are, but this is critical to Spokane's future."

I saw the muscles in her jaw clench. "You don't owe them anything. Why do you still look for forgiveness from a town that shut you out?" Sadie abruptly moved her bonnet to the other side of the blanket, "Why, for God's sake?"

I looked out across the river and bit my lip. "I yearned to be forgiven. I needed to forgive myself."

"But why? You followed every protocol," said Sadie. "Bigger cities with better systems couldn't stop their fires. You told me that yourself."

I rubbed the back of my neck and tried to push out the tension. "I don't know. Yes, I do." I turned. "I needed to do something that got me away from despair. Is it not better to forgive? Is it not better to turn a negative into a positive? On Christmas Eve, when we were in each other's arms after being apart for weeks, I found my way back from the darkness." An ache ran through my knee; I rubbed it until it dissipated. "I have to do what I am capable of doing for Spokane, for me, and for you. You're my whole world," I thumped my chest with both hands. "It's my responsibility to create a new life for us. Besides, it's the right thing to do."

"Calm down," said Sadie, her eyes brimming with concern. "Are you sure you're strong enough to handle their rejection?"

I hung my head low and took a deep breath. "There's a difference between fault and responsibility. True, I did not start the fire or create the fire conditions, but I do have responsibility for the water system. The truth is, the system responded slower than it should have. I should have done so many things that would have made a difference."

"Like what?"

"Like ask for a phone to be hooked up in the pump house for emergencies. I should have replaced pump three. I should have asked for a relief worker to cover mealtimes. "That night when Thomas went to the pump house, Akin was on his dinner break."

"You would have battled for all those things with the city council and probably lost. You know that's true."

"I should have tried." I dropped my head again and felt my heart beating. The whole topic never failed to upset me. A torrent of emotions—fear, rage, insecurity—racketed in my gut. "I want to change my legacy. I don't want to be known as a scapegoat. I don't want to be known as a coward." I took Sadie's hands and held them. "I want to be known as a man of vision. You deserve that. My children deserve that. Tell me you disagree?"

Sadie got up and walked from the blanket, her arms crossed in front. "Stop worrying about what others think."

"I've got to try to make the people of Spokane see that this is the answer to stopping future fires."

Sadie kneeled and cradled my face between her hands. "What if they reject your proposal? I've heard stories from Mrs. Clifton. She told me how they treated you—horrible. I've seen the scars on your back. My children and I need a man who is in one piece, not one in the depths of despair. Are you so concerned with their opinion that you're willing to be irreplaceably broken?"

Daniel popped his gun at a bird flying over. "I think I got one, partner."

Hazel Blue flinched and looked about.

I reached out to grasp Hazel's hand. "I can handle it, Sadie. I'm strong. If there is ever another fire in Spokane, I will rest easy knowing I did everything I could to prepare them."

"You warned them before, and they ignored you," said Sadie.

We gazed into each other's eyes awhile before resting our foreheads together.

"Rolla, let's put this whole thing behind us, not stir it all up again."

"I know, but what's the worst they can do, fire me?" I said, "I don't work for them. Spit on me? I can match any man in a spittin' contest."

Sadie paused for a moment, cracked a smile and leaned over to pick up a rock the size of a baseball. "Okay, but if they lay a hand on you, I'm throwing this rock through their window," She woofed out a little chuckle at the ridiculousness of her statement. "Yeah, big bad Sadie's got a rock." She threw it down, it landed with a good thump. She then sat down on the blanket and rolled on top of me. Daniel jumped in, too, squirming his way between us. I tickled the two of them until shrieks of laughter rang out. Even baby Hazel joined in by kicking her legs.

****

On the morning of my meeting with the mayor, Cyrus was saddled up and ready to go. I walked out with the blueprints and my wide-brimmed hat. Sadie followed with Hazel Blue on her hip, and Daniel trailed behind. Securing the prints in the side satchel, I untied the reins and mounted Cyrus. I looked at Sadie with gratitude. Although she wished I wouldn't do this, she understood my quest and stood with me. Her support was everything.

Sadie cocked her head to one side. "You're sure about this?"

I leaned down, kissed her and baby Hazel, and waved to Daniel.

"Don't worry; I'll be all right. I have to do this." This act may be the most critical lesson of integrity I could ever give my family. They wouldn't remember it, but they'd read about it in our family notes. Our lives are longer than the years we live in.

She laid a hand on my knee. "Rolla Allan Jones, I love thee with all my heart."

****

I rode straight to the newly built City Hall. The building stood austere and uncompromising in its stone veneer. I tied Cy to a post, thanked him with a fresh carrot, grabbed my satchel, and bounded up the steep steps two at a time. I held my shoulders square, my fists clenched and listened to my footsteps strike the stone floor as I walked the long inside hallway. When I reached the city council door, I paused. A queer confidence came over me. I was sure this was the right path regardless of the outcome. On the other side of the door, good old Mrs. Smithey greeted me.

"Good morning Mr. Jones," said Mrs. Smithey.

"Morning, ma'am," I said, doffing my hat. "I have an appointment with the mayor and the council."

"I'm sure you do, but let me just check the log," said Mrs. Smithey as she ran her crooked finger down the appointment page. "No, I'm sorry, I don't see your name."

"Please, check again. I have the right day, I'm sure of it."

She ran her finger down the page more slowly. "Here it is, sorry. My grandson, who works here twice a week, has atrocious handwriting. I'll tell them you've arrived."

I nodded in relief.

She waddled to the chamber door opened it with a yank, leaving it swinging shut behind her. A few muffled voices, a shout or two, and she was back. "Yes, they're expecting you, but they asked for a few minutes to conclude their current business."

Minutes later, three laborers stormed out the door into the waiting room.

"Their kind always cheats labor," said a burly man with thick a beard that grew above his cheekbones.

Another man—wiry and pale walking like a cowboy, said, "Yep, can't never trust 'em."

"This won't hold the men for long," said the third man, who was tall and looked more like a landowner than a laborer.

I was itching to know what they had disagreed about and hoped to read about it in the paper.

Mrs. Smithey appeared fearful. She hurried to the council door, popped her head inside, and returned with another request to wait. A few more minutes passed. I had waited long enough. I stood from the chair.

Mrs. Smithey rose. "You can't go in there. They're not ready for you."

"I'll tell the council you couldn't stop me."

At the door, I straightened my vest and tie, cleared my throat, and twisted the doorknob. Three times the size of the old room, the new chambers looked expensive and important.

"He's just trying to squirrel his way back into our good graces. What could he possibly offer us?" said Rossiter.

Jeb Thomas raised his hand and blurted, "Why do you persist in blaming him?"

Fred Nicholls, badly in need of a haircut and beard trim, stood and held out his hand. "Mr. Jones, please come in. We apologize for the delay." He pointed to a chair. "Labor representatives from the expo insisted on a meeting; everyone wants more money. Have a seat. How are your wife and children?"

Five other council members sat around the newly appointed oak conference table: Smith, Follet, Franzen, Krakenberg, and Bender, only one absent. I should have felt honored by their attendance. I set down the rolled plans on the glossy table and loosened its strap.

"Very well," I bowed, "thank you," I took a seat at the edge of a turned oak chair.

"I understand you have a proposal for us," said councilmen Bender.

"Yes, I do. Mayor, council—Thank you for agreeing to see me."

Rossiter fiddled with his pipe. "I can't imagine what's so pressing that we must meet amid an insurmountable rebuilding process."

Nicholls leaned toward Rossiter. "Will you please?"

My shoulders tensed. "I'll get right to it. I've been researching similar events in cities around the country."

Jeb Thomas cleared his throat. "By events, do you mean whole towns burning down?"

"Yes," I sighed, "but bigger cities with more advanced systems. Cities with a full-time fire department and new equipment, as in Seattle and Chicago."

I heard a snicker. "Let me guess—you found the city council to be at fault," said Rossiter.

"I am not here to point fingers, are you?" I said, trying to quell my inclination to retaliate.

"Of course not," said Rossiter, digging out his pipe, "that matter is fait accompli."

I turned to Mayor Nicholls." I am here to put forward a bold solution to stop further catastrophes from happening."

"Catastrophe, that's a good word for it," said Rossiter.

Ignoring him, I spread out the blueprints. "This is the time to be forward-thinking."

The mayor and the councilmen stood and looked over the prints. Rossiter remained seated and continued to clean his precious pipe.

"What I have designed is a straight gravity-fed dam. It would be the first dam to be built on the Spokane River. I call it the Upriver Dam."

"If it was approved, where would it be built?" said Franzen, the newest member of the council to wear mutton chops.

"Five miles up the river, off Upriver Road," I said.

"What are the particulars?" said Krakenberg, a council member who rarely spoke a word, preferring instead to write out his thoughts and opinions.

"Mature timber, two hundred logs, and three thousand pounds of backfill will be needed."

"Why a dam?" asked Nicholls.

I slid a hand in my front pocket. "A dam is the only thing that can provide constant water pressure even if firehoses have holes. It will also provide the city with seventy-thousand kilowatts of electricity per annum. As I am sure you're aware, the electricity demand is on the rise across the whole country."

"Seventy-thousand, you say?" said Thomas.

I tipped my head in agreement.

"That's impressive," said Nicholls.

"You've only just figured this out," said Rossiter from his chair. "Why didn't you know it before?"

I lowered my chin." That was not what I was hired to do. I was focused on another project as mandated by the city council of which you served as chairman." I paused and glared at Rossiter.

Rossiter made an ugly face at me. "Get on with it."

Yep, I was done being Rossiter's fall guy. I realized then he no longer had power over me. I didn't work for him or anyone else at the table. I was a free agent. I was doing my due diligence for a sense of integrity. It was no real skin off my back if he or they rejected it.

"The only way to stop a fire of great magnitudes, like the one we had, is to build a dam on the river. Only a dam will provide the kind of on-demand pressure necessary to extinguish a massive fire."

"Too bad hindsight's always right," said the mayor.

"Maybe so, but it's not too late to stop future fires," I said.

"Our buildings are now fireproof, made of stone and granite," said Thomas.

I looked to him, "Mr. Thomas, you're kidding yourself if you think any building is fireproof. There's no such thing."

Nicholls chewed on his pencil. "You may be correct, Mr. Jones, but at this time, we have to shelve all extraneous undertakings. There are too many other projects underway."

"I anticipated your resistance," I said. "I'll remind you, you shoveled that same hogwash at me about the fire department just before the great fire."

Rossiter turned away dismissively. Nicholls equivocated. The councilmen deflected my comment by continuing to assess the prints.

"A fire can happen at any time, in any place," I said. "You know, Rossiter, your stone house on the ridge would probably weather a fire, but between there and downtown, there are a lot of wooden structures where people live and work. So when you're ready to discuss real prevention, you know where to find me." God, it felt good to speak my truth.

"Got it. Now what's next on our agenda?" said Rossiter, lighting his pipe, the smoke rising to a steamy curtain.

As expected, Rossiter had tried to derail my presentation. For what reason? I had no more time to waste on such questions. I had held my own, firmly and with civility. I rolled up my plans, walked to the door, and turned back. "History has a way of revealing the truth of those who made bad decisions." Politely, I tipped my hat, opened the chamber door, and departed. Though my goal was unmet, ultimately, I knew I had won. I was free. Free to stay. Free to leave. Free to follow any path I dream. I carried my head high, knowing I'd done my very best for the people of Spokane Falls.

As I rode home on Cyrus, I felt in complete control. I had found myself no longer enslaved by tradition, expectation, or guilt. I could do what was best for my family and me. I would no longer be held down by what my father, or my siblings, or James Withers or Rossiter expected of me—no one. Sadie and I could do what we felt was right. It was my first taste of absolute independence. That day my life became my own. I could do things because I wanted to do them, not out of some obligation or guilt. I was no longer bound to what others wanted. I was free.

Chapter Thirty-Six

Weeks later, while Sadie and I were packing boxes in the front room to move to Coeur d'Alene, Benny cantered up the driveway on his horse and came into the house with a bang. "The workers have walked off," he said out of breath.

Hazel, sitting in her baby seat, let out a cry.

"Benjamin, you scared the baby," said Sadie in a huff.

Breathing hard, Benny wiped his forehead with his sleeve, bent down, and tried to calm Hazel. "I'm sorry, little Hazel."

Daniel, who was sitting at the table painting, stopped. Sadie had made him paints of beet, blueberry, and mustard seed.

I rose from a kneeling position. "What did you say?"

Benny tried catching his breath. "They're calling for every man to come down to the site with tools."

"Slow down and tell me what you mean," I said.

Ben let go of a heavy sigh. "All the workers on the exposition have walked off the job. The city and the contractor couldn't meet their demands for more money, said they'd been working day and night. Said they wouldn't continue unless they got more money, a lot more money."

"The day I went to City Hall, three of the reps stormed out," I said. "They just got a raise a few weeks ago."

"They want more, and the city doesn't have it," said Ben, tapping his fingertips together. "A whole lot of people are coming to our town."

"When?" I said.

"Opening day, October, first," said Benny.

Before I could respond, Sadie jumped in. "Well, we'll be in Coeur d'Alene. You can't go, Rolla. You're needed here."

Something inexplicable came over me, a fierce desire to help and preserve the town. I grabbed my hat and headed for the door. "Let's get some tools."

Sadie spun around. "Rolla?" Her hands held out in question.

I stopped. "I've got to help, Sadie. It would be cowardice for me not to."

She grabbed her forehead and held an expression somewhere between worry and disgust.

Just then, Sam Clifton rumbled up the driveway in his wagon. His sons were in the back, holding on to their hats. He called out, "Jones, have you heard?"

I kissed her on the cheek. "I'll be back. I love you. Come on, Ben."

Benny looked at Sadie timidly. "Go on, Benny, I'll put your horse away."

Benny and I departed. We were loading in the wagon when Daniel ran out the door. "Daddy, can I come too?" His chin puckered.

"Sorry, son, it's only for grown-ups." Daniel furrowed his brow as we took off down the driveway. I knew this boy would grow to be a good man, a good brother. I was so proud of him.

When we reached the expo, streams of men were walking in on the cobblestone streets from every direction—tools in hand faces lit with pride. Men from every line of work: bankers, shop owners, accountants, restaurant and saloon keepers, newcomers, and old-timers. Lady Colleen and a few of her cohorts headed toward the expo. A group of six or seven more women from the temperance union came charging down the street toting paintbrushes. Zhang Wei and his son joined the swarm. Three black soldiers climbed the stairs carrying saws.

The energy in the city was rousing. A delightful zoom whooshed through me with each breath. It felt good to be part of something again—to be contributing. Nobody said one crossword to me. We were just people united in a collective effort. It was impossible not to smile. Spokane Falls was a different town with showy new buildings and many street lights. But at its core, it was the same small town I had come to love.

With Clifton's clan, Benny and I climbed the stairs. We reached the Northwest Industrial Exposition Hall doors where Nicholls, Rossiter, and Thomas were poised, smiling proudly. They patted each other on the back and welcomed volunteers as they entered. Sam and his sons wandered off. Benny walked beside me when Rossiter and I locked eyes. I hoped he'd stay away. I was not in the mood to make friendly. I just wanted to work. But Rossiter couldn't let it go. He hiked up his trousers and intercepted me.

"Jones, the people of Spokane aren't ready to forget."

I squeezed my fists and tried to ignore him.

"Don't make a scene," said Rossiter. "Just leave."

Suddenly all patience in me vaporized. I had stored so much inside. Worked through the pain of being blamed, exonerated, and condemned again. Reconciled with the resignation rendered under duress. Rationalized that the people we thought were our friends couldn't help themselves. I was done apologizing and begging for forgiveness. Somewhere along the line, I had come to realize humans need a story that explains their predicament. They need to distance themselves from the pain, assign a scapegoat so they have a place to focus grief and anger. It's critical to contain their loss to wrap it up in a compact package and put it outside themselves like used milk bottles. A myriad of facts doesn't provide a fulcrum to understand loss. Only a myth satisfies a way to understand complicated and tragic events, a legend they've molded into their personal story. Blaming me served that need. No longer would I be anyone's scapegoat—most of all Rossiter's. In a loud voice, I said. "Get out of my way."

Nicholls stepped in, in his usual mollifying manner. "Rossiter, let it go."

"I will not," said Rossiter. "He's not welcome here."

That was it. The moment I could no longer ignore. No longer could I be civil to this man. I had had all that I could take. If I was to be thrown out of town, never to set foot in this place again, so be it. I had endured much worse and survived. I put down my toolbox and came up with an upper left to the jaw, a right punch to the gut, and a jab to the nose. I felt his nose break and saw the blood gush as he fell back.

Jeb Thomas's eyes were big. An odd smile spread across his face. He put out his hand to me. "He's been deserving that for a long time. Well done."

I shook his hand. "Man alive, that felt good."

With a look of dismay, Nicholls stood over Rossiter, who was out cold on the floor.

Benny bent over his bleeding father. "Ooh wee, he's gonna have some nice shiners." Benny stood, slapped me on the back. "Come on, let's get to work, brother."

Thirty feet away, a group of men, including the man who had saved my life that fateful night, was climbing ladders and hanging light fixtures. I approached. "Excuse me, you saved my life. Do you remember me?"

The Slavic man scratched his chin. "Yah, I remember. I see you're still in one piece."

"Yes, I am." I said.

"Know how to wire lights?" said the man.

"Yes, sir, I do."

"Good," he said in a Slavic accent. "Name's Johann Zilka, I'm happy to have your help. We've got twenty-four more fixtures to hang."

****

A crew of three hundred people worked around the clock for the next thirteen days. No one complained. No one fought. We worked. We got it done. Again, I was part of the community—part of Spokane, its people, and its scars.

The morning of October 1, 1890, the expo was completed. We filed out onto the steps in silence as dawn's light poured over the eastern horizon. A resplendent light spread over the fertile land, unlocking its majesty. Though our bodies were exhausted, our spirits were resolute. A sense of peace that comes only from a well-done job filled us. The townspeople, who I had worked alongside for thirteen days, and I shook hands. Finally, and without pomp or circumstances, we walked to our wagons. We headed for home to ready ourselves for the day's festivities.

On the way back, I broke down and cried like a baby. Benny watched in silence. I had survived when I wasn't sure I would. I had gained a strength that would take me through any trial life could throw my way, as I was sure there would be others. I was as tough as steel and as soft as wool. Everything that killed me before—my sibling's deaths, Sadie's leaving, being betrayed by friends and co-workers—no longer held the devastating hurt it once had. I pardoned them, just as I forgave myself. I released my limits, my failings, and my humanness. When I forgave, a real sense of self-respect shepherded its way into my heart.

Chapter Thirty-Seven

That same day, I drove back to town with my family—Sadie, Daniel, Hazel, and Benny—to the town celebration. I saw Jeremy and Francis standing on the street corner. They waved. I waved back. I saw Johann Zilka walking proudly with his wife Mary down Howard Street and tipped my hat. Men who had once worked for me digging trenches doffed their hats. My leprosy had healed, the exile was over. I was one of them again.

Sadie tugged on my arm. "Do you see it?"

We exchanged a look.

Flags flew high on the magnificent expo center. Thousands of visitors from all over roamed the newly paved streets. Photographers snapped pictures. Crowds went in and out of the freshly appointed dress shops and other retail establishments. The streets were full of townspeople dressed in their Sunday best. A band played John Phillip Sousa's "Washington Post March" on the front steps.

I saw Mayor Nicholls and Rossiter with his bandaged nose and black eyes. Jeb Thomas and the other city council members milled about, shaking hands and laughing easily.

Sadie looked at me—her eyes brimming. We stopped in the road to let people cross. She clutched my arm.

"Rolla, did you see the faces, the expressions?"

The sky was Prussian blue and the sun shone through clumps of cotton ball clouds. "See what?"

She tilted her head, sure, I was teasing. "I know you saw it."

I clucked Cyrus to move along. "Tell me what you saw."

She laid her head on my shoulder and took a deep breath. “We don’t need to move away, this is home.”

I smiled and pulled back on the reins for Cyrus to halt. One by one I gazed into the glowing eyes of Sadie, Benny, Daniel and little Hazel Blue. “Our home is here.”

We must make our homes centers of compassion and forgive endlessly.
-Mother Teresa

Epilogue

Three years later

And then one day, vindication wandered on to the lair. I thought I had stopped waiting for it long ago. Only a small part of me hoped it would one day arrive. I received a request for my presence at City Hall to discuss my dam proposal. Would other dam proposals be considered, or was mine the only one? Why a public meeting? A meeting three years after the great fire of 1889, and one year after the expo, the pride of Spokane, burned to the ground. The building that had brought together a town in the midst of reclaiming itself and told the nation: Spokane remains a prosperous city that contributes wholly to the agricultural and industrial revolution. The expo had garnered the heart and tenacity of all Spokanites to build a new future.

I went to the meeting, but not before stopping at the mighty falls to hear its wisdom and feel its pulse. I needed silence. I needed to listen to its current and the rushing whisper that comforted me so many times before. On that day, it spoke of patience, of endurance, and it spoke of peace.

So much had happened over the past three years. We lost Daniel to scarlet fever in '91 at the age of five. We buried him next to our other son on our homestead. Our boys will remain at rest, and one day Sadie and I will join them. Our girls Hazel and Mabel were thriving. I learned a lot about people during those difficult years after the fire. I learned about myself, who I am, what I truly care about.

I discovered that like a miner who just needs a pick and a light to do his job, at my essence I am an undemanding man with skills I want to put to use. I don't need to conquer the world to find joy. I derive satisfaction from designing systems, solving problems, and inventing new tools. I want to grow food on the land that sustains my ancestry. I want my family to be proud of who I am and who they are. I want them to be proud with where they originate. To know where they belong, to have a place in this world, where they feel anchored. All other regalia are window dressing for societal approval. I once had grand plans, endless energy, and an unquenchable desire to build something, to make something of myself. But my road took unexpected detours. Now, I can see it as a blessing.

****

That afternoon City Hall was full of townspeople and council members. Mayor Nicholls opened the meeting. I focused on a spot on the wall behind him so he thought I was engaged. Protecting myself required a promise not to grovel ever again, but the need to be absolved never wholly evaporated no matter how I tried. I removed my coat and laid it over one shoulder. My sweat let off a pungent odor just as Nicholls began to read.

"Three years ago," announced Mayor Nicholls, "during the reconstruction, Rolla Alan Jones presented a proposal for a dam on the Spokane River. His reasons were sound. If we are to stop a major fire within city limits, he said, we need a high-pressure water source. That element was not present in '89. And as we've come to know, cities around the country have fallen with bigger systems in place. Once a fire breaks out, stopping it is like trying to tame the devil himself. We've rebuilt our city from wood to stone, expanded our water system, and hired a highly trained fire department. The last piece of our survival is a dam. Therefore we propose awarding Rolla Jones and Company with building the first timber dam on the Spokane River. All those in favor say yea."

The yeas rang out.

"All those opposed say Nay."

One old-timer in the back stood. "So, we are to forget his previous negligence?"

Nicholls looked exasperated. "My good man, not only was he exonerated of all wrongdoing, the investigation found that the real problem was neither incompetence nor neglect but a burst hose. Now, if there are no other objections, I declare the yeas have it."

I wasn't looking at the spot on the wall anymore. I was watching the faces of the townspeople and the city council, deciphering if this was real. I tried to measure the strength of their intention from their expressions. I swallowed hard. There would probably always be people who'd blame me. For them, I was their scapegoat. Somehow it comforted them to condemn me. I had to live by the truth and let go of the minds that couldn't be changed. It wouldn't be easy, but I would prevail. I had to triumph for my family. One person at the back began clapping, and soon others joined, until everyone in the room was applauding. After the excitement died down, Mayor Nicholls said, "Mr. Jones, will you accept the contract?"

I scanned the sincere eyes of the townspeople, and at that moment, the need for redemption vanished. I hadn't admitted it to Sadie, let alone myself, that all the years I lived with this albatross of guilt, a new vantage point had been evolving.

I stepped forward and said, "Thank you for considering my plan. I will consult with my family and business partners and get back to you." With that, I tipped my hat, turned, and walked out the door with my head held high.

Made in the USA
Middletown, DE
28 August 2022

72377287R00215